THE LOST ANGEL

A CHARLIE MACCREADY MYSTERY

THE LOST ANGEL

A CHARLIE MACCREADY MYSTERY

James M. McCracken

CONTENTS

DEDICATION

To Anthony Theodore Huff
for being the best little brother ever
and for getting us through some
really hard times in life.

ACKNOWLEDGMENTS

With sincere appreciation to Dennis Blakesley, Melissa Ainsworth, Barbara Blair, Phyllis Jensen, Elizabeth Jones, and Michael Ann Maslow for their continued encouragement and support.

CHEATER

Charlie MacCready stood in the top of the bell tower, staring out the south arch at the mound in the distance known as Black Butte. Tiny beads of sweat dotted his forehead and dampened the tips of his unruly auburn hair. A tiny droplet ran down the back of his neck. He shuddered, hating the feeling of his tee-shirt sticking to his back. A momentary gust from a cool summer breeze provided some much-needed relief.

It was the start of Charlie's fourth summer at Saint Michael's Abbey and Home for Boys. At first, he was angry for being torn away from his grandmother and sent to the Abbey, but somehow over the past year that changed. He started to see the beauty of the hilltop, the colorful gardens and ponds that dotted the Great Lawn, the thick forest of evergreen trees that surrounded the monastery, and the spectacular view of the valley from his high perch in the tower. The Abbey had begun to feel like home and that stirred another feeling deep inside of him, guilt. For his first three years at the Home for Boys, Charlie had resisted becoming comfortable, saying that his parents would come for him and they would take him home and be a family. Feeling that the Abbey was home made him feel like he was betraying the parents he couldn't remember.

Across the belfry, peeking out of the north arch, were his friends Howard Miller, Gustav Kugele and Rick Walters.

"Wow!" Gus gasped.

Charlie turned to see the source of the excitement and saw his clumsy friend lean over the waist-high, arched window sill. In the distance a huge crane hoisted another steel beam into place on the new gymnasium being built on the site where the abbey's garages had stood.

"Did you see that?" Gus said.

"Yes! We're all watching. Now get back in here before you fall," Rick said, grabbing hold of the back of Gus's black cassock. He pulled his portly friend away from the window ledge.

Charlie turned back to his view of the butte. He pressed his palms against the brick sill and leaned forward on his arms, careful to stay inside the belfry. A strong gust of air tussled his hair, making it stick out a bit more than usual. He swiped at the hair that fell in front of his eyes.

"You're going to have to see Brother Simon about a haircut," Howard commented as he joined Charlie at the south arch. He stood beside Charlie and looked at the butte. "Still thinking about going back out there?"

"Nah," Charlie answered, and shook his head. He turned his back toward the butte and leaned against the brick wall beside arch.

"Then why so quiet and pensive?"

Charlie furrowed his brow and looked at Howard. "Where did you hear that?"

Howard laughed. "I heard one of the monks say it. I had to go look it up to find out what it meant. It's a good word, don't you think?"

"I guess," Charlie said, and shrugged his shoulders indifferently. "To answer your question, I was thinking about my grandmother and this." He pulled the chain from beneath the collar of his black cassock and looked at the Saint Christopher medal, a gift from his grandmother. Turning it over he squinted and read the etching that had puzzled him for two-and-a-half years. "I was so sure I would find whatever it is out there. Did I tell you, Mr. DeVries said it was a map to my family's fortune?"

"Yeah, but can you trust him?"

"I don't know, but he seemed to really want this medal." Charlie turned the medal so Howard could see. "I found the cornerstone with the 1984 on it. I even paced off the ten steps, but there was nothing there."

"Maybe you didn't go far enough," Howard suggested. "I mean, maybe whosever medal that was took bigger steps?"

Charlie shook his head. "No, there's nothing out there but a bunch of rocks and an empty field."

"Well, maybe it's like those treasure maps and whatever-it-is is buried."

Charlie's mouth dropped open slightly, his eyes sparkled with hope, but just as quickly, the spark was extinguished and his smile faded. "No," he said, shaking his head. "Remember, the ground caved in and Mr. DeVries fell through to the catacombs."

"Maybe it's in the catacombs?"

Again, Charlie shook his head. "No. Abbot Ambrose told me, 'What you're looking for is not out there.'"

Howard chuckled at Charlie's bad impersonation of the head of the abbey. He looked at the butte. Suddenly his eyes widened and a smile spread across his face. "That means *he* knows where it is!"

"I already thought of that. I even asked him but he won't tell me. It seems that everyone—my grandmother, Abbot Ambrose, Father Cecil, even Brother Simon—knows about my key, the medal and maybe even the watch; everyone except me. They all keep telling me, 'It's not safe for you to know yet.'" Charlie shook his head and tightened his brow. "Then why give me these stupid things in the first place?" He shook the chain around his neck. The old brass key clanked against the Saint Christopher medal and the locket that held the tiny pictures of his parents. "It's not fair."

"What about the watch's note? Did you ask your grandma about it?"

"Yes," Charlie answered. "She said she didn't know anything about a note. When I told her it was stuck inside the watch and made it not work, she said it was working when she wrapped it up for me."

"That means someone else must have put it in the there."

"But who?" Charlie said. "She sent it to Abbot Ambrose."

"Then it must have been him."

"What difference does it make? He won't tell me."

"True," Howard sighed and looked out at the butte. "Have you tried to find out what the Dark Angel is?"

"The only thing I could find in the library is a reference to the devil and I'm sure that's not right. I mean, here of all places?"

"I suppose so. Well, don't give up," Howard tried to sound positive. "We've got all summer to figure this out."

"I guess so. I just—" Charlie stopped and looked up at the sun. "Hey, what time is it?"

Looking at his wristwatch, Howard said, "It's almost two."

"Two!" Charlie nearly shouted. "We better get downstairs. Father Vicar is posting the course list at two. Hey, Gus—" Charlie caught himself when he noticed that both Gus and Rick were already gone. Quickly he and Howard climbed through the trap door in the floor of the belfry and down the stairs that hugged the outer wall of the tower. When they reached the small door that led to the fourth-floor stairwell, Howard carefully opened it, making sure no one was around to see them while they climbed out of the tower.

The bells in the tower struck two when they opened the heavy, double-paned fire doors.

"That was close," Howard commented. "We need to make sure we don't lose track of time when we're up there."

When the ringing stopped, the two friends heard a commotion coming from the lounge area. They picked up their pace, being careful not to run, especially past Saint Peter dorm.

The last thing they wanted was to have the prefect, Father Vicar, catch them and keep them from the signup sheets.

When they entered the lounge in the center of the students' wing, they saw a group of boys huddled around the bulletin board. Charlie felt a sinking feeling in his chest. *This can't be good.*

"That's not fair!" an angry voice shouted from the center of the huddle.

Charlie recognized it immediately and pushed through the boys until he stood in front of Travis Bleckinger, one of Dougary Duggan's thugs from Saint Peter dorm. He was dressed in the purple surplice and black cassock of his dorm.

"You can't sign other people's names to the list," Travis protested.

"Why not, you did," Gus challenged, stepping forward and coming within inches from Travis's face.

"What's going on?" Howard asked, looking back and forth between Gus and Travis.

"Travis is mad because he was too busy signing Austin and Dougary up for photography class that he forgot to write his own name down. Now the class is full."

Howard tried not to laugh.

"You cheated," Travis hissed, glaring at Gus. "You know I was supposed to be in that class."

"What's all of this about?" a deep voice asked from outside the huddle.

The boys froze and were silent. Charlie recognized the voice of their dean, Father Mark. A path to the center of the huddle opened up as the other boys stepped aside. Father Mark, a tall, thin, blonde-haired, blue-eyed monk with gold wire-rimmed glasses walked up to Gus and Travis.

"I will ask one last time, what is going on here?" His voice was stern.

Gus began to sweat. He looked at Howard and Charlie for help.

"Gus cheated. He signed Miller and MacCready up for

photography class."

"Well, you signed up Duggan and Fuller first!" Gus found his voice. "You're only mad because you were too stupid to sign your own name."

"Master Kugele," Father Mark said, deepening his voice and shaking his head in warning.

"What's the problem here, Mark?" another voice asked, this one devoid of any emotion.

Charlie looked over his shoulder in time to see Father Vicar reach the center of the huddle. Father Vicar was a gaunt monk whose face was pasty white. His eyes resembled black pearl beads and his nose was crooked and beaklike. He straightened his back and stretched his neck in an attempt to appear taller and more imposing than Father Mark.

"I've got it under control, Vicar," Father Mark answered. His tone belied his displeasure that Father Vicar was attempting to usurp his position, again. He turned back to the boys.

"Since you both are guilty of signing up others for a class, the solution is simple. Neither of you will be allowed to participate in that class."

"But—" Gus started to protest, and shot Howard and Charlie another glance as if asking for help.

Father Mark stepped forward and took a pen from beneath his black robes. He crossed out Gus's name on the course list.

"This course is filled," he announced to all standing nearby.

"Don't worry, Gus," Rick said, and stepped forward. "I'll drop out of photography, too. We'll find a class together."

"Then I'll take his spot," Travis announced, and started toward the bulletin board.

"Not so fast." Father Mark snapped. Travis stopped. "I said, *you* are not allowed to participate in that class this year."

"But Walters took his name off. I'm just taking his place, not Porky's."

Father Mark's eyes widened. "That will be an hour of work crew for that remark."

"Come, come now," Father Vicar spoke up in a condescending tone. "What's the harm in allowing Master Bleckinger to take Master Walter's place?"

"Vicar, as Dean and your superior, I have made my decision and expect you to uphold it."

Father Vicar's gaunt, stony face went cold. His eyes narrowed in an angry glare. His jaw tightened. "Yes, Father," he answered. "Master Bleckinger and the other boys of Saint Peter, back to the dorm at once!"

"But I—" one boy started to protest but was silenced by Father Vicar's icy glare.

Charlie watched Father Vicar turn and seemingly glide above the floor on his way to Saint Peter dorm. There was a rustling as the boys dressed in black cassocks and purple surplices scurried like rats after their Pied Piper.

With his attention on Father Vicar, Charlie did not see Father Mark leave. One moment he was there and the next he was gone. Only Howard, Rick, Gus and a few other boys from the other dorms remained.

Howard stepped forward and looked at the papers tacked on the bulletin board. He smiled and turned around.

"I can't believe it," he said. "I'm finally getting to take photography."

Charlie glanced at the sheet and saw his name beneath Howard's. The bottom spot was blotted out, making the amount of pupils for the class one short and an odd number. He turned toward Gus and smiled sympathetically. "Thank you, Gus. I'm sorry you can't be in the class with us."

Gus shrugged. "It's okay. I know how much it meant to Howard, and I was only trying to help."

"Thanks, Gus, but—"

"Don't worry about us," Rick interrupted Howard and stepped forward. He put his arm around Gus's shoulders. "We'll find another class to take together. We'll have a great summer. You'll see."

Gus nodded but Charlie could see the disappointment on

his face.

THE ABSENT DEAN

The next morning, the four boys met in the belfry. Once again, Charlie stood staring out at Black Butte. The voice of his great-uncle kept ringing in his ears, "What you are looking for isn't out here."

"Still trying to figure out your mystery?" Howard asked, walking over to Charlie.

"Yes," Charlie admitted and let go of it. The medal fell against his chest with a faint tink sound when it tapped against the key and locket.

"I've been doing some thinking about it, too. Remember how you said the Abbot told you what you are looking for wasn't out there?"

Charlie nodded.

"He's giving us a clue without telling us."

"What?" Charlie's eyebrows pinched. He gave Howard a confused look.

"Well, for starters, he didn't say you misread the engraving. So, you were right. Whatever it led to *was* out there."

"But I already told you, there was nothing out there."

"I know. I know," Howard said, and shook his head. "Maybe it was *moved*."

Charlie felt a jolt of excitement fill his chest, but like a skyrocket exploding on the fourth of July, it vanished.

"How are we going to find out where it was moved to when we don't even know what *it* is? I can't ask Abbot Ambrose."

"True. What we need to do is find someone who was around back then, before the abbey burned, and ask them what it was."

"Easier said than done. Do you know how old they would have to be?"

"I don't know, at least forty I would guess," Howard answered.

"More like in their seventies," Charlie said.

"Hey, guys," Gus called from across the belfry, interrupting the two. "You gotta see this!"

Charlie and Howard hurried around the bells hanging from the rafters in the center of the belfry to the north window. They looked across the Great Lawn to where Gus was pointing.

Slowly making its way along the road on the west edge of the Great Lawn was a police car, followed by four black cars.

"Who are they?" Charlie asked.

"I don't know for sure," Howard answered. "But I think the Archbishop has a car like that one." He pointed at the second car.

"If it is, why the police?" Rick asked in his usual patronizing tone.

"I don't know, Rick. Maybe you can enlighten us?" Howard's tone was sarcastic and filled with contempt.

"Come on, guys, knock it off," Charlie spoke up. He stepped between them and cautiously looked down at the motorcade. "What do you suppose they want?"

"Beats me," Howard answered. He glanced at his watch. "We better get to class."

The boys made their way down to the fourth floor. Gus, the last one out of the bell tower, closed the small door behind them. The four dusted off their black cassocks and straightened their white surplices, the uniform of the Altar Boys Club members.

"So, what class did you two guys settle for this summer?" Charlie asked while they started down the stairs.

"Rick signed us up for a stupid class." Gus groaned.

"It was either that, or tracing our family history in a genealogy class," Rick said.

"Like that really worked out for me last year," Gus lamented.

Charlie immediately thought about Gus's cousins and how they promised to adopt him, then left him at the start of the previous summer.

"So, what class did you two decide on?" Howard spoke up, sounding exasperated by their chatter.

"Basket weaving with Sister Beatrice," Rick said.

Charlie shuddered. He had heard stories about the nun. She was the female version of Father Vicar and had no qualms about striking a boy or grabbing him by the ear and giving it a sharp twist. One boy claimed she pulled him around the room by his ear for missing a stave while weaving the side of his basket.

"More like the wicked witch of the hilltop," Gus said. The disappointment in his tone was clearly heard.

"Maybe it won't be that bad," Charlie said, trying to sound positive. "It could be fun."

"Really? How fun is sitting around weaving a basket while a crazy nun walks behind you carrying a reed, ready to smack you with it if you make a mistake? I heard the stories," Gus said. "And I believe them."

Charlie bit his tongue and tried not to laugh at his friend's frightened expression. "I'm sorry," he said.

"Don't worry about us," Rick chimed in. "We'll be just fine and we'll make it fun." He put his arm around Gus's shoulders in a one-armed hug.

The boys reached the first floor. Charlie glanced down the main hall, toward the center of the building where Abbot Ambrose and Father Mark had their offices. A man standing outside Abbot Ambrose's office door, dressed in a dark suit, caught his eye.

"Howard," Charlie whispered and motioned with a nod of his head in the direction of the man.

Howard looked down the hall. "Hey, Gus, Rick, we'll see you at lunch. Come on, Charlie, we'll go this way."

Before Charlie could stop him, Howard started down the hall toward the main entrance. Charlie quickly followed. He kept his eyes on the man who was, in turn, watching them.

"Morning," Howard greeted the stern looking man.

The man did not answer, but locked his eyes on Howard.

"How's the Governor this morning?" Howard asked.

The man gave a visible jolt and looked a bit surprised.

"You best run along," he said. His voice was deep and surly.

Howard nodded and kept walking. Charlie followed close behind him. They passed through the large wooden doors that separated the students' wing from the abbey's grand foyer. The chandelier high above their heads glistened like the sun. The white-marble tiled floor shined like glass. The boys went through the double front doors and down the steps under the portico. The four black cars Charlie saw from the tower were parked alongside the curb, their drivers huddled together at the edge of the Great Lawn smoking cigarettes and talking.

Charlie picked up his pace until he was walking beside Howard.

"How did you know he was with the Governor?" he asked.

"Simple," Howard answered. "I saw the security badge clipped to the pocket of his suit. It has the state seal on it. So, I guessed."

"I didn't see a badge. I can't believe I missed that," Charlie lamented.

"Don't feel bad," Howard said with a chuckle. "I recognized him from the news actually."

"Oh you!" Charlie playfully bumped Howard with his shoulder. "What do you suppose the Governor wants with Father Abbot?"

"I don't have the foggiest," Howard answered. "But I aim

to find out. Let's get to class."

The boys walked around the corner of the abbey and down the steps to the side, basement entrance of the abbey wing. Howard opened the door and the boys entered. It took a moment for Charlie's eyes to adjust to the dim light. Even though he was familiar with that part of the basement, being assigned to help Father Ignatius with setting up a new museum a few months ago, he stopped just inside the door until he could see clearer.

"This way," Howard said and tugged on Charlie's arm. They turned right and headed down a short corridor toward their classroom.

The windowless room was well lit by several florescent tube lights that hung above the two rows of three desks each. Charlie was relieved to see they were the first to arrive. He quickly sat down at the last desk on the left. Howard claimed the one on the right.

Austin Fuller and Dougary entered the room and stopped inside the door. Austin's smile faded when he saw Charlie and Howard. Dougary scowled at Charlie and took the desk in front of him. Austin sat in front of Howard.

There was one more student yet to arrive. Charlie looked at the two empty desks and wondered who it would be. A noise in the hall caught everyone's attention. Charlie looked at the door and his jaw dropped in disbelief.

"What are you doing here?" Howard demanded, jumping to his feet and knocking over his chair. It hit the floor with a loud bang.

"Mind your own business, Miller," Travis snarled. He slipped into the seat in front of Dougary.

Charlie noticed that Austin appeared to be as surprised as he and Howard were. Before he could speak up, Brother Claude walked into the room.

Charlie had never seen Brother Claude before and guessed he was new to the abbey. Brother Claude was younger than any of Charlie's other teachers. Based on his youthful complexion and that he wasn't wearing a postulant's habit, Charlie figured the monk was at least in his early twenties. That would make him close to ten years older than Charlie who was fifteen, soon-to-be sixteen. Brother Claude's head was shaved but Charlie could still see the brother's hairline. He also didn't appear to be much taller than Charlie.

Brother Claude took off his wire-rimmed, circular glasses and rubbed the lens with a white cloth he pulled out of the pocket of his black habit before putting them back on. He stood in front of his desk at the head of the class room and leaned back against it.

"Good morning, boys," he greeted them and then his eyes met Travis's. He pulled out a paper from his briefcase and appeared to be taking roll. He looked again at Travis with a puzzled expression. "Master Bleckinger, I don't appear to have you down for this class. In fact, Father Mark informed me that you were not permitted to take this class this summer."

"Yeah, Bleckinger," Howard snarled.

"For your information, Howie, Father Vicar got permission from Abbot Ambrose," Travis said smugly. "You can ask him yourself, if you don't believe me."

"All right, that will be enough," Brother Claude interrupted. "I will check with Abbot Ambrose about that later. For now, you are excused. Please leave."

"Can't you just call the Abbot?"

"He's in an important meeting right now and I will not interrupt him."

"But that's not my fault," Travis whined.

Brother Claude appeared to be thinking while he stared at Travis. "Fine. You may stay, for now."

Travis slumped in his chair and, turning around, grinned at Howard.

Charlie leaned closer to Howard who was obviously upset. "Just ignore him. Don't let him ruin the class for you. You've waited a long time for this."

Howard looked at Charlie and after a few seconds, nodded.

The morning passed quickly with a brief lecture about what

they could expect from the class and a tour of the darkroom. Even Brother Claude's final lecture on the history of the camera seemed interesting but Charlie couldn't keep his mind from wandering back to the puzzling medal and ominous message from the pocket watch. *What was out there? Where is it?* So many unanswered questions kept distracting him.

"Tomorrow," Brother Claude said in a tone that pulled Charlie out of his daydreaming. "We will go over the features of the camera and how to take a proper photograph. Then you will each be assigned a camera for the summer. Class is dismissed for the day."

Travis, Dougary and Austin were the first to leave the room. Charlie looked at the clock on the wall above the green chalkboard. It was nearly time for lunch. Then he noticed the writing.

"When did he do that?" he whispered. He quickly scribbled down the writing in his notebook, thinking it would be important but unsure of what it all meant.

Howard stood up and turned to Charlie. "What are you doing?"

"Writing down the stuff on the blackboard."

"Why?"

"It could be important?" Charlie answered, and finished writing.

"Weren't you paying attention?" Howard asked.

"Yes," Charlie lied. He closed his notebook and stood up.

"Come on. I'm going to talk to Father Mark about Travis," Howard said while they left the classroom.

"Howard, let it go. I don't think talking to Father Mark is going to do any good if Abbot Ambrose gave him permission," Charlie said. "Besides, we didn't sign up for the class. The only reason we're here is because Gus cheated."

"So what? Fuller and Duggan didn't either."

"Let Brother Claude deal with Travis. He's the teacher. Let's just enjoy our summer. Hey, you finally made it into the photography class," Charlie said, giving Howard a playful slap on the back while they walked up the side steps outside the abbey building. "Don't let him spoil it for you."

"I suppose you're right," Howard admitted.

~§~

Lines had already begun to form outside the refectory doors on the first floor of the student wing by the time Charlie and Howard arrived. They quickly took their places and stood quietly with the others.

Brother Owen, the prefect for Saint Thomas dorm, opened the refectory doors and walked back inside. The boys silently filed into the dining room.

The dining hall appeared different. The décor, portraits in ornate gold frames of Abbots-gone-by still adorned the walls. But something had changed. When Charlie reached the end of his dorm's long table, he stopped causing the boy behind him to bump into him.

"Keep moving," a boy behind him whispered.

"Sorry," Charlie answered and resumed walking.

When he reached his chair beside Howard's he fought the urge to tell Howard the table was shorter. Instead, he looked at the head table. The dark, navy-blue velvet curtain still hung on the wall behind the table. In the corner opposite the entry doors, a gold crucifix affixed to the top of a matching gold pole stood in its stand. A bouquet of fresh flowers sat in a vase on the floor in front of it.

Charlie looked at the dorm prefects as though taking roll. Brother Owen stood at his place at the end nearest the entry doors. Brother Simon, Charlie's dorm prefect, was next. The chair where the dean normally sat was empty. Father Mark was curiously missing. Father Vicar, who appeared more sinister than ever, stood staring at the boys from his dorm. Brother Conrad, prefect of Saint Sebastian dorm, was the last. He stood, glaring at Charlie.

Brother Owen said Grace, then the boys took their seats.

Charlie looked across the table at Rick and Gus while he waited for the clap from the block of wood at the head table—the signal that it was okay to talk—but it didn't come. Charlie looked at their prefect, Brother Simon.

Brother Simon, a tall thin monk that could pass as Father Vicar's twin, except he wasn't as gaunt or sinister, sat with his eyes fixed in a cold stare at the wall in the back of the refectory.

Without warning, Rick raised his hand. Charlie noticed Brother Simon's back tense. He discreetly motioned for Rick to put his hand down. Rick complied with a puzzled look in his eyes.

Charlie nudged Howard but Howard just gave him an I-don't-know shrug.

The boys ate their lunch in silence. Afterward, there were no announcements. Brother Simon closed the meal with the usual prayer and dismissed the boys. There was a rustle from their uniforms as the boys quickly filed out of the refectory and into the hall.

"What is going on?" Rick asked when the four of them entered the hall. "Why couldn't we talk? Where's Father Mark?"

"I don't know," Howard answered. "But I am going to find out." He headed straight for the main hallway with Charlie close behind.

"Something is seriously wrong here," Charlie said, while keeping pace with Howard.

They stopped in front of Father Mark's office door, across from Abbot Ambrose's. Howard knocked calmly and listened for a reply.

Nothing.

He knocked again a little louder.

Again nothing.

He was about to rap on the door a third time when Abbot Ambrose's door opened.

"Boys," Father Mark said, eyeing them.

Howard turned around. "There you are," he said, taking a

step toward the dean.

Father Mark held up a halting hand. "I'm really busy right now. Why don't you both run along and we'll talk later."

"But—"

"Come on, Howard," Charlie interrupted, tugging on his friend's arm. "Let's go for a walk."

"That's a good idea," Father Mark said before retreating back into the abbot's office, closing the door behind him.

Charlie could tell that Howard was not pleased at being put off. He pushed the door to the foyer open with such force Charlie braced himself for it slamming against the wall, but it didn't. The stopper attached to the top of the door had prevented it. Charlie hurried out the front door after his friend.

"Wait up, Howard," he called and rushed down the front steps.

"Why did you pull me away?" Howard said turning around when he reached the Great Lawn.

"Because, I saw someone else in the office with Abbot Ambrose."

"You did? Who?"

"I don't know."

Charlie noticed Howard look around.

"There aren't any cars here. Was it a monk?"

"No. He was in street clothes."

Howard bit his lower lip while he looked from side to side. "There's definitely something strange going on," he said. "I'll see what I can find out from Brother Gregory." He rushed back into the abbey.

"I'll do the same with Father Cecil," Charlie called after him. Charlie sensed a feeling of dread begin to grow, a feeling all too familiar to him since coming to the Abbey's Home for Boys.

Moments later, Charlie stood outside Father Cecil's cell door. The memory of their first meeting was still fresh in his mind. He blushed when he remembered how shocked he was to learn Father Cecil was blind. It was something that still tickled the middle-aged monk but embarrassed Charlie a little each time the priest brought it up. Even so, it was hard to for him to explain why, but Charlie felt a connection with the monk. They were more than just an Altar Boy and his assignment, they were friends.

The door opened. Father Cecil smiled and stepped aside. His chin was raised and his milky-blue eyes stared over Charlie's head. "Master MacCready, come in. How was your first class in photography?" He felt the wall beside the door and flipped the light switch on.

"It was okay," Charlie answered, walking into the small room. "Brother Claude gave us a tour of the classroom and lectured today. Tomorrow we'll get our cameras."

Father Cecil closed the door and slowly made his way across the small room to his chair in the corner. "I think that is what I miss the most about not being able to see," he said, while he sat down. "I used to love taking photographs. I had so many photo albums I had to put up a shelf that spanned the whole width of the room just to store them." He motioned toward the ceiling above the door.

"You did?" Charlie said, a bit confused. There was no shelf on any of the walls and no marks in the wall from where one might have been. "What happened to them?"

"A few years ago, I had Simon put them in the attic. They're useless to me and their presence was a constant reminder of what I lost."

A memory flashed in Charlie's mind. His first year, when he was staking out the attic with Howard, he saw Brother Simon putting some books in a trunk. He had speculated they were the old yearbooks from when his father was there but when he found the yearbook on his bed at the end of his first year, he was not as sure.

"I bet I could find them," Charlie said.

"No," Father Cecil answered. His voice was firm but at the same time gentle. He put his hand up as if to halt Charlie. "It's best they stay where they are for now."

"But—"

"You best get started," Father Cecil said. He picked up the large book that was on a small table between his chair and bed and opened it. Charlie watched while Father Cecil's fingers moved across the page, feeling the tiny bumps embossed in the paper.

Charlie set about making Father Cecil's bed and tidying up the small room, careful not to move any of the chairs or furnishings. When he was finished, he sat down on the chair beside the table.

"Father, may I ask you something?" Charlie said.

"Sure." Father Cecil closed his Bible and set it aside.

"Have you heard anything strange going on?"

"Strange? What do you mean?"

"This morning, before class, there were men from the Governor's office here. They had a meeting with Abbot Ambrose and Father Mark. Do you know what it's about?"

Father Cecil shrugged and shook his head. "I have no idea," he answered. "I would imagine it would have something to do with the boys who are wards of the state."

"What?"

"The boys who were sent here instead of a juvenile home for delinquents."

"Oh, you mean like Dougary and his goons."

Father Cecil smiled. "I suppose. It's the reason I can think of as to why someone from the state would be meeting with Abbot Ambrose. I wouldn't worry about it. It's probably nothing."

"I guess." Charlie slumped in his seat while more questions flooded his mind. "Father, do you mind if I leave a bit early?"

"No, not at all," Father Cecil answered.

"I'll see you tomorrow, and maybe we could go for a walk or something."

"That will be fine."

Charlie headed straight to Saint Nicholas dorm on the fourth floor of the student wing. The dorm was quiet, as Charlie had expected, since most of the boys had gone home for the summer a week ago.

"You're back already?" Charlie said when he reached the cubicle he shared with Howard. "What did you do now?"

"Nothing. Why would you say that?" Howard said, looking over the top of his comic book at Charlie. Howard lay on his bed on his back with his knees were drawn up so he could rest his book on them.

"Forget it," Charlie answered, though he remembered how Howard had accidently knocked Brother Gregory into one of the ponds that dotted the Great Lawn on their first meeting. He also recalled the other times the poor monk was the subject of Howard's clumsiness. "So, did you find out anything from Brother Gregory?"

"No." Howard shook his head. He closed his comic and rolled onto his side, facing Charlie. "What about you?"

"Same here, pretty much. Father Cecil thinks it might have something to do with the boys who are juvenile delinquents," Charlie said. He sat down on the edge of his bed. "I did find out something interesting though."

"Oh yeah?"

"Remember when we were staking out the attic my first year here? We saw Brother Simon putting some books into a trunk."

Howard sat up and tossed his comic book onto his nightstand. "Yeah."

"Father Cecil told me he used to take tons of pictures before he went blind. He had a lot of photo albums. He said a few years ago he had Brother Simon put them in the attic."

"Oh," Howard said, sounding confused. "What's that have to do with what's going on now?"

"Nothing, maybe. When I asked if I could find them for him, he said no. Isn't that odd?"

"No. It's not like he can see them, he's blind. Why do you think it's odd?"

"Because the way he said it. It was like he was afraid I'd

see something."

"Like what?"

"I don't know, but maybe he has a picture of whatever was out there. I mean, he is older."

Howard laughed. "But he's not *that* old. You said it, yourself. He would need to be in his eighties."

"I still think he's hiding something, after all, he had them locked in a trunk."

"We don't know that's what Brother Simon was doing."

"But we don't know that it was not, either."

Howard drew his eyebrows tight and looked puzzled. "Fine. I'll admit, it does sound suspicious."

"I wonder what he's trying to hide from me?"

"From you?" Howard asked, his voice sounded shrill. "What makes you think it has anything to do with you?"

"Because—"

Howard looked at Charlie and stifled his laughter. "We should just forget about that for now. We have enough mysteries to solve already with finding out about that note in your pocket watch and why the Governor was here."

Charlie gave a heavy sigh. "I suppose you're right."

The bell in the hall rang out, startling Charlie.

"I wish they wouldn't do that."

Howard laughed. "Then how would we know when it's time for dinner? Come on," he said, and stood up. "Maybe there'll be an announcement?"

"Don't hold your breath," Charlie said while he followed Howard to the door.

PHOTOGRAPHY CLASS

The next morning, Charlie sat at his desk in the photography classroom, feeling a bit annoyed that Travis was still there. Brother Claude had explained that Father Vicar had gone over Father Mark's head to weasel the goon into the class. Goon was Charlie's word, not Brother Claude's. Charlie imagined that Father Mark was not pleased about it either, but what could he do, Abbot Ambrose was *his* superior. Still, Charlie thought, it is not fair.

"Now, each of you will be assigned a specific camera," Brother Claude said in the conclusion to his lecture on the different features of and how to operate the camera. "Keep it with you at all times. Do not leave it lying around where someone can take it or mess with it. And for God's sake, don't lend it to anyone."

While Charlie listened, he felt the key beneath his cassock and remembered the similar warning his grandmother had given him the day she gave it to him. She seemed frightened and slightly worried. But, about what?

"If you have a problem with your camera," Brother Claude continued, "bring it directly to me. Do not try to fix it yourself. You will only make matters worse. Is that understood?"

"Yes, Brother Claude," Charlie answered with the rest of the class.

"Very well," Brother Claude said. "There's one more thing. Film is not cheap. Neither are the chemicals used to develop and print your photographs. Do not waste either. Is that understood?"

"Yes," the boys answered in unison.

"Very well," Brother Claude said. He took a seat at his desk and pulled out a thin, wide book from the top drawer. Taking a pen from the breast pocket of his habit, he opened a ledger and clicked his pen. "When I call your name, please come up and receive your camera. Master Miller." Brother Claude reached down into a box beside his chair. He took out a camera and wrote in his ledger.

Howard rushed up to the front of the room and stood in front of Brother Claude's desk. When he received his camera, he slipped the strap around his neck and looked through the lens. "Thank you," he said, before returning to his desk.

"Master MacCready, you're next." Brother Claude announced.

Charlie went forward and received his camera. Returning to his desk, he looked it over.

"They all look the same," Howard said when he saw that Charlie's camera looked identical to the one around his neck. "How is he going to keep track of whose is whose?"

"There's a number on the bottom," Charlie answered, turning the camera over and pointing to the engraving. "I noticed Brother Claude wrote it next to my name in his book."

"Oh," Howard said, sounding a bit disinterested. He was already aiming the empty camera at various points around the room and squinting while he looked through the lens.

Charlie looked at his camera. There were numbers on the ring around the lens and buttons on the top and back. He regretted not paying better attention during Brother Claude's lecture. He looked at Brother Claude right when Travis was handed his camera. He clenched his teeth.

Brother Claude closed his ledger. Standing, he picked up a small box. "Now, before I dismiss the class, are there any questions?" Brother Claude asked while he placed a small plastic canister containing a roll of film on each of the boys' desks.

Charlie raised his hand.

"Master MacCready?"

"Could you show us one more time how to load the film?"

"Certainly." Brother Claude returned to his desk and picked up his camera.

Charlie watched intently while Brother Claude opened the back of the camera. Taking the canister of film, he placed it into the camera and showed the class. He closed the back. A whirring sound was heard and then Brother Claude smiled. "That's all there is to it," he said. "Now, you try."

Charlie opened the back of his camera and placed the small canister into it just as Brother Claude had done. He closed it but his camera didn't make a sound. All around him he heard the other cameras loading. He raised his hand.

"Yes?"

"What if your camera doesn't make that sound?"

"Then open it up and make sure you have enough of a tail of film for the winder to catch."

Charlie opened his camera and adjusted the canister. He pulled a bit more film out, making sure it reached the small cog before closing the back. This time he heard the whir. His anxiety waned slightly.

"Your first assignment will be to take pictures of things that interest you. Pay attention to lighting and composition just like we discussed."

Brother Claude glanced at the clock behind him. It read five minutes before noon.

"Class is dismissed for the day," he announced.

Charlie followed Howard into the hall.

"So, are you excited about getting your camera?" he asked.

"Yeah," Howard answered. "I can't wait to get out and take

some pictures. Maybe after lunch we could—"

"We can't," Charlie interrupted. "We have to see our monks, remember?"

"Oh, yeah," Howard said. "Well, maybe Brother Gregory will want to go for a walk or something."

"Maybe," Charlie agreed.

~§~

After lunch Charlie headed for Father Cecil's cell. For the second day in a row, Father Mark was missing at the head table and the boys ate in silence. Something was going on, and the lack of news fueled Charlie's curiosity.

"Come in, Charlie," Father Cecil invited, stepping back and opening the door to his room wider.

"Hi, Father," Charlie said.

"Uh-oh, what's the matter?" Father Cecil asked, while he walked across the small room to his chair.

"I don't know," Charlie answered and closed the door. He sat down at the small table to the left of the door and across from the monk.

"Photography class going okay?" Father Cecil asked.

"Yeah."

"Your friends, they're all okay?"

"I guess so."

"Charlie, I'm blind but that doesn't make me a mind reader. You've got to help me out a bit. What's bothering you? Did something happen?"

Charlie took a deep breath and let it out. "Today, Brother Claude told us that Travis gets to stay in class."

"Oh?"

"Father Vicar went to Abbot Ambrose."

"I see," Father Cecil said and nodded.

"I bet Father Vicar lied to the Abbot."

"Now, now."

"Well, why else would he let Travis stay in the class? It's

not right. Gus shouldn't be the only one punished. Travis signed up Dougary and Austin, first. It's not fair."

"Aye, that is rough. Charlie, as you get older, you will find there are a lot of things that don't seem fair. Some people manage to get all the breaks, as it were. The main thing is not to let it get you down. You can't control everything. So, focus on what you can and keep doing the right thing. Then you will have no regrets."

"I guess you're right," Charlie slumped in his chair. He could not see any way to change what had already been decided. Father Vicar and his goons won again.

"I know you're disappointed, but don't let it ruin your enjoyment of the class. Now, tell me, how did the rest of photography class go?"

"We got our cameras today," Charlie said and held up the camera that hung from the strap around his neck.

"You did? What kind?" Father Cecil asked, staring across the room in the direction of the door.

"It's a Canon, thirty-five millimeter," Charlie answered.

"Nice. I'm partial to Pentax myself. I found it easier to use."

"Brother Claude said someone donated these to the Abbey."

"That was generous of them. Canon cameras aren't cheap by any means. So, have you taken any pictures yet?"

"No." Again Charlie slumped in his chair. "We're supposed to take pictures of things that interest us, but I can't think of anything."

"Really?" Father Cecil cocked his head to the right. "There's nothing that interests you? I find that hard to believe."

"I just can't think of anything worth taking a picture of."

"What about your friends?"

"Well—I suppose."

"Charlie, don't overthink things. Pictures are physical manifestations of your memories. Right now, you have to rely on the images you have in your head of your friends and things that happened, but those memories tend to fade quickly. Taking a photograph of someone or something preserves it for years to come. So, tell me who are some of the people you would want to remember?"

"You, Sister Margaret Mary from the kitchen, Howard, Brother Simon, Gus, Rick—"

"I see. Well, why not take their pictures but don't let them know it. See if you can catch them doing something."

"Like what?"

"Anything—working, playing, standing around—the main thing is don't let them know you're doing it. That way you can capture the *real* them and not a posed them."

Charlie thought for a moment. It sounded like it might work. "Okay, I'll try it."

"Good," Father Cecil said.

After tidying the small room, the afternoon was free for Charlie to put Father Cecil's idea into action.

On his way back to his dorm, he slipped into the kitchen and ducked behind a tall food cart. He readied his camera and waited for the right moment. Sister Margaret Mary hummed while she kneed a large mound of dough on the flour covered, wooden bakery table. She had her white apron on over her black habit and her white forearm cuffs over her sleeves. Charlie watched while she tossed a handful of flour onto the table and then dropped the dough in the middle of it. Instantly a white cloud puffed up into her face. Snap. He had his shot.

"One down, eleven more to go," he said while he slipped away.

By the time he reached Saint Nicholas dorm, he needed to take one more photo. Rick was in Gus's cubicle. They were talking to each other. He readied his camera and was about to snap the shutter when Rick looked at him.

"Oh, no you don't!" he snarled and held up his hand to block the lens.

"Fine!" Charlie said and lowered the camera. He walked up to the foot of Gus's bed. "What are you guys talking about?"

"Sister Beatrice grabbed Gus's ear in class today."

"She yanked it!" Gus said, covering his left ear.

Rick rolled his eyes and shook his head. "He's afraid she broke it."

"She did," Gus insisted. "Look it sticks out now." He lowered his hand.

"You look fine, Gus, honest," Charlie said, pretending to examine Gus's ear and trying not to laugh.

"Are you sure?" Gus asked.

"Yes," Charlie answered. "Trust me."

"I do."

"What? I've been telling you the same thing all afternoon." Rick said.

Charlie slipped away, leaving the two to sort out their own issues.

Peeking around the end of the divider that separated their cubicle from Gus's, Charlie saw Howard laying on his bed with his comic book held in the air above his face. Charlie quickly raised his camera.

"Don't you dare," Howard said without looking.

Snap.

Howard sat up on his bed.

"What did you do that for?" he asked.

Charlie laughed. "Don't worry. I don't have any film," he lied. Suddenly the camera made a whirring sound as it automatically rewound the film into the canister.

"Liar!" Howard shouted and sat up.

"Sorry," Charlie said. "I just needed one last picture to finish my assignment. Did you get yours done?"

"Yeah, Brother Gregory and I went for a walk. I snapped off the roll then. Killed two birds with one stone."

Charlie took the strap from around his neck and set his camera on his nightstand. Howard tossed his comic book back onto the stack of others on the lower shelf of his nightstand.

"Did—" they both said together and then laughed.

"Did you find out anything from Brother Gregory about

what's going on with the abbot and the governor?"

"Nah, he doesn't know, or else is being tight lipped like everybody else."

"Yeah," Charlie sighed and slumped while he sat on his bed. "I wonder what the big secret is?"

"Well, one thing is for sure, it's not going to be good."

"Why do you say that?"

"Usually when it's good news word leaks out somehow. There's always one monk who slips and spills the beans."

"Oh," Charlie said. "I wish there were some—" A memory flashed in his mind of how while they were in the attic, they could hear through the vents. "I have an idea, but I need to check it out. See you at dinner."

"Okay," Howard said. "But don't be late. They're still handing out work crew for being tardy."

Charlie was already in the hall before Howard finished his warning. He looked the left then turned right and slipped through the door into the central stairwell.

~§~

At dinner, everyone was surprised when they entered the refectory. The four prefects were standing at their places at the head table as usual, but this time Father Mark was with them. After the prayer, he smacked the wooden block against the table, signaling it was okay for the boys to talk.

Howard leaned closer to Charlie.

"So, where did you go this afternoon?" he whispered.

Charlie glanced across the table at Gus and Rick before watching their server, a younger member of their dorm, begin to make his rounds.

"Not here," he whispered to Howard. "We'll talk in the bell tower after dinner."

"Fine," Howard said and sat back in his chair. "Since when did you get all tight-lipped?"

Charlie smiled. "I don't want anyone to overhear."

When the meal was finished, Father Mark made a few mundane announcements, not offering any explanation as to where he had been, and then closed with a prayer.

"See, nothing. He might as well have skipped dinner," Howard said while he walked into the main hall outside the refectory with Charlie.

"That's okay, I think I found a solution," Charlie said. "Come on."

The two made their way up the stairs. As they neared the fourth floor, they slowed, letting the other boys pass them. When they reached to landing outside the fire doors, they let the few remaining stragglers go by before Howard opened the small door to the bell tower. The two quickly entered the dark landing with Charlie closing the door behind them.

Even though they had been sneaking up to the belfry for nearly two summers, Charlie still found it a bit unnerving. He sat with his back pressed against the wall beside the small door, staring at the large hole in the center of the wooden plank floor. The ropes from the bells above dangled freely through the opening to the ground below. Charlie kept reminding himself that the floor was not tipping, that he was not moments away from being sucked through the hole and falling four stories to certain death. Once his eyes adjusted to the dim light, Charlie stood and pressed his back against the wall. Following Howard, he made his way to the stairs leading up to the belfry.

"So, what is the big secret?" Howard asked while they stood among the bells.

"I found a way we can hear what's going on in Abbot Ambrose's office."

"You did?" Howard said.

"Yes," Charlie answered, not sure what to think of the surprised and almost shocked expression on Howard's face.

Howard's gaping mouth stretched into a grin. "You're becoming quite the little Sherlock."

"Well, don't get too excited. There's a bit of risk involved. If we get caught, we will be in big trouble."

"Count me in," Howard said.

Even though they were alone in the bell tower, Charlie leaned closer and whispered in Howard's ear.

"We can test it out tomorrow," Charlie said, stepping back.

Howard nodded. "What a brilliant idea."

CAUGHT

After morning Mass, Howard and Charlie headed for their photography class while Gus and Rick went off to their class.

"Poor Gus," Charlie said when they parted. "He's not enjoying making baskets at all."

"Yeah," Howard answered. "Sister Beatrice really likes his ears."

"It still irks me that Abbot Ambrose agreed to let Travis take the course. How could he turn on us like that?"

"I don't know," Howard answered. "I can't even get near his office to see him, let alone ask."

"Me, neither," Charlie said. He felt resentment toward his great-uncle for caving into Father Vicar and his goon, surely, he had to know what was going on.

The boys rounded the corner of the abbey building and noticed the motorcade parked against the curb in front of the Abbey. Neither of them said a word while they passed. Charlie tried to discreetly look into the back seat of the last car but the tinted windows only cast his reflection back at him.

"Maybe if Brother Claude lets us out of class early, we can see if my idea works," Charlie said when they entered the side basement door.

"Good morning, boys," Father Ignatius greeted while he stood in front of the door to the museum.

"Good morning, Father," they answered in unison.

"Hey, Father," Charlie said, pausing for a moment. Howard continued on his way to class. "How's it coming?"

"Oh, good, good," Father Ignatius answered while he unlocked the door. "Just finishing up some of the displays. The museum should be ready for our grand opening at Oktoberfest."

"I can't wait. If you need any more help, let me know."

"I will, Master MacCready."

The old monk entered the dark museum and closed the door behind him. Charlie waited until he saw the light turn on through the opaque glass window in the door before he continued on his way to class.

Howard was sitting by himself in the back of the room while Dougary and his two goons yammered on about nothing important. Charlie ignored them and took his seat.

"So, what's up with Iggy?" Howard asked.

"Nothing. He said the museum is going to open in September. Hey, I wonder if he might know what was out on Black Butte?"

"He is the historian around here. You should ask him."

"I will," Charlie said and looked at Travis, Austin and Dougary. "What's going on here?"

"They're just being obnoxious. I have half a mind to drop out of this class."

"Howard, you can't!" Charlie gasped. "You've wanted in this class for years."

"I know, it's just these imbeciles are ruining it for me."

"Ignore them," Charlie said.

Brother Claude entered the room and the noise died instantly. Travis, Austin and Dougary took their seats.

"Good morning, boys. Did you all finish your assignments?"

"Yes, Brother Claude," everyone answered.

"Splendid. Today we will go over the steps of developing

your film. Everyone, take out your manuals and we'll begin."

Charlie found it hard to concentrate. He kept mulling over Howard's threat to quit the course. Howard had been trying to get into this class for as many summers as Charlie knew. It was all he talked about. Quitting was never an option for him in anything, even when it resulted in him getting in trouble. Charlie couldn't help but think there was something else bothering Howard.

The morning slipped by without anyone developing their film. Brother Claude lectured and then read from the manual before giving everyone a second tour of the darkroom. With the lights on, the darkroom appeared as big as their classroom. There were two workstations set against each of three walls. A supply cabinet with the developing solutions and another of photo paper and unexposed film sat against the fourth wall to the right of the door. The boys quickly claimed their stations. Howard and Charlie took the stations on the wall opposite the door, Dougary and Austin claimed the two stations on the wall to the right, leaving Travis the station of his choice on the remaining wall.

"Whenever you enter the room to develop your roll of film or make prints, lock the door behind you." He closed the door and locked it. "Since light will destroy your film, the first thing you will want to do is prepare your station. Make sure you have your film canister, scissors and developing tank with the lid off and the reel removed. Set them out so you can easily find them in the dark. Then, turn off the lights," Brother Claude instructed while he flipped the switch. The room was plunged into darkness. Charlie heard a rustling sound. "It's all right," Brother Claude continued. "Your eyes will adjust to the darkness in a few seconds. In the dark, you will open your small canister of film and carefully transfer the film to the developing tank reel. Once the film is on the reel, put it into the tank. Then put the lid on and turn it until it locks in place. Your developing tank is now light-tight and it's safe to turn on the lights." Brother Claude flipped the switch and the bright lights came on. "Now, what did I say?"

One at a time, the boys answered by repeating the instructions back until Brother Claude was sure they had it.

"There is a lot of money in supplies locked up here," Brother Claude said and patted the supply cabinet door. "Heads will roll if these instructions aren't followed. Is that understood?"

The boys answered in unison. "Yes, Brother."

After practicing the transferring process several times using exposed film, class was dismissed. Howard and Charlie headed outside behind the others.

"I don't know if I'll ever be able to work in the dark," Charlie said.

"Brother Claude said we will practice some more before we use real film. You'll get the hang of it."

Once they reached the corner of the abbey, they noticed the motorcade was gone but Rick and Gus were sitting on the front steps under the portico.

"Wonder what they're doing?" Howard said.

"Dunno," Charlie answered.

As the boys drew nearer, Rick and Gus stood up.

"It's about time!" Rick said, sounding impatient.

"We just got out of class," Howard said. "And why aren't you guys still in your class?"

"It was canceled," Gus answered.

"Canceled?" Charlie asked.

"Yeah, Father Mark took three of the guys out, that just left Gus and me. So Sister Beatrice canceled the class for today," Rick said.

"Who did he take?" Howard asked.

"Toby from Saint Sebastian and Eric and Frank from Saint Thomas."

"Wonder what he wanted them for?" Howard said.

"I don't know, but they came out a while ago with suitcases and a car took them away." Rick said.

"What kind of car?" Howard asked.

"One with wheels."

"Don't be a smart ass, Walters," Howard said.

"Well, how should I know. It was dark green. There was a logo of a pine tree or something on the door."

"What's going on?" Gus said, looking at Charlie and then at Howard.

"How should we know?" Charlie asked.

"I thought you two had an in with Abbot Ambrose?"

"You know we haven't been able to see him. And no, we don't," Howard answered, sounding annoyed.

"We're just as much in the dark as you guys," Charlie said. "Have you ever seen that car before? Is there anything else you remember about it?"

"No. Oh, it was a station wagon."

"What about the driver?" Howard asked.

"It was a woman, sort of heavyset and ordinary, just your type, Howie," Rick said and laughed.

The bells in the tower began to strike.

"We better get to lunch."

The boys climbed the front steps and rushed down the hall to the refectory. They made it just as Father Vicar opened the doors. He scowled at Charlie and Howard as they passed in front of him.

After the prayer, the boys took their seats. Charlie looked at the head table. Most of the chairs were empty, and only Brother Simon and Father Vicar were present. Charlie waited for the clap from the wooden block that sat in the center of the head table, but it didn't come. It was going to be another quiet lunch. He settled back in his chair and watched the servers make their rounds with the trays of food.

With his eyes fixed on Father Vicar, Charlie leaned closer and whispered to Howard, "What is going on?"

"Beats me," Howard said quietly. "Maybe after lunch there will be an announcement."

The boys ate their meal in silence. After dessert of chocolate chip cookies, some of which Gus hid in the pockets of his cassock, they turned to face the head table.

Father Vicar stood behind his chair as did Brother Simon. They looked at the handful of boys at each table before Father Vicar opened his mouth to speak.

"There will be no announcements," he said and then offered the closing prayer.

Once Charlie, Howard, Rick and Gus were outside in the hall, Howard turned around to look at the refectory doors.

"No announcements? Can you believe that? Three boys abruptly leave and there's nothing?"

"Yeah, and where was Father Mark and the other two prefects?" Rick said.

"Let's go see if he's in his office," Howard said and led the group down the main hall.

When they reached Father Mark's office door, Howard was about to knock.

"Boys?" Brother Simon said, halting Howard's fist just inches away from the door.

"Yes, Brother Simon," the four responded as one.

"Shouldn't you be attending to your Altar Boy duties?"

"Yes, Brother Simon."

"Then, get to it."

The four boys slowly walked back down the hallway toward the refectory and staircase.

Charlie glanced over his shoulder just in time to see Archbishop Gavin and another man in a dark blue suit enter. Abbot Ambrose's office. Another man in a suit stood in the hallway outside the door. Charlie grabbed Howard's arm, stopping him.

"What?"

"You guys go on ahead," Charlie said to Rick and Gus. "We'll catch you later."

Rick turned around on the first landing and looked at them. "Oh, no you don't," he said, pulling Gus by the arm and leading him quickly back down to the main floor. "You're up to something and we want in."

Charlie looked at Howard who shrugged his shoulders as if giving in.

"Fine. Come with me, but keep quiet," Charlie said and hurried up the stairs. When they reached the second floor, he stopped and looked around the stairwell to be sure they were alone.

"What?" Howard asked.

Cautiously, Charlie walked over to the fire doors that led to the seminary classrooms. Since the fire, the glass panels had been covered on the inside with heavy sack paper to prevent prying eyes while the monks worked to repair the damage. Ignoring the sign taped to the outside of the door that warned no entry, Charlie pulled the door open a crack and listened. Silence.

"What are you doing?" Rick protested. "We can't go in there."

Charlie let go of the door, letting it close, and turned around sharply. "Hey, it was your idea to come along," he whispered harshly. "Now, keep your voice down." He turned back to the door.

Howard stepped beside Charlie. "I hate to say it, but Rick is right. What are we doing?" he whispered loud enough for only Charlie's ears.

Charlie looked at Howard. "Remember when we were in the attic, how we could hear people talking near the vents?" Howard nodded. "Well, there's a vent in Abbot Ambrose's office that joins with one on this floor. We can hear what is being said."

For a moment, the idea appealed to Howard. He smiled, but then it faded. "I don't know, Charlie. This is serious. If we are caught—"

"Since when have we let that stop us? Come on but be quiet," Charlie said and looked over his shoulder at Rick and Gus. He pulled the door open and before anyone could stop him, slipped inside.

Howard followed, as did Gus and Rick.

"I guess it was bound to happen," Howard said as stood

beside Charlie.

"What?" Charlie asked while they waited for their eyes to become accustomed to the dim light.

"You've become me."

Charlie smiled at the compliment and looked around. The entire floor of the college wing had been gutted. Only the outer walls and a row of square, steel, support pillars that ran down the center of the floor remained. The scent of stale smoke still lingered in the air and took a bit of getting used to. Gus coughed which earned him a glare from Charlie and Howard.

"I'm sorry," he whispered.

Turning away, Charlie said. "It's over there." He pointed across the floor to the grate on the wall near the exit door at the other end.

Quietly, they made their way toward it. As they drew nearer, they began hearing voices. Charlie was right. The four crouched down beside the vent in the wall and listened.

"Please have a seat," they heard Archbishop Gavin say. "Over the last several weeks, we have been discussing the problem of what to do and how to move forward. These have been rough years."

"Your Excellency," Father Mark spoke up. "The problems we have faced in the last two years have been totally unrelated. The attacks on the boys two years ago was from the father of one of our 'at risk' students. As for the fires, had the previous institution the boy attended been forthcoming with his records, we would never have permitted his enrollment. These are two random events."

"If you take out the MacCready factor," Father Vicar growled. His voice appeared louder than the others which Charlie surmised was because he was nearest to the grate downstairs.

"Pardon me?" Archbishop Gavin said, sounding confused.

"Forgive me, Your Excellency. If we look at the record of the Boys' Home you will see that our problems began when we took in Master MacCready, three years ago."

"Don't exaggerate, Vicar," Abbot Ambrose chided. "It is just a coincidence."

"Is it?" Father Vicar challenged. "The first year he was here he was nearly dropped out of the attic window on his head."

"Is this true?" the Archbishop asked.

"Yes, Your Excellency. However, what Father Vicar failed to mention, we had an uninvited guest that night who was mentally unstable. It was nothing that Master MacCready caused."

"What was he doing out of bed after lights out?" Vicar persisted.

"Vicar, that is enough!" Father Mark said sharply.

"If I may interrupt, Your Excellency," an unfamiliar deep voice spoke up. Charlie assumed it must be the Governor. "While this is all very interesting, I fail to see what it has to do with boys in my charge?"

"It's quite simple Governor, if Master MacCready were sent to a juvenile home, then our problems would cease to exist."

"Vicar, I said, that is enough!" Father Mark snapped.

"Men, brothers, please," Archbishop Gavin said, trying to calm them.

"It is obvious, you have some internal issues," the governor spoke up. "I'm not here to debate those issues. I'm here because I have met with the director of the Department of Corrections about this matter and a decision has been reached. The State is revoking your license for the Boys' Home. The boys in my charge will be relocated to another Home for Boys by the end of next week. As for the orphaned boys, they will be transferred to the facility run by the Sisters of the Blessed Virgin."

"What about our other students?" Abbot Ambrose asked calmly.

"Your license to operate your seminary high school is in place. Those boys who wish to pursue a religious life can stay."

"Does that include the boys in your charge?" Father Mark asked.

Charlie looked at Howard. He was stunned. In his wildest of dreams, he never suspected this.

Gus coughed again. All three boys cringed and looked at him.

"Sorry," he said, forgetting to whisper.

"Shhh! They can hear you!" Charlie whispered back.

"Excuse me, Father Abbot. I'll be right back."

Charlie's eyes widened at the sound of Father Vicar's voice. He jumped to his feet.

"I'll be right back, too, my apologies," Brother Simon said.

Charlie and Howard quickly made their way toward the door they had entered. When they were halfway there, one of the doors moved.

"Vicar!" Brother Simon's voice called out.

The door closed again.

Not waiting to hear what was being said, Charlie turned around and the boys rushed out the other exit to the central stairway. They didn't stop hurrying until they reached their dorm two floors up.

When they walked into Saint Nicholas, Howard sniffed the air. "Is it me or do we smell like smoke?" he asked.

Charlie sniffed his surplice. "I don't know. We better change just in case."

"That was close," Howard said while he pulled his white surplice over his head.

"I'll say. Thank heaven for Brother Simon," Charlie said as he buttoned his fresh cassock.

"Yes, it was a good thing."

The sound of Brother Simon's voice sent a jolt through Charlie's entire body. He turned around and with wide eyes looked at his prefect standing behind Howard.

Rick and Gus, dressing in front of their lockers on the same wall but on the other side of the dorm doors, tiptoed toward the exit.

"I'm not going to ask what you boys were doing on the second floor because I already know," Brother Simon said through pursed lips. "Masters Kuegle and Walters, get over here."

Gus jumped at the sound of his name and looked surprised. "How did he see us?" he whispered to Rick as they joined Howard and Charlie.

"I'm really disappointed in the four of you."

"I—"

Brother Simon held up his hand, silencing Rick. "After your hour with your assigned brothers, you boys will spend every afternoon for the rest of this week and next in work crew."

"But—"

Again, the hand raised and halted Howard this time.

"Master Miller you will be helping Brother Francis in the pig barns. Master Kuegle, you and Master Walters will report to Brother Luke in the orchards. MacCready, you will see Father Ignatius in the museum. Now, get to your duties, your brothers are waiting."

"Brother Simon, please," Charlie said, stepping away from the others and closer to the prefect.

Brother Simon stopped and turned back around. He didn't say a word. He stood, chin up, lips pursed, looking down at Charlie.

"This is all my fault," he said. "It was my idea. Don't blame the others."

Brother Simon looked at the three boys standing together behind Charlie. He took a deep breath and Charlie thought he looked as if he were thinking it over. Brother Simon looked back at Charlie. "I have spoken," he said and left the dorm.

"Damn it!" Rick cursed. "I knew it wasn't a good idea to go on the second floor. This is all your fault." Rick glared at Charlie.

"Back off, Walters. No one twisted your arm into going. In fact, you insisted on being a part of it," Howard said, defending his bunkmate. "If anyone is to blame, it's Gus."

Gus's mouth gaped open.

"Stop it, guys. No one is to blame but me. I knew the risk.

I'm sorry. It's my fault. I shouldn't have taken you there," Charlie said.

The angry look on Rick's face softened and his shoulders relaxed. "Forget it. It's not all on you. We all went along with you. It's okay. Besides, we found out what's going on."

"True," Charlie said while the four of them entered the hallway. "But we can't tell anyone what we heard, and that goes for you, too, Gus. No slip ups. If word leaks out on this, we will all be blamed. And I don't think there are enough weeks in a year for the amount of work crew we'll get. Two weeks of work crew will seem like nothing."

"Charlie's right," Howard said before they entered the monastery wing. "Not a peep."

"You got it," Rick said. "No one will hear it from me."

"Me, neither," Gus said.

"Good." Howard nodded and opened the door.

Moments later Charlie was standing outside Father Cecil's cell. He knocked on the door and it opened almost immediately.

"Hi, Father," Charlie greeted.

"Charlie?" the blind monk responded, sounding a bit confused.

"Yes, it's me."

"I, Charlie. It is I," Father Cecil corrected. "Come in."

"Thank you."

Again, Father Cecil's eyebrows pinched. He closed the door and returned to his chair. "So, why do I smell a trace of smoke on you?"

"Oh," Charlie said and sniffed his clothes. "Sorry about that."

"No apologies. I'm looking for an explanation."

"Today, three boys were called out of Gus and Rick's class. They packed their things and left with some lady. At lunch, we were hoping to find out what was going on, but Father Vicar wouldn't say. Howard, Rick, Gus and I went to ask Father Mark about it but he told us to run along. So, we snuck up to the second floor and listened through the air vent," Charlie admitted.

"So, you were eavesdropping?"

"Yes, but before you get upset with me, Brother Simon caught us," Charlie said quickly. "We all have work crew every day for two weeks."

"I see. Is that why you're upset?"

"No—well, part of it. When we were listening, I heard the governor tell Father Abbot, due to the issues here, he's closing the abbey's home for boys and sending them away."

"Oh my," Father Cecil gasped.

"But I also heard Father Vicar blame me for all of the trouble going on. Abbot Ambrose didn't say a word in my defense. Only Brother Simon told him to shut up."

"Shut up?" Father Cecil repeated.

"Not in those exact words, but that's what he meant."

"Son, don't judge Abbot Ambrose too harshly. I'm sure he has his reasons for not speaking up. Don't think it means he agrees with Father Vicar."

"Okay," Charlie answered but sounded less than fine. "The governor did say the abbey can still run its seminary high school."

"That's good," Father Cecil said.

"I suppose," Charlie said.

"What's wrong?"

"I'm worried that Howard, Gus and I will be sent away. Howard's dad doesn't want him, Gus is an orphan, and everyone thinks I'm one, too."

"Oh, dear, that is a predicament," Father Cecil said. "But I'm sure Abbot Ambrose will think of something to keep as many of you as he can."

"I hope so."

"I'm sure he will. Why don't we skip the chores today and go for a walk? I think the fresh air will do us both some good."

"Sounds good," Charlie said.

As Charlie led Father Cecil down the front steps, he noticed Father Ignatius struggling with a large flat package wrapped in brown paper.

"Father Cecil," he said to the monk holding onto his arm. "I think Father Ignatius could use a hand. Do you mind waiting here?"

"No," he answered. "Go ahead." Father Cecil gripped his cane and stood by the concrete post at the foot of the steps.

Charlie rushed down the walk to catch up with the curator. "Looks like you could use some help with that," he offered.

"Oh, Master MacCready, you are a godsend," the elderly priest said.

Charlie took the large, flat package and found it surprisingly lighter that he expected. "Another exhibit for the museum?" he asked.

Father Ignatius grinned. "Yes. I found the most amazing photograph from the night the second abbey burned. It will complete our history exhibit nicely." He led Charlie down to the basement and held the door for him.

"I can't wait to see it," Charlie said. "Maybe when I'm finished with my walk with Father Cecil, I could come down and give you a hand hanging it?"

"That would be splendid. Go ahead and set it down by the door. I can manage it from here," Father Ignatius said while he fumbled with his keys.

"Okay. I'll see you soon," Charlie said and hurried back to Father Cecil.

"What was all of that about?" Father Cecil asked while the two walked across the driveway to the Great Lawn.

"Father Ignatius has the final piece for the history exhibit in the museum."

"Oh?"

"He said it's a picture from the night the second abbey burned."

"Sounds interesting. I wish I could see it."

Suddenly Charlie felt bad for his friend. "Oh, I'm sure it's not all that great," he said, trying to backpedal and downplay the picture.

"Don't feel sorry for me," Father Cecil said. "It was only a comment."

"Okay."

The rest of their walk consisted of stopping by one of the ponds and smelling the flowers, passing by the construction zone while Charlie explained the workers' progress, and pausing to listen to the sound of baby birds calling out to their mother high up in a tree. After returning Father Cecil to his room, Charlie said his goodbye and rushed down to the museum.

"Oh, good, you haven't hung the picture, yet," he exclaimed when he entered the museum and saw the package still wrapped and laying on top of the display case in the history corner.

"I should say not," Father Ignatius said, sounding a bit offended. "I told you I would wait, and I did. Now that you're here, shall we have a look?"

Charlie stood in front of the display case while Father Ignatius walked around to the other side.

"I've been waiting for this for months. I was hoping it would be here before we opened. Just wait until you see it," Father Ignatius explained. Grabbing a corner of the wrapping he gave it a yank and ripped off a large portion of it.

"Ah," he said, and continued to unwrap his treasure. "There now. What do you think?"

Charlie's eyes widened is surprise. The picture was of a three-story building engulfed in flames. Even though it was black-and-white, Charlie could feel the intensity of the fire. He looked behind Father Ignatius at another large photo and then back at the new one.

"This the Abbey?" he asked.

"Sadly, yes. As you can see, it was taken the night of the fire that destroyed it."

"I can't believe someone actually took a picture of it."

"Oh, yes. It was big news back then. One of the town's residents was a reporter for a newspaper. He heard the sirens and followed them to the abbey. He took several pictures. After the paper ran the article, he sent the abbot the prints and negatives."

"That's incredible," Charlie said as he continued to examine the details. "Who's that?" he asked pointing to a dark figure in the lower left corner standing near the flames.

"It is not a who, it is a what. That was the statue of Saint Michael the Archangel, for whom the abbey is named."

"A statue?" Charlie said sounding confused. "But it's not in that picture." He looked up at the picture on the wall behind Father Ignatius and pointed at it.

"That's because this picture was taken before the statue was installed. See here." Father Ignatius pointed a pile of bricks beside the building. "The abbey was still under construction. If you look closely," Father Ignatius said, pointing at another spot on the photo, "you'll see the brothers were still working on the pedestal."

Charlie thought about his excursion to the ruins on Black Butte and became puzzled.

"What happened to it? Was it burned up too?"

"It might as well have been," Father Ignatius lamented. "After the fire was out, the statue was so scarred by the heat and soot that it was ruined. The abbot wanted to have another one sculpted to replace it but there wasn't the money at the time. Then, when we had the money, the sculptor had already passed away."

"I'm sorry," Charlie said, still staring at the picture. "What happened to this one? It's not there now."

Father Ignatius cocked his head and furrowed his brow while he thought.

"As I recall, several years ago, a group of students from the town's high school carried it off, though I don't know how. It must have been terribly heavy."

"Why would they do that?"

"There has always been a playful rivalry between the town's school and the abbey's. A little game of war that was usually played out on the soccer field. When we no longer had enough boys for a sports team, the rivalry ended," he answered. "I think they viewed our statue as a sort of trophy and since their school still had a soccer team, they were claiming victory and wanted it," Father Ignatius said then turned around to look at the wall. "I'll hang it up here. Hand me the hammer and the nail. They're in the box over there."

Charlie retrieved the tools and helped the old priest hang the picture. They stepped back on the other side of the display case and admired it.

"Father, do you know of something called the dark angel?"

Father Ignatius turned and gave Charlie a surprised look. "Where did you hear that?"

"I found a note stuck inside a pocket watch my grandmother gave me. On it was written, the dark angel."

"How interesting," the monk replied.

"The only thing I could find is it being a reference to Satan,"

Father Ignatius chuckled. "That's true," he said, "but, after the fire, some of the boys started calling the scarred statue the dark angel."

Charlie looked at the picture again. "Really?"

"That was until the abbot heard it and put a stop to it. He couldn't bare hearing our beloved St. Michael called by such an awful name."

"Father, did the abbey get the statue back from the boys who stole it?"

"No. Everyone the police talked to denied taking it and a search of the school property didn't turn up anything. So, without any proof, they escaped punishment and we lost our angel."

"Oh," Charlie said, feeling his hope of solving the mystery of the note disappear.

"Well, I can't stand around here. I still have work to do."

"I can give you a hand if you like."

"Splendid. You can sweep and mop the floor for me. I need

to get some more items from the attic."

"I'll get right on it," Charlie said.

An hour later, Father Ignatius returned, carrying a box of things wrapped in old newspapers. "It's looking good. If I had you for a helper, we'd be ready for our grand opening for sure." Father Ignatius said after setting the box down on a display case across the room.

"Actually, Father, you will," Charlie admitted.

"I will?"

"For the next two weeks, anyway. I got work crew and Brother Simon assigned me to help you."

"I see. Well, I won't ask what you did, but I'm glad you are here. Oh my, it's almost time for Vespers," Father Ignatius gasped as he looked at his watch. "We should lock up."

"I'm almost finished mopping," Charlie said. "I'll finish, then put the mop and bucket away. I can lock up for you."

"Oh, thank you, Master MacCready. As I said earlier, a godsend. Now don't forget to lock the door."

"I won't," Charlie said as Father Ignatius left the museum.

Charlie looked at the clock on the wall. He had a half an hour before it was time for dinner. He quickly finished his chore and stopped for one last look at the picture of the lost angel before locking the door behind him.

~§~

At dinner, Charlie was surprised when he saw Father Mark and all four prefects standing at the head table. His smile quickly faded when he saw Father Vicar glaring at him.

After the prayer, Father Mark gave the signal it was okay to talk but the boys ate their dinner in silence. Charlie stole a glance at the head table, even they weren't talking to each other. Charlie wanted to point it out to Howard but didn't dare risk it. Instead he ate his dinner and willed the hour would pass quickly.

At the end of the meal, Father Mark stood behind his chair.

Charlie felt his heart beat faster with anticipation. However, instead of an announcement, Father Mark offered the closing prayer and dismissed the boys.

"How'd it go for you guys this afternoon?" Rick asked while the four walked up the stairs.

"How do you think it went?" Howard answered. "I was up to my ankles in pig shit."

"Howard!" Charlie gasped.

"It's true. Who knew pigs shit so much?"

"Will you stop saying that before Father Vicar or Brother Simon hear you."

Howard laughed. "I don't care. Let them shovel it all afternoon and then see if they don't call it like it is."

"Well, we're in enough trouble already. We don't need any more."

"You worry too much, Charlie."

"What about you guys, how was it working in the orchards?" Charlie asked changing the subject.

"I can't believe Brother Simon would give us that assignment, the two weakest guys in the school," Rick lamented.

"We had to carry big tubs—"

"Bushels," Rick corrected Gus. "They're called bushels not tubs."

"Whatever they're called, they were still heavy," Gus said.

"What was in them?" Charlie asked.

"Apples, of course," Rick said. "Basket after basket of apples."

"What are they doing with them?" Charlie asked.

"Beats me," Gus answered. "We just had to load them onto a truck. What did you do?"

"I swept and mopped the floor. Oh, and I also helped Father Ignatius hang a picture," Charlie said.

"O-o-oh, sounds like hard work," Rick mocked.

"Hey, I said I was sorry."

"Yeah, well, forget it. I just hope these next two weeks go

fast."

Once they reached their cubicle, Howard plopped down on his bed and put his head on his pillow. Charlie sat down on his bed across from him.

"You were quiet," he said to Howard.

"Yeah, just tired."

"You're not mad at me, are you," Charlie asked.

Howard looked at Charlie. "Why would you think that?"

"Rick sounds a bit sore." Charlie glanced across the dorm in the direction of Rick's cubicle.

"Yeah, well, Rick's a big baby. He whines about everything."

"Hey, I found out something today," Charlie said.

"You did? About what?" Howard asked, still looking at Charlie.

"Hey, you two," Rick interrupted, standing at the foot of Howard's bed.

"What now, Walters?" Howard said, sounding disgusted.

"Well, if you are going to use that tone—"

"Don't pay any attention to him," Charlie said. "He's just tired from shoveling manure all afternoon. What's up?"

Rick walked into the cubicle, followed by Gus. He sat down on the bed beside Charlie and leaned forward.

"We just overheard two guys from Saint Sebastian talking. One was telling the other that Toby was transferred to Haven Wilderness Center for Boys. I assume that's where Eric and Frank went too, since they all went together."

"That must be where they are going to send all of the juvenile delinquents," Howard said.

"That was my guess, too," Rick said. "So, it's already begun. Shouldn't they make an announcement or something?"

"Who knows and who cares?" Howard said and stared at the ceiling.

"Well, you should care," Rick said. "I mean, I'm staying but you two. . .."

"Yeah, well, what can any of us do about it? It's not like

we can march in there and tell the governor or archbishop what to do," Howard said.

"You don't have to get all mad at me," Rick said. "I was just telling you what we heard."

"And thank you for that," Charlie said. "At least we know where they are sending some of the guys."

"I suppose the three of you will be going to the convent orphanage," Rick said.

"Maybe, maybe not," Howard said. "You don't know everything. Just go away."

"What do you mean by that?" Rick asked.

"I mean, get out of our cubicle!" Howard shouted and sat up, throwing his legs over the edge of his bed and bringing his face within inches of Rick's.

"Fine, shoot the messenger," Rick snapped, and stood up.

"Don't tempt me," Howard said while he watched Rick turn to leave.

"Come on, Gus," Rick said to Gus who was standing at the foot of Charlie's bed.

"But I didn't say nothing," Gus whined.

"I don't care," Rick said. "Come on. We'll find something else to do."

Once Rick and Gus were gone, Howard turned and lay back down on his bed.

"What did you mean?" Charlie asked. "About maybe?"

"Nothing. I just said it because Rick's a prick."

"Howard!" Charlie gasped.

"Well, he is," Howard defended himself.

"I know, but still . . . Hey, remember those three guys who left? They were here because it was either here or juvenile hall."

"Yeah."

"So, maybe Dougary and his goons are next," Charlie said, and grinned.

"Wouldn't that be nice."

"You don't think they'll send us away before them, do you?" As the words left Charlie's mouth, a feeling of dread swept over him. "I can't go away. How will my parents find me?"

"I don't know but don't start freaking out," Howard said, sensing Charlie's growing anxiety. "Besides, if they were going to send us away, Brother Simon wouldn't have given us two weeks of work crew."

"Hey, that's right," Charlie said. He felt his shoulders relax a bit.

"So, what was your afternoon really like?" Howard asked.

"Not bad. I was going to help Father Ignatius out anyway. So, it's not really a punishment."

"Don't let Brother Simon hear you say that."

"Oh!" Charlie gasped. "I can't believe I forgot. Here, here." He motioned for Howard to sit up and lean closer.

Howard did what Charlie wanted and sat up.

"I found out what the dark angel is," Charlie whispered, then sat back and grinned.

"You did? How?"

"That picture I helped Father Ignatius hang—it was of the second abbey on fire. There was a statue of an angel. . .." Charlie pulled the Saint Christopher medal from beneath his cassock. He turned it over and looked at the engraving. "It stood where this said."

"It did?"

"Father Ignatius said it was damaged by the smoke and soot from the fire, and some of the boys started calling it the dark angel."

Howard's eyes widened. "I assume it wasn't out there. I mean, you said there was nothing."

"Yeah, it's not. Some guys from town stole it."

"Oh," Howard said and frowned. "Guess that's another dead end."

"Yeah," Charlie agreed. "So, did you see any pigs today?"

"Besides Rick?" Howard said with a laugh.

Charlie shook his head. "Yes."

"Yeah, I saw some. There are two sows about ready to have

piglets."

"Really?"

"Yep. Brother Francis even said if it were to happen when I was there, I could give him a hand."

"I don't know if I would want to do that. My grandma's cat once had kittens and seeing that was enough for me." Charlie shuddered and gagged, pretending to nearly vomit.

"You're such a wuss. I think it sounds pretty cool. I might even take pictures of it."

"Oh gross. Who wants to see that?"

Howard laughed out loud and then a serious look came over him. "Oh crud, I forgot about our photo assignment." He grabbed his camera from the nightstand.

"What assignment?"

"We're supposed to take pictures of things, no people."

"Where was I? I didn't hear anything about an assignment?" Charlie said while he grabbed his camera from his nightstand.

"We still have a few minutes of light left outside. Come on."

"I need a roll of film," Charlie said as he hurried after Howard.

TRAVIS

A week passed. Charlie was kept busy in the museum unpacking the boxes that Father Ignatius kept bringing down from the attic, even though the curator said they were nearly ready for the grand opening. Charlie was beginning to wonder where they were going to display the stuff. They were running out of room.

Howard was having similar luck in the pig barns. The two pregnant sows still had not given birth. Howard said he was beginning to think they were just fat but Brother Francis assured him they were definitely pregnant.

Staring out the south arch of the belltower, Charlie's thoughts turned back to the mystery of the lost angel.

"Still fretting about the statue?" Howard asked as he walked across the belfry and joined Charlie.

"Yeah. I can't believe it's over and it's gone. I mean, Mr. DeVries said it led to my family's fortune."

"Didn't you tell me the police didn't find the statue at the school in town or on the property of any of the guys who took it?"

"Yeah, so?"

"So, that means it never left the abbey's property. You said

Father Ignatius told you it was heavy. Maybe they got part way and abandoned it?"

Charlie's eyes lit up with the prospect that the mystery was still alive but then it faded. "Black Butte is still off limits, and I promised Abbot Ambrose I wouldn't go out there again."

"Honestly, Charlie, sometimes I think you worry too much," Howard said, shaking his head and laughing quietly. "You said so yourself, nothing is out there, that means the statue's not there. So, we wouldn't have to go back to Black Butte. We just need to search *around* the butte."

"Oh, I get it," Charlie said.

"We could even combine our searching with taking pictures for Brother Claude's class. Kill two birds with one stone, as it were," Howard said, obviously proud of himself that he thought of it.

"Well, we can't do it today," Charlie said. "This afternoon I have to take Father Cecil for a walk and then help Father Ignatius again."

"Yeah, I have pig barn duty. Honestly, who cleans the *manure* out when I'm not there?" he said, purposely editing his comment so Charlie would freak out. "Maybe if Brother Claude lets us out early?"

"He hasn't been," Charlie lamented. "I guess we'll just have to wait until next week, when we are through with work crew."

"Yeah," Howard agreed. "Well, let's get to class."

Just as Charlie expected, Brother Claude kept them in class until the last minute.

"Honestly," Howard said while he and Charlie headed to the refectory for lunch. "I'm beginning to think B. C. likes to hear himself talk. I mean, he could have told us how to use a zoom lens in five minutes. How could he make it drag on for an hour?"

Charlie laughed. He had to agree. After the third time repeating the instructions to the class, Charlie's mind had wandered off to thinking about the lost angel. He couldn't wait for the chance to start looking for it. He even started imagining what his family fortune might be.

When they reached the refectory, the doors opened and Brother Simon stood holding it. The boys quietly filed into the dining room and took their place behind their chair at their dorm's table. Charlie looked at the head table and felt a jolt deep inside. He nudged Howard, who nodded that he had noticed, too.

Once everyone was in their place, Abbot Ambrose led them in saying Grace. The sound of wooden chairs being pulled back then scooted forward filled the refectory momentarily, then the silence returned. Charlie waited for the signal that it was okay to talk but it never came. He leaned toward Howard and was about to whisper to him when he saw Brother Simon watching him intently. Brother Simon slowly shook his head and Charlie settled back in his chair.

He looked across the table at Rick and Gus. They appeared as uneasy as he. Instead of scarfing down his lunch, Gus was taking small bites of his ham and cheese hoagie. Rick was staring at the head table while he picked at the crust on his sandwich.

Father Mark clapped the wooden block against the table, startling Charlie. All eyes turned toward the head table. Abbot Ambrose stood. Slowly he walked around to the front of the table. Charlie noticed that none of the prefects were smiling.

This is it, he thought.

Abbot Ambrose looked at the faces of his young charges and smiled but Charlie could tell it was forced. There was no joy in his great-uncle's eyes.

"I'm sure that all of you have noticed, for the past several weeks Father Mark and I have been absent from your meals due to meetings. The governor, the archbishop and the faculty have been discussing the future of our boys' home."

Charlie looked at the back of Howard's head and then Rick and Gus. They were staring intently at the Abbot. Gus looked afraid.

"I am here to inform you that some rather painful decisions have been made. The decisions affect every member of our community here."

The refectory was deafeningly silent. An overwhelming feeling of anxiety rose inside Charlie even though he knew what was coming. He began to fidget in his seat. He glanced at Rick and Gus before looking back at the abbot.

"It pains me to say, but we will be closing our boys' home."

Audible gasps echoed throughout the refectory followed by looks of confusion on many faces.

"I know," he said and blinked the tears back. "After the closing prayer, you are all to meet with your prefects in your dorm. They will provide you with further details and instructions."

Rick's hand shot into the air. Abbot Ambrose tried to ignore it but Rick began wiggling his fingers. Exasperated, Abbot Ambrose relented.

"Yes, Master Walters?"

Rick stood up. "What about those of us who are students? Is the school closing too?"

"Your prefects will answer your questions. That is all."

Charlie watched his great-uncle walk back to his chair behind the head table. Abbot Ambrose held out his hands and raised his palms toward the ceiling. The boys stood and bowed their heads.

After the prayer the boys were dismissed. Charlie looked at the head table but Abbot Ambrose was already gone. He scanned the crowd of boys leaving the refectory but didn't see his great-uncle anywhere.

"Where are you going?" Howard called to Charlie when they reached the main hall.

Charlie stopped and turned around.

"I need to talk to Abbot Ambrose," he answered.

"But we're supposed to meet with Brother Simon in the dorm. We can't miss it or we'll be in big trouble. We can see the abbot later. Okay?"

"Fine," Charlie relented. He followed Howard up the stairs.

Once in the dorm, the two headed for the lounge in the center. Brother Simon stood, back straight, head held high and a clipboard in his hands. He made a checkmark motion on the paper when he saw them.

"Hello, Brother Simon," Howard said as he slipped past the prefect. He stopped in front of his favorite chair and stared at the younger boy who was sitting in it. The boy hesitated for a moment and then jumped up and claimed the other chair at the opposite end of the sofa.

Charlie sat down on the end of the sofa nearest Howard. Gus plopped down between Charlie and Rick. The remaining four boys either sat on the floor stood behind the sofa. No one said a word. They all looked worried and a bit fearful of what Brother Simon was about to say.

Brother Simon looked down his crooked nose at the boys and gave a hint of a smile. He set the clipboard down on the old steamer trunk that served as a coffee table and then straightened back up. He clasped his hands together as if he were about to say a prayer but quickly hid them beneath his habit.

"I see you are all present, so we can dispense with roll call," he said in his usual cold tone.

"You all heard Father Abbot's announcement, so I am left the task of informing you of what this will mean. The Abbey is in the process of restructuring. We will no longer serve as a boys' home. This means that the following boys will be leaving us tomorrow: Master Campbell, Master Edwards, and Master Thompson. The three of you will need to pack your things tonight. Tomorrow you will be taken to Haven Wilderness Center."

"A juvie home?"

"Yes, Master Thompson," Brother Simon said. "I know it's not to your liking but it has been decided."

"But the judge said—"

"You will need to take it up with your parents or attorney. The fact remains, Saint Michael's will no longer operate a Boys

Home. Now, may I continue?"

"Yes, Brother. I'm sorry."

"The second change," Brother Simon continued, "is we will no longer serve the state as an orphanage." He paused anticipating another interruption but none came. "This means that those boys will be leaving us to go to a facility run by the Sisters of the Blessed Virgin. You will be informed as to when you will need to pack. For now, you needn't concern yourselves."

Charlie looked at Gus whose chin was quivering as though he were about to cry at any moment.

"Finally, the Abbey's high school will be renamed to Saint Michael's Seminary High School. It will be for young men who are contemplating a vocation to religious life. Are there any questions?" he asked and looked at Rick. "Yes, Master Walters."

"Brother Simon, if an orphaned boy was considering a vocation, would he have to leave?"

"That all depends, Master Walters. The boy would have to be of high school age and would have to make his intentions known to his counselor. Then, it would be up to a judge."

"Oh," Rick said.

"Any other questions?" Brother Simon asked and looked at each boy. "Very well. I will be in my office if any of you should think of something." He turned and left the dorm.

"Gus, you don't have to leave," Rick said and nudged his buddy.

"But I don't want to be a priest," Gus said, sounding almost ready to cry.

"Well, if you don't say you want to stay, then you'll have to leave," Rick said.

"I don't want to go, either."

"Then tell your counselor you're thinking about being a priest," Rick said. "Then you can stay."

"You mean, lie to a priest? Won't I go to Hell if I do that?"

"It's either that or you'll have to leave."

"I don't know," Gus said and shook his head.

Howard stood up and left for his cubicle. Charlie jumped up and followed.

"What's the matter?" Charlie asked.

"That's why all the pressure from my counselor," he said, putting his hands to his forehead and looking at the floor. He let out a heavy sigh. "Damn it, why couldn't he just tell me why he was asking."

"What are you talking about?"

"My counselor kept asking me if I was thinking about the priesthood," he answered, turning around to face Charlie.

"Howie, a priest? That's a laugh," Rick said and gave a boisterous, forced laugh.

"It's no funnier than you becoming a priest without any teeth," Howard said, clenching his fist and taking a step toward Rick.

Rick backed up, bumping into Gus.

"What about you, Charlie?" Gus asked.

"I don't know. I can't leave. What if my parents came for me? How would they find me?"

"Face it, Charlie," Rick said, standing behind Charlie, just outside of the cubicle. "If they haven't come for you by now, they never will."

"You don't know that, Walters," Howard said, raising his voice and scowling at him.

Rick looked at Howard and shrugged indifferently. "Fine, continue to stick your head in the sand, but the truth is still the truth."

"Just go away before I knock *your* head off," Howard said. "You don't know what you're talking about."

"That's what you think," Rick answered.

"Why are you being so mean?" Charlie asked.

"I'm sorry if the truth hurts."

"Well, if you don't leave, you'll be the one who's hurting," Howard said, lunging at Rick.

Rick again stumbled backward, then turned around and

quickly retreated to his cubicle on the opposite side of the dorm.

Howard returned to his bed and sat down. "Don't listen to him, Charlie. He's just a know-nothing prick."

Charlie looked up at Howard. "What if he's right? What if all of this time I've been hoping for nothing?"

"Hey, don't let him get to you."

Charlie turned away. "I need to talk to the abbot."

Before Howard could stop him, Charlie was gone.

As soon as he reached the fire doors by the stairs, Charlie heard yelling coming from inside Saint Peter dorm. The doors flew open causing Charlie to retreat to the corner between the fire doors and the broom closet.

"This is bull shit!" Travis yelled as he stormed into the hall. He slammed his fist into the wall opposite the dorm, then turned around.

"Master Bleckinger, get back in that dorm and watch your language," Father Vicar said sternly, appearing in the hallway before the dormitory doors had a chance to close.

"Why does he get to stay and I have to go?" Travis continued to yell.

"Master Bleckinger, lower your voice!" Father Vicar said calmly.

"This is a load of crap and you know it!"

"I'm warning you."

"Why? What are you gonna do? Give me work crew? Ha! I leave tomorrow."

"There are other ways to teach you respect," Father Vicar said.

Charlie was surprised by how calm Father Vicar seemed in the face of an enraged Travis.

"You still haven't answered my question."

"Since when is Master Duggan's affairs any of your concern?"

"He's my friend. Why isn't he being sent away? Why does he get to stay?"

"The decision is out of my hands. Lodge your complaint

with the Governor's office if you think it will do you any good. In the meantime, get back in there and pack your bags. You and the others are to be ready by morning."

Father Vicar stood, back rigid and straight, neck elongated for maximum height, pointing at the doors of Saint Peter dorm with his long bony fingers while keeping his other hand hidden beneath his black habit. Charlie imagined it was clenched in a fist. Luckily both were too engrossed in their argument to notice Charlie cowering by the stairwell doors.

"Fine," Travis snarled. He pushed away from the wall and went back inside the dorm.

Father Vicar started to follow but stopped. "Suppose you're happy now," he said, without turning to face Charlie.

"Me?" Charlie said. "No. Why would I be happy?"

"You've managed to single-handedly ruin what it has taken years and many people to build here. I hope you are proud of yourself." Father Vicar turned his head and glared at Charlie. "Because no one else is."

Charlie watched the priest disappear back into Saint Peter dorm. Once the doors closed, he slowly continued on his way. When he reached the first floor, he turned away from the main hall and headed for the back door. His mind was swirling with conflicting thoughts. Could Father Vicar be right? Could it be true, he was the reason for all of the changes and the boys leaving? A feeling of guilt started to grow in his chest. No matter how many times he tried to tell himself it was not true, he could not stop the feelings that began to bubble up inside of him. He looked around at the empty baseball field and forest not knowing where to go or what to do. The sound of people talking set Charlie moving in the opposite direction.

"What happened to you this afternoon?" Howard asked

while waiting in line outside the refectory doors.

"Nothing," Charlie answered, still feeling depressed.

"Well, what did Father Abbot say?"

"I don't know. I didn't see him," Charlie answered.

"He wasn't in his office?"

"I don't know."

"So, what happened?"

Charlie glanced at Travis, standing in line with the other boys from Saint Peter. He still looked upset. He wasn't talking to either Austin or Dougary. "I'll tell you later," he answered Howard. "We can talk in the bell tower after dinner."

The refectory doors opened and Father Vicar stood back, his head tilted back, his lips pressed thin, his eyes looking down his nose at the boys. Slowly, the lines began to move. Charlie avoided looking at the prefect but felt the heat of his burning glare as he passed by him.

Glancing at the head table while he stood by his chair at the Saint Nicholas table, Charlie saw the faces of the other prefects and dean. They all appeared to have the same, accusing expression. He felt his stomach tighten and his appetite vanish. Instead, the thought of eating made him feel nauseous.

"Amen," the boys said in unison and took their seats.

The clap from the block of wood against the head table came instantly. The waiter boys quickly brought the trays of food to their respective tables.

"What's up with you?" Rick asked, looking across the table at Charlie.

"I guess I'm not hungry," he answered.

"Why? What's wrong?"

Charlie looked at Rick. "I'd rather not talk—"

"You're no friend!" Travis shouted, jumping to his feet and knocking over his chair. Everyone turned to look at the Saint Peter table. "You're a traitor!" He threw a biscuit at Dougary but missed. The biscuit hit Charlie in the chest, instead.

Father Vicar appeared instantly beside Travis, his hand gripping the boy's arm tightly. "That will be enough of that," he said through clenched teeth.

Travis pulled and twisted against the prefect's hold. He shoved Father Vicar, causing the priest to lose his balance and fall backward into Brother Simon, who had come to the prefect's aid.

"Master Bleckinger, that is enough!" Father Mark said, stepping between the prefect and the boy.

Travis doubled up his fists, raring for a fight.

"I would not advise that," Father Mark said sternly.

Without saying a word, Travis swung at the priest. Father Mark ducked and grabbed Travis's arm, quickly twisting it and turning Travis around. He bent Travis over. Travis's face landed in his plate. "You're lucky you're a minor," Father Mark said. "Otherwise you'd be picking yourself up across this room."

"Let me go!" Travis screamed, his face still in his plate.

"Once the police arrive," Father Mark said.

"No! I'll be good," Travis said, sounding frightened and no longer pulling against Father Mark's grasp.

"It's too late for that."

"Please," Travis pleaded.

"When I let go of you, you will go quietly with Father Vicar to your dorm. You will collect your things and wait in the main foyer. Is that understood?"

"Yes!"

"Yes, what?"

"Yes, Father Mark."

"Very well." Father Mark gradually eased his hold on Travis's arm, letting the boy stand up.

Snickering was heard at the other tables when the boys saw Travis' face dripping with gravy and mashed potatoes. He quickly grabbed a napkin from the table and tried to wipe his face clean but only managed to smear it.

"Come on," Father Vicar growled, taking hold of Travis's arm and leading him out of the refectory. Brother Simon followed after them.

"Wow," Rick said, turning back round. "Father Mark can

sure move fast."

"He should," Howard said. "He was the state boxing champ for three years in a row when he was in college."

"Really?" Gus said, looking at the head table.

"How do you know?" Rick asked in his usual belligerent tone.

"Because, I looked him up in the library, last year," Howard said.

"Oh," Rick said. He resumed eating his meal.

"Are you okay?" Howard asked leaning toward Charlie and whispering.

"Yeah," he answered, wiping the front of his white surplice with his napkin.

The rest of the meal was uneventful. Father Mark closed with prayer and the boys were dismissed. Howard and Charlie headed straight for the attic, not telling Rick or Gus where they were going.

Charlie went straight for the north arch and looked down. The portico over the front steps blocked the view of what was beneath it.

"Do you suppose the police already took Travis away?" he asked while Howard walked up behind him.

"Probably. He sure lost it," Howard said. "I wonder what brought that on?"

Charlie turned away from the arch and walked around the bells to the south side of the belfry.

"Charlie, what's the matter?" Howard asked while he followed. "I know something's up. You haven't been this quiet since your first summer here."

"True," Charlie said. He took a deep breath and looked out at the butte. "Do you think it's my fault the abbey is having to close the boys' home and send everyone away?"

"Your fault?" Howard repeated and looked puzzled. "Why would you say or think that?"

"You heard Father Vicar."

"Yeah, but I don't pay any attention to him. He's a

pompous ass."

"Howard!" Charlie said sharply and looked at him.

"It's true. Ask anyone."

"Still. . .." Charlie shook his head. "This afternoon, when I was on my way downstairs, I saw Travis and Father Vicar arguing."

"You did? About what?"

"Travis was—is upset because he's leaving in the morning but Dougary isn't."

"He's not?" Howard interrupted, sounding shocked and surprised.

"That's what Travis said," Charlie answered and shrugged. "Anyway, Father Vicar saw me watching. Before he went back into Saint Peter dorm, he said it was my fault the abbey has to close the home and send everyone away."

"Don't be ridiculous. You don't have that kind of power. You heard the governor yourself. He decided to close it down."

"But, Brother Conrad—"

"No. Charlie, listen. You are not the cause of this. As time goes on, things change. It's no one's fault. It's just life."

Charlie nodded but still could not silence the guilt he felt.

SLIPPED

The next morning, the boys and prefects gathered on the front steps. Charlie did not sleep much the night before. He could not stop thinking that he was to blame for what was happening. He stayed back, standing to the side of the front doors at the top of the steps, watching the boys huddled on the sidewalk, their belongings in boxes or suitcases.

The sound of a bus engine growing louder caused the boys to fall silent. Across the Great Lawn, Charlie spotted the drab green school bus. He watched as it made its way along the driveway on the east edge of the Great Lawn, finally coming to a stop beneath the portico in front of him.

The door folded and two men—one dressed in a white shirt and tie, the other in a tan jumpsuit—stepped out. Abbot Ambrose shook their hands and appeared to introduce Father Vicar and Brother Simon to them. Charlie wished he could hear over the rumbling of the idling bus.

The man in tan walked to the back of the bus and opened the door. Charlie noticed there was another person inside the bus. Through the windows, he could see the man was also dressed in a tan jumpsuit. The boys lined up and one at a time, handed the man their belongings. The man passed them to the other inside the bus. Then the boy walked to the front, passing the sign painted on the side, Haven Wilderness Center, and boarded the bus. With each boy, Charlie felt worse. He saw Austin and watched him stop on the first step inside the bus. He turned and waved at someone then continued on. Charlie looked toward his right, where Austin had been directing his wave, and noticed Dougary standing away from everyone toward the west end of the abbey.

"They're really going," Howard said as he climbed the front steps to join Charlie. "It's sort of a mixed blessing. I mean, it's going to be great not having Travis and Austin here but we still have Dougary."

Charlie felt a sinking feeling in his stomach. He watched the last of the boys board the bus. The man in the tie shook Abbot Ambrose's hand again and then he boarded. The door unfolded and the engine revved. Slowly, the bus pulled away from the curb and turned around. Charlie watched it pass in front of them for the last time before it headed back up the driveway and out of sight.

"What's the matter?" Howard asked. "You look sad."

"Aren't you forgetting," Charlie said. "We're next."

"Don't remind me." Howard said, the excitement in his voice draining away like a deflating balloon. "We better head to class."

Charlie walked down the front steps with Howard, avoiding the prefects and Father Abbot. They headed to the left, toward the east end of the abbey and the side, basement entrance.

"You need to talk to Abbot Ambrose," Howard said. "Find out if there's a way we can stay here."

"I know," Charlie said. "I will try after class."

When they entered the photography lab, Dougary was already sitting at his desk. He ignored them as they took their seat. Brother Claude opened the ledger he had placed on his desk. Picking up one of the two cameras in front of him, he it looked over before writing in his ledger. He then placed the camera into a box on the floor beside him. After he finished with the second book, he closed his ledger and stood up.

"Good morning," he said, but his voice belied the cheerfulness of his greeting.

"Good morning, Brother Claude," Howard and Charlie answered.

"Please, place your assignment canister in this box and I will give you a new roll of film," he said, and handed Dougary a small box.

Dougary dropped his spent roll of film into the box and passed it back to Charlie. Brother Claude collected it from Howard, after handing him a small silver canister that contained a new roll of film.

"For your next assignment," Brother Claude said as he returned to his desk. "I want you to take pictures of something no one else has thought of or maybe even seen. That means no more pigs, Master Miller."

Charlie looked at Howard and quietly chuckled.

"And Master MacCready, try to get a little closer to your subject. Picture of landscapes are nice now and again but not every assignment and not always of the Great Lawn. Might I suggest exploring the woods or even some remote place here on the hilltop?"

Brother Claude looked at them and then at the clock that hung on the wall above his desk. "I guess that will be all. Spend the rest of the class working on your assignment. Remember, something no one else has seen."

"Yes, Brother Claude," the three answered.

Dougary didn't dawdle. He grabbed his camera and roll of film, and left the lab without another word. Howard and Charlie followed but at a distance.

When they reached the outside, Howard said, "You know, I really hated Dougary and his goons, but now, I sort of feel sorry for Dougary. Did you notice how quiet he was in there?"

"Yes," Charlie answered. "He wouldn't even look at me when I walked past him. Do you think he blames me for his two buddies leaving today?"

"Who cares? He's no one to us," Howard said.

"So, where should we go?" Charlie asked when they reached the outside.

"Maybe we should start looking for your lost angel," Howard suggested.

"But where to begin?"

"Where was it seen last?" Howard asked.

"Out on Black Butte."

"Then, we should start there."

"But we will get in more trouble if we're caught," Charlie said.

"You heard Brother Claude. He practically gave us permission. I mean, surely no one has taken pictures on Black Butte before."

"I don't know," Charlie said while he continued to follow Howard to the road that led out to the butte.

"Honestly, Charlie, sometimes you worry too much," he said and slipped past the gate and sign that read no trespassing.

"It's my job," Charlie said with a laugh as he quickly followed, glancing over his shoulder to make sure they were not seen.

"It sure seems like it," Howard teased while they made their way along the overgrown road.

The trees eventually gave way to an open field as the road dipped down and started up again. At the top of the mound was the location of the second abbey and its burned-out remains. The boys stopped before reaching them. Howard raised his camera and focused on the mound of stones beneath the collapsed arch that was once the main door. Charlie heard the click and wished he had thought of it first.

"Brother Claude's gonna be so happy to see this. Though I think I will go by the barns and snap a couple pictures of some pigs, just to tease him," Howard said and laughed.

"Hey, any news on the piglets?"

"No, Brother Francis is still insisting it should be any day now," Howard said, "but, I'm not holding my breath. He said that last week."

"True," Charlie said. "So, now which way do we go?"

"Well," Howard said looking around. "If I were stealing a statue, I would avoid the road. It's too easy to get caught. I'd go. . .that way." He pointed east, downhill toward the forest. "It looks like a truck could fit through there."

"Okay," Charlie said.

The boys headed across the side of the butte toward the spot Howard had pointed out.

"You said Father Ignatius told you the police couldn't find the statue, so I'm guessing they would have ditched it somewhere on the hill," Howard said to fill the void while they clomped through the tall grass and weeds. "Hey, watch out," he warned. "There could be snakes out here."

A shiver ran up Charlie's back. He loathed snakes almost as much as spiders. Now on high alert, he searched the ground around them as they walked.

They reached the woods and started along what appeared to be a trail.

"See, what'd I tell you?" Howard said.

"We haven't found it, yet," Charlie reminded him. "Besides, this path is too narrow for a truck, or haven't you noticed?"

Howard frowned at Charlie. "Yeah," he said.

The two walked in silence while they trudged through the undergrowth, following the narrowing path as it headed back toward the abbey. Charlie stopped and grabbed Howard's arm. He put his finger to his lips and then pointed at a deer in the distance. Slowly he raised his camera and snapped a picture. The deer looked at them and then ran away.

"That is so cool," Charlie said. "I bet no one else will have a picture of a deer."

"Except me," Howard said. "I hope it turns out."

"Howard," Charlie groaned.

The two continued along the path. Before they knew it,

they were at the back of the new seminary building built on the side of the hilltop at the east end of the abbey building. Howard glanced at his watch.

"Time for lunch," he announced.

"That was some walk," Charlie said when they reached the sidewalk in front of the new building. "I still have five pictures to take."

"We can get those after lunch, and after you see Father Abbot," Howard said.

~§~

The refectory was shockingly empty. Charlie felt his guilt return when he saw how few boys there were left. He took his place at the Saint Nicholas table. There were only six boys including him at the table. There were fewer at the Saint Thomas and Saint Sebastian tables. Saint Peter table had the most boys with eight. Charlie's appetite began to wane.

After the prayer, Charlie took his seat. He looked at the head table and noticed a stereo had been placed on a stand beneath the curtain. Father Mark turned it on and instantly the soft sound of an instrumental recording filled the room.

"You may visit while you eat your meal," Father Mark said to the boys before taking his place at the head table.

"Wow!" Howard said. "Everything is changing so fast."

"Because of the stereo?" Rick scoffed.

Charlie glared at Rick. "Why do you have to be such a jerk about everything?"

Rick looked at Charlie with a shocked expression. "I don't know what you mean? I'm not being jerk."

"Yes, you are," Charlie said. "If you can't say anything nice, then don't say anything at all."

"Or how about, just don't say anything, period," Howard said.

"I wonder where they got that stereo?" Gus asked.

"It's not mine, if that's what you're thinking," Rick said.

"Yeah, it's a lot nicer," Howard said.

"Not funny, Howie," Rick sneered.

"Hey, Gus, how was basket weaving class?" Charlie asked.

"It's over," Gus said. "Sister Beatrice decided to cancel the rest of the class. She doesn't think we're good enough."

"Really? She can do that?" Howard asked.

"Apparently, so," Rick answered. "She's funding the class and sells the baskets at Oktoberfest. Since it's just Gus and me left, she thinks the sisters would do a better job making baskets on their own."

"I'm sorry," Charlie said.

"I'm not," Gus said. "She's mean."

The boys finished their meal and after the prayer, were dismissed.

Howard and Charlie headed straight for Abbot Ambrose's office. Charlie felt nervous. His hand trembled when he knocked on the door.

"Ave," came the response from inside.

Charlie looked over his shoulder at Howard.

"I'll wait out here," he said. "Go."

Charlie took a deep breath and opened the door.

"Ah, son, come in," Abbot Ambrose said in a cheerful voice.

"Hello," Charlie said and entered the office.

Howard sat down in one of the chairs by Father Mark's office, across the hall from the abbot's. He closed his eyes and before he realized it, was asleep.

"Come on, Howard," Charlie said, shaking Howard's shoulder.

"Wha—what?" Howard said as he awoke. "You're done already?"

"Yeah, it's been nearly half an hour. You fell asleep."

"I just closed my eyes for a second," he said. He stood up and looked at his watch. "Wow, I guess I did."

"Come on. Let's go outside and get some fresh air," Charlie said.

"Well, someone is sounding more cheerful. I take it things went well in there?"

"Yeah," Charlie said and pushed the front door of the abbey open. "Father Abbot said I'm not a ward of the state. My grandmother signed over guardianship of me to my—Abbot Ambrose."

"My?" Howard stopped and looked at him. "Is there something you aren't telling me? Is there some connection between you and Abbot Ambrose?"

Charlie looked around nervously. He could not believe he made that mistake. He looked at Howard. "Let's get walking. I'll explain."

The two headed down the stairs and then across the Great Lawn. The sound of a car on the driveway heading to the abbey caught Howard's attention.

"Look at that beauty," he said.

Charlie looked at the car and shrugged.

"It's a Cadillac DeVille. Man, would I love to have one of those," Howard said.

"You?" Charlie said. "I didn't know you were into cars."

"Not just any car. Cadillacs," Howard said. He watched until the car passed out of sight. Turning around, the boys resumed walking. "So, what's the deal with you and the abbot?"

Charlie swallowed. "If I tell you, you have to promise not to say a word to anyone."

"Sure, okay," Howard said.

"No, promise," Charlie said.

"Fine, I promise."

"Cross your heart and hope to die?"

"What? Am I two, Charlie? I said, I promise."

"Fine," Charlie said. "Abbot Ambrose is my great-uncle."

"What?" Howard said and stopped. "No, he's not. You're pulling my leg."

"No, I'm serious. He's my grandmother's brother."

Howard's mouth gaped open. He looked back at the abbey and then at Charlie. "Seriously? He's your uncle?"

Charlie nodded. "But he told me not to tell anyone, especially Rick."

"Oh, yeah, Rick would love this. No, your secret is safe with me," Howard said.

The boys continued walking past the new gymnasium site and across the driveway to the woods.

"Did Abbot Ambrose say anything about me?" Howard asked.

"No."

"Did you ask about me?"

"Yes, but he wouldn't say," Charlie answered. He raised his camera and took a picture of a bird sitting on a tree branch. "But, remember last night, Rick told Gus he needed to tell his counselor he was thinking about being a priest so he could stay."

"Yeah, I remember," Howard answered, sounding depressed.

"That's what you need to do, tell your counselor you want to be a priest."

"I can't. Remember I said my counselor kept asking me that?"

"Oh, yeah."

"Well, I was adamant and told him there was no way I wanted to be a priest. So, I'm doomed."

"You can tell him you changed your mind," Charlie said, trying to sound positive.

"No," Howard said and shook his head. "He'd never believe me."

"Then you can tell Abbot Ambrose."

"Abbot Ambrose is my counselor," Howard said.

Charlie felt his jaw drop. He looked at his best friend and didn't know what to say.

Howard nodded when he saw Charlie's expression. "I'm doomed."

"Maybe not," Charlie said. "Talk to him. Tell him you want to stay."

"Okay, but I'm not going to hold my breath," Howard said.

He looked at his watch. "Oh, no. It's time for work crew. We better get going."

The boys turned around and headed back to the abbey.

Helping in the museum wasn't as much fun as it had been. Charlie kept thinking about Howard and his predicament. Heading back to his cubicle after helping in the museum, Charlie stopped at Abbot Ambrose's office. He knocked and listened for a reply but none came.

Walking up the stairs to the fourth floor, he thought of another idea. With renewed hope, he picked up his pace. Moments later he was standing in front of Brother Simon's office. He knocked. The door opened almost immediately.

"Master MacCready," the stern-looking monk said when he saw Charlie.

"Hi, Brother Simon. May I talk with you a moment?"

"Sure, come in," he answered and walked back into his office.

Charlie followed him, closing the door. The office hadn't changed at all since Charlie visited last. The end of the large oak desk sat against the wall to the left of the doorway, creating a narrow passageway into the rest of the room. Behind the desk, covering the entire wall, was a built-in bookcase with doored cabinets along the bottom. There were no plants, personal photographs, or knickknacks of any kind, only a few books. Charlie recognized Brother Simon's prayer book and Bible. The binding was the same as his great-uncle's.

"Have a seat," Brother Simon said, standing behind his desk and gesturing toward the two chairs beneath the window across from the door.

Charlie sat down.

"Now, what did you want to speak to me about?"

"I just have a question. The other day when you told us about the changes in the school, you mentioned—" Charlie suddenly felt nervous and looked at the floor.

"You want to know if you are leaving?" Brother Simon

offered.

"No," Charlie answered and shook his head.

"Okay, then what is it?"

"If a person who said he doesn't want to be a priest, now says he changed his mind, would he be able to stay?"

"Is this about Master Miller?"

Charlie looked surprised. "Yes," he admitted.

"It would depend on his motives, I supposed. Is he just saying it now because he doesn't want to leave, or is he truly genuinely considering a vocation? Chances are it's the former, in which case he would not be permitted to stay."

"So, his leaving isn't for sure?"

Brother Simon frowned and looked at Charlie. "It's really none of our business."

"But he's my best friend—"

"I'm aware of that and I'm sorry, but this change is hard for us all."

"Yes, Brother Simon."

"Now, if that is all. . .."

Charlie jumped to his feet. "Thank you, Brother Simon," he said and left.

Howard sat up on his bed when Charlie walked into their cubicle.

"So, how was the museum?" Howard asked.

Charlie sat down on the edge of his bed. He looked at the floor and then at Howard. "It was okay," he said. "How about the pigs, any piglets yet?"

"No, but one of the sows is getting close," Howard said.

"How can you tell?"

"I can't, Brother Francis said she was."

"Oh," Charlie said. "So, any thoughts about what you are going to do about. . .?"

"I stopped by Abbot Ambrose's office."

"You did? I knocked on his door but there was no answer."

"That was you?" Howard said.

Charlie looked surprised. "You were inside?"

"Guess so."

"So, what did he say?"

"He said he's working on it. Whatever *it* is," Howard said.

Charlie smiled. "I knew he wouldn't send you away."

"Yeah," Howard said. He pulled out a tattered comic book from the stack on the lower shelf of his nightstand. Opening it, he rolled onto his back and held it above his face.

Charlie put his camera down on his nightstand and pulled out his pad of stationary. Settling down on his bed, he began a letter to his grandmother.

By the time Charlie had finished his letter, it was time for dinner. He sealed the envelope and placed a stamp on it. Tucking it into the pocket of his cassock, he and Howard headed for the refectory.

Music from the stereo greeted the boys when they walked into the dining room. Charlie was surprised to see the tables were no longer in long rows. They were separated and placed randomly around the main floor. Only the four tables nearest the head table were set for dinner.

Charlie followed Howard to where the Saint Nicholas table used to be. They were joined by the other four members from their dorm. The other boys looked confused but stood by their respective tables.

At the head table, Father Mark turned the stereo off before facing the boys. He offered no explanation for the change in the table arrangement but said Grace, after which the boys took their seats.

"What's going on?" Rick asked, leaning over his plate.

"Beats me," Howard said.

"I don't like this," Gus said. "What's happening?"

"It's going to be okay, Gus," Howard said.

"Did you talk to your counselor?" Charlie asked.

"Yeah," Gus answered. "I don't want to talk about it."

"What did he say?" Rick asked, pressing the issue.

Gus didn't look at him. Instead he used his fork to move a piece of cooked mushroom toward the edge of his plate. "He said I should probably prepare myself to leave, but he would do what he could.”

“What sort of answer is that?” Rick snapped.

“The same one everyone is getting, I guess,” Howard said. “Just because you say you want to stay doesn’t mean you get to. A judge or someone still has to agree to it.”

Rick looked at Charlie. “So why aren’t you worried?”

“He’s staying,” Howard said. “His grandma gave Abbot Ambrose legal guardianship of him.”

Charlie looked at Howard, his mouth open in shock.

“Interesting,” Rick said. “So, why is that? I mean, what’s the connection?”

“Drop it,” Charlie said.

“Oh, defensive,” Rick said, eyeing him suspiciously. “There must be something—I mean, your grandmother must know the abbot.”

“You’ll never figure it out,” Howard said. “So, do like Charlie said and drop it.”

“You know!” Rick said. “You and the abbot are related.”

“No,” Charlie said but heard his voice crack.

“Aha! What is he, your uncle? No, that can’t be right. He’s too old. He’s your great-uncle?”

“Drop it, Walters,” Howard said.

Charlie felt anxious. His stomach fluttered and he felt weak and on the verge of panic. He was not supposed to tell anyone.

“I’m right!” Rick announced.

“Keep your voice down,” Howard growled after glancing at the head table. “Or I’ll bust your nose.”

“You don’t scare me, Howie,” Rick said, but lowered his voice. Turning back to Charlie, he said, “Why didn’t you tell us? That explains a lot.”

“Does it?” Charlie asked. “Just what does it explain?”

“How, after being here for only two months, you were named to the Altar Boys Club, for starters.”

“Big deal,” Howard said.

“It is a big deal, Howie. Gus had to wait—”

"Leave me out of this," Gus interrupted. "I don't care if he is or isn't, Charlie."

"Thanks," Charlie said.

The refectory door opened and a brother walked, going directly to the head table. He whispered something to Father Mark. Father Mark looked in the direction of the Saint Nicholas table and whispered something back. The brother then came over to Howard.

"Master Miller, Brother Francis wants you to come to the pig barns immediately. It's time," he said.

"Oh!" Howard gasped. "Here, Gus, you can have the rest of this if you want." He pushed his plate toward the center of the table. "I'll catch up with you later, Charlie. Don't let Walters bully you."

"Not to worry," Charlie said, and watched Howard rush out of the refectory.

FRIENDS

At breakfast the next morning the refectory was back to normal. The boys laughed and talked freely while they ate. Even Rick seemed in a better mood, kidding with Gus and not grousing about some insignificant issue.

"I wish I hadn't used up all my film taking those pictures in the woods yesterday," Howard lamented while he dipped the tip of his toast into the wet yolk of his fried egg. "One of the sows finally gave birth to eight piglets."

"When did you get back to the dorm?" Rick asked.

"It was late. After lights out."

"I know," Charlie said. "I heard you come in but I was too tired to wake up."

"Sorry about that."

"So, how many babies did the pig have?" Gus asked.

"The sow had eight piglets. Brother Francis said it was a small litter. Her last one was twelve."

"You are joking!" Rick said.

"Nope. It's true," Howard said. "Brother Francis thinks the other sow will have her litter soon, and since she's younger she might have a lot more."

"Wow," Gus said and picked up a piece of bacon. He

started to take a bite, but stopped and stared at it.

"What's the matter?" Rick asked.

Gus looked at him. "You don't think this is one of the pigs, do you?"

"Yes," Rick answered.

Gus dropped the bacon back onto his plate.

"Where do you think bacon comes from?" Rick said with a laugh.

"I know where it comes from, but I didn't think it was from someone I might have met."

"Eat it, Gus," Howard said. "I'm sure it wasn't from any of the pigs we've seen. When they butcher a pig, it takes a long, long time before it's ready to eat."

"Really?" Gus said and looked at Howard.

"Yes," Howard said and took a bite of his bacon.

Gus hesitantly took a bite.

The rest of the meal passed uneventfully. After the closing prayer, Charlie and Howard grabbed their cameras and headed to their class.

"So how long does it really take before pig meat is ready to eat?" Charlie asked.

"Not very long, maybe a week or two," Howard said.

"So, you lied to Gus?"

"It was either that or have him never eat ham again," Howard said. "Today, I'm gonna ask Brother Claude for an extra roll of film to have on hand for when the sow gives birth. Brother Francis said he's going to let me know."

"Cool," Charlie said.

The morning seemed to pass quickly for Charlie. He developed his roll of film and was only halfway through making prints of them when Brother Claude announced it was time to clean up. When Howard asked Brother Claude for an extra roll of film, Brother Claude announced to all three of them he would no longer be handing out film. If they wanted film, they just needed to help themselves from the rolls in the supply cabinet.

As they headed up the walk from the basement, Rick

came running up to them. He was out of breath and looked worried about something.

"What's the matter with you?" Howard asked.

"There you are!" he said, panting and out of breath. "Where've you been?"

"We had photography class, remember?" Charlie said.

"Oh, who cares about that," Rick snarled. "Honestly, you two are such clods. The whole world could be caving in and you'd be standing by taking pictures."

"What's your problem?" Howard said.

"Gus is in his cubicle, packing."

"What? Why?" Charlie said.

"Why do you think, because he's leaving," Rick said. "But I thought. . ."

"Well, do something!" Rick said and looked at Charlie. "Like what?"

"Talk to your great-uncle. Get him to let Gus stay."

"I don't have—"

"Don't play dumb," Rick interrupted. "Everyone knows he'll listen to you. You have to do something or Gus is leaving for good."

Charlie looked at Howard for help but Howard only shrugged.

"Give it a try," he said.

"Okay," Charlie agreed. "I don't know if it'll do any good."

"It has to. He's my friend," Rick said.

When they reached the first floor of the student wing, Charlie stopped in front of Abbot Ambrose's office and knocked.

"Ave," came the familiar response from inside.

"We'll see you at lunch," Rick said and tugged on Howard's arm.

"Cowards!" Charlie whispered loudly then opened the door. Abbot Ambrose was seated in one of the two chairs across from his desk. The floor lamp between the chairs was on and he had an opened book in his lap. He closed it and set it on the small table beneath the lamp. Charlie stepped inside and closed the door behind him.

"May I talk to you?" he asked.

"Of course, son. Have a seat." Abbot Ambrose motioned to the empty chair beside his.

Charlie sat down but leaned forward resting his forearms on his knees.

"So, how was your morning? Did you and Master Miller visit the newborn piglets this morning?"

"No. We had to develop our film from yesterday."

"Oh, I see," Abbot Ambrose said and ran his hand over his short, white beard. He looked over the top of his half-moon spectacles at Charlie.

Charlie felt a wave of nervousness sweep over him. He rubbed his hands together and looked at the floor. "Father Abbot, can I ask you a question?"

"You may."

"Why is Gus leaving?"

Abbot Ambrose removed his glasses and set them on top of the book on the table beside him.

"Have you talked with Master Kuegle?"

"No," Charlie admitted.

Abbot Ambrose frowned sympathetically. "You should talk to him."

"But I thought if someone said they wanted to be a priest they could stay."

"Son, as I said before, it's complicated and there's a lot more to it than just making the statement," Abbot Ambrose said. "When a boy makes that claim, I petition the court for legal guardianship of him. The judge will interview the boy as well as his counselor before he makes a decision. It could take months. While the petition is pending, the boy will be permitted to stay here."

"So, why is Gus packing?"

Abbot Ambrose smiled again. "I understand your

concern, son. Truly, I do. That is something you should ask Master Kuegle.”

“But you can’t send Gus away, he’s my friend.”

“Son, I’m not sending anyone away. Master Kuegle asked to leave. He has made it clear that he doesn’t want to pursue a vocation and that he would be happier moving on.”

“No,” Charlie said.

“I’m sorry, that is the truth.”

“Can’t you stop it?”

“I’m sorry, there is nothing I can do.”

“I thought you were my friend. I thought you understood,” Charlie said and stood up. He headed for the door.

“This is out of my hands, son. Surely you see that?”

“I guess,” Charlie said jerked the door open and nearly slammed it shut behind him. He ran down the hall to the stairs. When he reached the fourth floor he was out of breath and still upset. He could not understand how his great-uncle could sit idly by and do nothing to stop his friend from leaving. Charlie had to see Gus to let him know that he tried.

Rick met Charlie at the door, frantically wringing his hands and looking harried. “So, how did it go? What did he say? Is he going to do something?”

“Nothing,” Charlie said.

“What? What do you mean, nothing? He said nothing or isn’t going to do anything?” Rick said, looking confused.

“Guess you were wrong. I don’t have an in with the abbot,” Charlie said and took a step away from Rick. “He said he can’t do anything to stop Gus from having to leave.”

“No. No. No. No. No,” Rick repeated, becoming more distressed. “He has to do something. Gus is my friend. He can’t leave. You’re lying!”

“No, I’m not,” Charlie answered and noticed Gus standing in the lounge. Charlie felt his anger at Abbot Ambrose wain. “I’m sorry, Gus. I tried.”

“You have nothing to apologize for,” Gus said. “I didn’t ask you to talk to him.”

"I know," Charlie said. "He told me you asked to leave."

Gus nodded. "I did."

"What?" Rick shrieked. "Why would you say such a thing?"

Gus took a step back. "Because it's true. Remember last year, I was ready to leave. I didn't want to be here."

"But you didn't leave. You are still here," Rick said.

"But my feelings haven't changed. Rick, I don't want to be a priest. I'm not like you. I'm here because my parents are dead. This isn't my home and I don't want it to be."

"But—"

"There's no use in putting off the inevitable. I want to get it over with. That's why I'm leaving tomorrow morning when a group of us move to the new place. Besides, everything is changing here. It's not the same."

"But, Gus, you're my friend," Rick protested. His voice quivered as his eyes filled with tears.

"It's okay. We can still write to each other."

"Of course, we can and will," Charlie said.

~§~

After lunch, Howard disappeared. He told them he would see them in the bell tower. Minutes later, Charlie stood, looking across the Great Lawn at the north arch of the tower with Gus and Rick.

"I'm really going to miss not being able to see them finish the gym," Gus said. "You'll have to take pictures and send me some," he said to Charlie.

"You can count on it."

"Hey, there's that car again," Gus said, pointing at the Cadillac driving along the east edge of the Great Lawn.

"Again?" Charlie asked. "How many times have you seen it?"

"Oh, nearly every day this week," Gus answered.

"Funny, Howard and I saw it for the first time, yesterday."

"I wonder who it is?" Rick said, leaning out to watch it until it disappeared beneath the portico below.

"Well, whoever it is, they must see either Father Mark or the abbot."

"How do you know?"

"I saw him go into the student wing yesterday."

The sound of someone coming up the steps below caused the three to turn around. Howard poked his head up through the trap door. He looked around and spotted them.

"Can I get a hand here?" he asked. He hoisted a paper bag through the opening and set it on the floor of the belfry.

Charlie quickly retrieved it.

"Here," Howard said and handed another bag up.

"What is this?"

"It's a little something from Sister Margaret Mary," he said while he finished climbing into the belfry. "This bag is for you to take with you," he said to Gus. "And this bag is for us all, now."

Gus opened the bag. His eyes lit up. "Really? All of this is for me?"

"Yes," Howard said, and laughed. "Sister Margaret said she couldn't send you away on an empty stomach."

Gus took a large sugar cookie from the bag and bit into it.

"You just ate," Rick complained. "How can you still be hungry?"

"I'm a growing boy," he said with his mouth full.

Howard and Charlie laughed.

The boys spent the rest of the afternoon playing tag on the Great Lawn and poking around the construction site.

"Too bad they closed up the tunnels," Gus said. "I would have loved to take another look at them."

"After the fires, it was too dangerous," Howard said. "Plus, when they dug for the foundation, part of the tunnel caved in.”

"I know," Gus said. "Oh well."

The four headed back to the abbey.

"You know what I'll miss the most?" Gus said while they walked.

"What's that?" Howard asked.

"Helping you and Charlie solve your mystery."

"Mystery?" Rick scoffed. "Don't be ridiculous. No one cares about Charlie's stupid note or his key."

"Tell that to Mr. DeVries," Howard said. "Or Mr. Duggan, or Mr.—"

"All right, all right," Rick interrupted. "So, a few losers but no one else."

"Don't worry, Gus, I'll write to you about what's going on and when we do solve it, I'll let you know."

"Good," Gus said. "Hey, have you found out any more about the dark angel?"

Charlie filled Gus in on the statue and how he and Howard have been combing the woods looking for it.

"How do you even know it's still on the hill?" Rick asked in a condescending tone.

"We don't know for sure, but the police didn't find it at the boys' high school at any of their homes, so it must still be here somewhere."

"I think you're nuts. If you ask me, you are wasting your time."

"No one is asking you, Walters," Howard said and took another cookie from the bag.

~§~

That night, while Howard climbed into his bed, Charlie rolled over onto his side and looked at him.

"That was a really nice thing you did," he said.

Howard pulled his blankets over himself and took a deep breath. "Yeah, I guess. I'm really going to miss him."

"Me, too."

"I just wish it were Walters who was leaving. I'm sick of his snide remarks and attitude. He seems to think he's better than us because he has parents."

"Yeah, but they're getting a divorce," Charlie said.

"I don't blame them. They're probably doing it to get away from him!"

Charlie quietly snickered. "That's horrible."

"Charlie, I really hope Father Abbot won't make me leave," Howard said. "I really want to stay here. This is my home."

"I know," Charlie said. "I feel the same way. Maybe you could talk to him again?"

Howard yawned. "Yeah, well, goodnight."

~§~

The next morning, the summer sun rose over the top of the trees to the east. The dew on the Great Lawn glistened. The air was scented with the exhaust from a bus that idled beneath the portico. The Blessed Virgin's Home for Children was painted in black letters along the side, beneath the windows.

Charlie stood beside Howard with Rick and Gus, away from the other boys. A stocky nun, wearing a short, brown veil and matching brown dress that came to her mid-calf, stepped down from the bus. She shook Abbot Ambrose's hand and then looked at the boys gathered behind him. Charlie couldn't hear what was being said. The nun continued to smile so it couldn't be too bad.

"She looks nice," Rick said to Gus.

"Yeah," he answered, less than enthused.

A few minutes later and the boys who were leaving were seated on the bus. Gus looked out the window and waved at Charlie, Howard and Rick. They waved back. The bus began to move. Charlie watched it until it disappeared behind the gymnasium. He looked at the handful of boys still standing on the front steps.

"You should get to your classes," Father Mark said in a loud voice. "Master Walters, I could use your help."

The boys dispersed quickly. Charlie and Howard headed to the photography lab.

"I can't believe he's really gone," Howard said while they walked.

"I know," Charlie answered. "Did you notice how few of us are still here?"

"Yeah," Howard said. "Makes me wonder what will happen to the school."

"It will be smaller, that's for sure."

CHANGES

That afternoon, after lunch, Charlie headed straight to Father Cecil's room. Since Gus left after breakfast, Charlie had been purposely avoiding returning to his dorm. He did not want to see Gus's empty cubicle.

Charlie knocked on the door. As always, it opened immediately, as though the monk were standing on the other side waiting for him.

"Master MacCready, come in," the blind priest greeted.

Charlie followed him into the room, closing the door behind them.

"I hear you had a pretty rough morning," he said and sat down in his comfortable chair by the window.

"Gus and the other boys left today," Charlie answered and sat down on the chair at the small table to the left of the door.

"Master Miller?"

"He's still here. Howard said Abbot Ambrose told him he's working on something. So, it appears Howard's going to get to stay."

"Well, that's good news." Father Cecil smiled but continued to stare at the wall above his bed.

"Yes."

"But something is still bothering you." His smile faded.

"Gus said something yesterday that struck a chord. He said with all the changes happening here, it no longer felt like home."

"Is that how you feel?"

"Yes."

"Son, in life, change is the one thing you can count on. Nothing ever stays the same. For example, when you came here, you were twelve, right?"

"Yes."

"Now, you're nearly sixteen."

"In a couple months," Charlie interjected.

Father Cecil smiled again. "Yes. The point is, you've changed since you've been here. You're not the same, are you?"

"I guess not," Charlie said, though he felt the same, inside.

"The same is true for everything around you. Look at the hilltop. Is it the same?"

"No."

"Exactly. So, change is just part of life."

"I suppose so. It's just that it hurts, sometimes."

Father Cecil nodded. "Yes, it does. But consider this, when you lived with your grandparents, it was just you and them. When you came to live here, you had to adjust to living in a dorm with several other boys. It took time to get used to your changed circumstance. And, it will take time now."

"Is it always going to be this hard?"

"That depends on you, son," Father Cecil said. "If you resist change in your life, it will always be hard, but if you embrace it, you will find it easier to take."

Charlie nodded as he let the priest's words sink in.

"You are going to be okay," Father Cecil added. "Trust me on this."

"I do," Charlie said. "I guess I should get busy."

After his time with Father Cecil was finished, Charlie hurried downstairs to the basement to help Father Ignatius in the museum. He was excited, because this was his last day of work crew, and in two short hours he would free again.

Father Ignatius was outside the museum, locking the door when Charlie entered the basement. He looked up and smiled. "Hello, Master MacCready. I won't be needing you today. The brothers just gave the floor a final polishing. We're all set for the grand opening at Oktoberfest."

"Really?"

"Yes, indeed. You have been a tremendous help."

"But I still have two hours of work crew."

"Consider it done," Father Ignatius said. "You have completed your task. If anyone should ask, refer them to me."

"I will," Charlie said, grinning happily.

"Enjoy your afternoon," the curator said. "I must be going."

Charlie rushed out the door and into the bright sunlight of the afternoon. He couldn't wait to tell Howard. He rushed up path to the sidewalk and suddenly stopped.

Parked beside the curb at the edge of the portico was the Cadillac. Charlie did not know why but the sight of the car made him feel uneasy. Slowly he walked toward it. He glanced through the windows at the interior. It was neat and clean but there were no clues as to who owned it. He headed inside.

When he reached the abbot's office, he paused and listened. Muffled voices were coming from inside but Charlie could not make out what they were saying. He continued on his way to his dorm.

The dorm looked the same as it had that morning with the exception of Gus's cubicle and a couple of the others. The beds in them were stripped of their sheets and blankets. Only a naked pillow remained. Charlie felt his mood sinking. He thought about what Father Cecil had said, that how he looked at change made it easier or harder. He decided to write Gus a letter.

When he finally sealed the envelope and put a stamp on it, he noticed it was time for dinner and Howard was still not back from the pig barns. He wondered if the sow had finally had her litter and that was why Howard was late. He put his writing pad and pen in the drawer of his nightstand and headed downstairs to wait outside the refectory.

As the boys began to gather, Charlie saw for the first time just how few of them were left. When Rick arrived, Charlie turned to talk to him.

"Have you seen Howard?" he asked.

"No. It wasn't my turn to keep track of him," Rick answered in his usual tone and turned his back toward Charlie.

"Where were you this afternoon?"

Rick turned and looked at Charlie. "That's none of your business."

"Oh, I didn't mean anything by it," Charlie apologized. He noticed the whites of Rick's eyes were red. "Are you okay?"

"What's with the interrogation?" Rick said and moved away.

Charlie looked at the other boys who had gathered for dinner. Dougary stood in the Saint Peter line in front of Ted Wilson. He looked different. His usual sneer was gone, replaced by a calm expression. In Saint Thomas line there were three boys, and another three in the line for Saint Sebastian. Dale Kaufman smiled at Charlie but did not speak. Charlie looked over his shoulder toward the back door.

"Howard, where are you?" he said to himself.

"What?" Rick snapped.

"Nothing," Charlie said.

The rustle of robes and the sound of shoes on the concrete floor caused Charlie to look down the main hall. To his relief, Howard came running into view. He pulled on his white surplice over his half-buttoned cassock and took his place in line in front of Charlie.

"Where have you been?" Charlie asked.

"Later," Howard said as the refectory doors opened.

Father Mark stepped into the hall.

"Since there are so few of us," Father Mark said. "We will have only two tables for meals. You may sit at either table but once you decide, that will become your table for the duration of summer. Please form a single line and we shall go inside."

With a little shoving and pushing, the boys came together and formed a solitary line as instructed. Father Mark turned and entered the refectory. Charlie quickly followed Howard and claimed the chair beside his, facing the head table. He watched to see who would join them.

"No," he whispered to himself when he saw Dougary heading toward them.

Dougary quietly claimed the chair at the end of the table beside Howard. Ted followed and took the chair at the other end. Dale smiled and stood at the chair across from Charlie.

"Very well," Father Mark said. "It appears everyone has made their decision."

Charlie looked at the other table and was surprised to see Rick. He was about to whisper to Howard when Father Mark started Grace.

After sitting down, Charlie nudged Howard and motioned for him to look at the other table. Howard did.

"Good," he said.

"Good? He's our friend," Charlie said.

"Look, just because he's sitting over there doesn't mean he's not our friend. It just means we won't have to listen to him whine all through dinner."

Charlie glanced at Rick again.

Dale returned from the kitchen with a tray. He set it down on the table, then placed bowls of green beans and mashed potatoes in the center. The platter of meatloaf he handed to Dougary, who took a slice and handed it off to Howard.

"What's this?" Charlie asked.

"F-f-f-family-style," Dale answered, and returned to the kitchen.

"Gus was right," Charlie said, taking the platter from Howard. "Too many changes."

"I sort of like this one," Howard said while he dished up a mound of potatoes.

"Hey," Ted said from the end of the table. "Remember there are others here who might like some too."

"I am," Howard answered, and passed the bowl to Charlie.

"So, why were you so late tonight?" Charlie asked Howard.

"The sow finally had her litter."

"That's what I figured."

"She had twelve, can you believe it?" Howard sounded amazed.

Dale returned from the kitchen and set the gravy boat and warm dinner rolls down. He set the empty tray on the chair beside him and sat down across from Charlie.

"Wh-wh-what are you t-t-t-talking about?"

"A sow had piglets today," Charlie answered.

"C-c-c-cool."

"Hey," Charlie said, turning toward Howard. "I almost forgot. When I was returning from the museum, I saw that Cadillac again. I wonder who it belongs to."

Howard seemed disinterested. He was focused on his dinner.

"I heard someone in Abbot Ambrose's office when I passed by but I couldn't hear what was being said," Charlie whispered so only Howard could hear.

"I'm sure it's nothing," Howard said.

"Well, aren't you even curious about who it is?"

"Honestly, Charlie, not everything is a mystery that needs to be solved."

Charlie sat back in his chair. "Okay," he said and pretended to eat.

"Oh, don't be like that," Howard said. "Of course, I'm curious. It's just we have a bigger mystery to solve, remember?"

Charlie nodded and relaxed.

When the boys were nearly finished with their dessert, the refectory doors opened and Abbot Ambrose walked into the room. He went straight to the head table and sat down beside Father Mark. Brother Owen brought Abbot Ambrose a piece of cake and poured him a cup of coffee.

Charlie started to say something to Howard but stopped. He did not want Howard to think he was searching for another mystery. He watched the abbot and the dean talk and laugh while a feeling of dread began to build inside him. Abbot Ambrose's presence could only mean there were more changes coming. Charlie looked at his piece of yellow cake with pineapple chunk frosting and decided he was full. He wished Gus were still there. Gus would have loved a second helping of dessert.

Once the tables were cleared and the serving boys had returned to their seats, Father Mark stood up. He turned off the music and the refectory became silent. He deferred to Abbot Ambrose who stood and walked around the table to the front. He smiled at the boys.

"Why all the worried looks?" he said. "I know this summer has been rough for you, for us all. That is why we are all taking a trip to the coast for a week."

The sound of surprise rose from the boys and brought a smile to the abbot's lips. He raised his hands to quiet them.

"The abbey has a beach house we will be staying at. While there, you will have plenty of time to enjoy the ocean and explore the town. I ask only that you behave in a manor befitting the dignity of our school and abbey."

Charlie was in shock. It was not bad news after all.

HOWARD

The afternoon sunlight filtered through the branches of the tall fir trees while Charlie and Howard made their way along a narrow path. The abbot's announcement the night before still filled Charlie with excitement.

"I still can't believe we are going to the coast," Charlie said while he followed behind Howard.

"Yeah, it'll be fun. In all the years I've been here, we've never gone to the beach," Howard said. "It'll be nice to get off this hilltop and see the outside world."

"I'll have to write my grandma."

"You do that," Howard said. "Oh, maybe you can even send her a postcard from the beach."

The boys walked a bit further, searching the woods on either side of the path.

"I honestly don't know how anyone could have carried or drug a statue through here," Howard said. He stopped suddenly and raised his camera. He aimed it at something above them. Charlie looked but couldn't see what it was. The click from the camera's shutter sent a bird flying away.

"How did you see that?" Charlie asked.

"You have to keep your eyes open."

"I am. I'm just looking for a statue."

"Well, remember, we also have an assignment due. Let's go."

A twig snapped on the path behind them. Charlie turned right as Rick, out of breath and panting, came running up to them.

"There you are!" Rick said, trying to catch his breath. "Abbot Ambrose wants to see you right away."

"Me?" Charlie asked.

"No, Howie."

Charlie looked at Howard.

"Me?" Howard said, sounding both surprised and confused.

"Unless there is another Howard Miller here—"

"Don't be a smart ass, Walters," Howard grumbled. "What does he want?"

"I'm sorry. The head of the monastery didn't feel the need to confide in me, today."

"Asshole," Howard snarled. "Stay with Charlie and make sure he finishes his assignment. Even though we leave Monday, Brother Claude wants us to turn it in."

"What?" Rick protested.

Howard stepped closer to Rick, his face within inches of Rick's. "You do it or else."

"Fine," Rick said and backed away, stepping off the path into the underbrush.

Howard turned to Charlie. "Keep looking and keep taking pictures."

"Okay."

Howard ran back up the path toward the abbey.

"So, what are you looking for?" Rick asked.

"The lost angel statue," Charlie said, looking around him at the trees and undergrowth.

"The lost angel statue? What's that?"

"It's a statue of Saint Michael according to Father Ignatius. It used to be outside the old abbey before it burned. Some guys from the high school in town tried to carry it off a few years ago, but evidently, they didn't make it. The police never found the statue when they searched the high school, or the homes of the guys."

"So, you think it's out here?" Rick said.

"I'm hoping."

"Why?"

"I think it's the same statue that the note I found in my pocket watch mentioned. If it is, it may be another clue to what this key is for."

"Oh, good grief, you and that stupid key," Rick said and shook his head.

They began walking down the path toward the bottom of the hill.

"Why does Abbot Ambrose want to see him?" Charlie asked Rick.

"As I told Miller, I don't know. When I was passing the abbot's office, Father Mark stuck his head out the door and told me to find Howard. This is nuts. How many pictures do you have left to take?"

"Three," Charlie answered.

"Let me see your camera," Rick said, grabbing the camera.

"We're not supposed to—Hey, wait a second, you're choking me." Charlie pulled the camera strap from around his neck.

Rick turned and snapped off the last three frames. "There, you're done," Come on or we'll be late for dinner and I don't want work crew because of you." He grabbed Charlie's arm and pulled him along.

In the refectory, Charlie looked at the empty chair beside him at the table. He had expected to Howard to meet up with him in line or, at least, show up a little late. As the hands on the clock continued to tick away the hour, he couldn't help but feel worried. He looked at his plate of spaghetti. It looked good but his stomach was in too many knots to eat.

"Wh-wh-what's wr-wr-wrong?" Dale asked.

Charlie looked across the table. "Nothing," he answered.

"You're worried because Miller isn't here?" Ted asked.

"Maybe," Charlie said, trying not to sound like he cared.

"Rumor has it he had a visitor," Ted said.

"A visitor?" Charlie repeated.

"Yeah, some guy," Ted said.

Charlie felt his body tense. His fork began tapping on his plate as his hand began to tremble. "Who? Wha'd he look like?"

"I don't know who," Ted answered. "As for what he looks like, I don't know, average, about Father Mark's age, I guess, dark hair. . ... He's been coming around for a few days. I've seen him before."

Charlie suddenly felt sick. He put his fork down and picked up his glass of water but his hand shook too much, splashing the table. He quickly put the glass down and began to mop up the water with his napkin.

"Is there a problem Master MacCready?"

Father Vicar's icy voice sent tiny bolts of electricity throughout Charlie's body. He looked up at the monk standing beside him and nervously shook his head.

"Very well."

"Fa-fa-father," Dale spoke up, halting the prefect from leaving.

"Y-y-yes, Master Ka-ka-kaufman?"

"D-d-do you k-k-know wh-wh-what happened to H-h-howard?"

Father Vicar looked at Howard's empty chair and smiled. "Yes, I do," he answered and walked back to the head table.

Charlie waited until Father Vicar resumed his seat. "Well, that didn't help matters."

Ted looked at Charlie and grimaced. "What did you expect him to do? Tell you?"

"No. Not really. But I thought he might," Charlie answered. He picked up a slice of garlic bread and nibbled on the crust.

Once the closing prayer was said and the boys were

dismissed, Charlie headed straight to his cubicle. When he entered the dorm, he glanced to his left at the lockers that lined the wall. Howard's locker was closed and locked. Charlie rushed to his cubicle. Howard wasn't there. His bed was still made and his well-read comic books were still stacked on the open shelf in his nightstand.

Charlie bolted from the dorm and headed to the bell tower. Howard had to be there. When Charlie crawled through the small door, he looked up and noticed the trap door in the ceiling was open. He quickly climbed the stairs.

"What's going on?" he asked when he saw Howard sitting on the floor in the corner between the east arch and the south arch. "What did Abbot Ambrose want?"

"My father," Howard answered.

"Your father? What did he want your dad for?"

"Nothing," Howard answered and shook his head. "My father wants me back."

"Wants you—but, then you're leaving?"

"I don't know."

"But, he's your dad," Charlie said and sat down beside his friend. "You have to go." The words stung Charlie's heart as he said them.

"My dad told me to think about it and let Abbot Ambrose know by tomorrow."

"Tomorrow?"

"Yeah, he's coming back then."

"Oh," Charlie said and let the idea of Howard leaving sink in.

"I don't want to go," Howard said after a bit of silence.

"But he's your dad," Charlie said even though his heart ached and tears began to fill his eyes. "You have to go."

"I told my dad I didn't want to leave you behind. If he wanted me to go, he'd have to take you. But Abbot Ambrose said no."

"He did?" Charlie said, sounding bewildered. He did not know what to say. He stared at the large metal bells that hung from the ceiling in front of them.

"It's almost time for the bells to ring," Howard said. "We should go." He stood up and held out his hand to Charlie. Helping him to his feet, the boys descended the stairs. Howard closed the trap door behind them.

"Let's go outside," Howard said when they reached the fourth-floor stairwell.

"Okay."

Once outside, the boys headed across the Great Lawn, past the construction site and into the thick woods beyond. Howard lifted the camera to his eye and snapped a picture of something. Charlie wasn't really paying attention. They walked a bit further and Howard took another picture.

"What are you doing?" Charlie asked.

"We have an assignment. I'm taking pictures and you should too."

"Of what?"

Howard let out a sigh and his shoulders slumped. "Who cares. Anything."

"I forgot to ask. How was your last day of work crew?" Howard said, changing the subject.

"Great," Charlie said. "When I showed up at the museum, Father Ignatius said it was all done and I didn't need to do anything. So, he canceled my last day of work crew."

"Lucky you."

"I suppose."

"Oh." Click. Another photograph taken. "You better hurry up and take a few pictures."

"Rick already finished my roll."

"He did what?"

"After you left, he grabbed my camera and popped off the last shots."

"I hope he doesn't get you in trouble. Remember, Brother Claude said no more landscapes," Howard reminded him.

"I know," Charlie said, now worried that Rick might have been too hasty.

They continued to walk along a narrow path until they reached the bottom of the hill at the entrance to the abbey. Howard took a picture of the sign beside the road.

"We better head back before the sun sets."

"Howard," Charlie said while they returned to the path. "Why does your dad want you to come home now? I mean, don't you find it strange how he shows up when other boys are leaving?"

"I don't know," Howard answered.

"Do you think Abbot Ambrose had anything to do with it?"

"He might, but who cares? Let's talk about something else."

Not knowing what else to say, Charlie walked behind Howard in silence.

Once they reached the Great Lawn, Howard stopped and turned around to face Charlie. "I'm going to tell Abbot Ambrose I don't want to go," he said

"You are?"

"Yes. You're my best friend, my brother. I can't leave you behind."

"But Howard, he's your dad."

"Who didn't want me and dumped me here. No, I've made up my mind. I'll tell Abbot Ambrose tomorrow morning. That way he'll know I thought about it."

Charlie nodded but still felt worried.

~§~

The next morning, Charlie waited in the sacristy for Howard. He had stopped to give Abbot Ambrose the news. Charlie glanced at Dougary who was busy pouring some wine into a cruet.

"Are you gonna help or just stand there?" he grumbled.

"Sorry," Charlie said. "I'll take it out." He picked up the small glass tray with the cruet of wine and another of water, along with a small cloth finger napkin. Slowly he made his way out to the small side-table in the sanctuary. He set it down and returned to the sacristy without looking at the congregation to see who had arrived early.

Charlie walked across the room to the hall door and stuck his head out.

"What are you doing?" Dougary asked.

"I'm looking to see if Howard is coming," Charlie answered.

"He's not scheduled for this Mass."

"I know, I just thought he'd let me know what the Abbot said."

"Forget about it and focus. We have our own duties to tend to. Now, come on."

Charlie turned away from the hall and joined Dougary by the door to the sanctuary.

Despite Dougary's order, Charlie could not focus. He mechanically went through the motions of serving Mass. His mind was fixed on Howard, worrying about what was keeping him and fearing it was not good. While the priest served Communion, Charlie searched the faces of the congregation but saw no sign of Howard.

Once the Mass was over, Charlie followed Dougary back to the sacristy. After receiving a blessing from the priest, Charlie quickly cleaned up the utensils and put them away.

"Done," he announced to Dougary who was talking to the officiating priest.

Charlie rushed back to Saint Nicholas dorm. He glanced at the lockers. Howard's door was open. The padlock, gone. He hurried to his cubicle.

Howard stood beside his bed putting the knickknacks from his nightstand into a large cardboard box.

"What's going on?" Charlie said.

"What's it look like," Howard answered while he picked up the stack of comic books. "You want these?"

"No. They're yours. Did you tell Abbot Ambrose you aren't going?"

"I did."

"So, what are you doing?"

"I'm packing."

"But you're staying."

Charlie could see the tears on Howard's cheeks and suddenly felt his own chest tightening. His mouth gaped. Howard became a blur as tears blinded him. "No, don't go," Charlie groaned.

"I have to." Howard said as his tears began to dampen his cheeks. "Abbot Ambrose said I have no choice."

"Then why did he say for you to think it over?" Charlie said as he became angry.

"It was a ruse. He said had thought I would decide to go with my dad. That's when he told me the truth, the decision was already made and I had no say. He told me to go pack my things, that my dad will be here soon to pick me up."

Charlie suddenly looked confused. Tears continued to stream down his cheeks.

"Please don't cry," Howard said through his own tears.

They grabbed each other and hugged. Neither heard Brother Simon walk up.

"Boys," he said, his voice strained.

Charlie and Howard let go of each other. They wiped the tears from their cheeks and stood at attention.

"Howard, your father is waiting downstairs."

"Okay," he answered and picked up his box. "Thank you, Brother Simon."

"Howard?" Charlie said when his best friend started to leave.

Howard stopped and turned back. "Please, write to me. I left you my address and my dad's phone number, in case you can call."

Charlie turned to look at his bed for the paper. Seeing it, he picked it up and said, "I will. I promise," he said and turned around.

Howard was gone.

Charlie made a start for the door but Brother Simon grabbed him.

"No, son," he said.

"But he's my friend," Charlie cried. "Howard, don't leave me here!"

Brother Simon wrapped his arms around Charlie and held him close.

"We have to let him go."

"No!" Charlie yelled twisting and pulling away from Brother Simon. Finally, he broke free and ran for the door.

"Charlie, stop!" Brother Simon called and ran after him.

Charlie didn't hear him. He raced down the hall and burst through the fire doors. Taking the stairs two at a time, careful not to fall, he hurried to the first floor. The soles of his shoes slipped on the polished concrete of the first floor. He caught his balance and ran for the lobby. Out of breath and gasping for air, he reached the top of the front steps beneath the portico in time to see Mr. Miller's Cadillac drive away and disappear behind the construction site.

"No!" Charlie screamed and fell to his knees while he wept.

Behind him, in the foyer, Abbot Ambrose stood watching his great-nephew. He quietly opened the door and walked outside.

"Son," he said.

Charlie turned sharply while he stood up. He glared at his grandmother's brother.

"I thought you were my friend," he said. "I thought you cared about me, but you're just like Uncle Chester. I hate you!"

Charlie saw Brother Simon coming up behind Abbot Ambrose. Not waiting, he turned and ran down the front steps and headed in the direction of the Grotto.

"Charlie!" Abbot Ambrose called out.

Charlie kept running. He didn't know where. He just knew he had to get away, to be alone.

When he reached the Grotto, he stopped and glancing back,

saw that no one was following him. He opened the wrought iron gate. The ground in front of the Grotto was covered in cobblestones with green moss growing between them. The ivy-covered stone fence had a built-in bench that faced an alcove made of larger stones. Charlie sat down and pulled his knees up to his chest. He looked up at the life-sized statue of Mary that stood in the alcove behind a newly installed sheet of Plexiglas. Her painted eyes seemed to look at him sympathetically. He buried his face in his arms and sobbed.

"I thought I heard someone," a gentle voice said.

Charlie gave a start and looked up. He wiped his eyes and tried to focus them through his tears.

"You look like someone who's lost his best friend," the young nun said.

Charlie didn't say a word. He just looked at her and tried to remember where he had seen her before.

"You know, Master MacCready, we have to stop meeting like this," she teased, her blue eyes sparkling and her pink lips spreading into a gentle smile.

That's it! She was the nun who thought I was smoking, Charlie remembered.

"Mind if I sit down?"

Charlie shrugged. He put his feet on the ground and moved over to give her room to sit even though there was already more than enough for her thin frame.

"I'm Sister Faith," she said.

Charlie looked at her. "Faith is my mother's name," he said.

"It's a fine name," she said with a smile. "So, am I right? Did you lose your best friend?" she asked, looking at him.

Charlie turned away.

"It was Master Miller wasn't it," she continued.

Charlie looked at her with surprise. "How did you know?"

"Well, it's obvious that it wasn't Master Walters because he's a student and still here. And Master Kugele has already left with the other boys."

"Yes, Howard's gone," Charlie answered and let his shoulders slump. He looked at the ground. "It's Abbot Ambrose's fault."

"Oh? Why's that?"

"Because he could have stopped it and didn't. Howard's father didn't want him. Howard told me so. So why let him have him now?"

"Well, maybe he had no choice."

"You always have a choice. At least that's what Brother Simon tells us. He's another one I'm mad at. I thought he was my friend, too. You know what he tried to do? He tried to stop me from following Howard. I didn't even get to say, goodbye. I hate them!"

"That's a bit harsh isn't it?"

"I don't care."

"Oh, but I think you do. You care very much and that's why you're so upset."

Tears returned to Charlie's eyes the more he thought about her words. His head bowed in defeat and he began to weep. "I can't go on without him, Sister."

Sister Faith moved a bit closer and put her arm around Charlie's shoulders. "You will, Charlie. You'll see. Oh, it won't be the same, true, but you'll make new friends."

Without any thought or hesitation, Charlie turned and wrapped his arms around her while he wept. She held him and let him cry.

"It's going to be okay," she cooed in a motherly tone while she patted him on the back. Softly she began to hum a song that stirred a memory in Charlie of a woman singing him to sleep at night when he was little.

~§~

The dorm was dark and quiet. Charlie had fallen asleep in the Grotto. When he woke, Sister Faith was gone. Had it been a dream? Slowly he made his way to his cubicle. Howard's bed had been stripped of its blankets, sheets and pillowcase. The sight jolted Charlie. He sat down on his bed and pulled his white surplice over his head and threw it at the partition on the other side of Howard's bed.

"Where have you been?"

Charlie looked at Rick standing at the foot of Howard's bed, dressed in pajamas. "What does it matter?" he said, sounding depressed.

"I know Howard's gone. I'm going to miss him." Rick said and ran his hand over the top of the footboard on Howard's bed. "But I'm still here. We're still friends, aren't we?"

"For how long?" Charlie said.

Rick looked at Charlie with a confused expression. "What do you mean by that?"

"Nothing," Charlie answered and shook his head. He didn't want to talk. "Just go away and leave me alone." Charlie turned his head away from Rick. I don't need any friends, he thought. They'll only leave me, anyway. He stood up and began to unbutton his cassock.

"Son," a deep but gentle voice spoke.

Slowly Charlie turned around. He looked at his great-uncle standing at the foot of the bed. Charlie clenched his teeth while his anger burned in his chest.

"Put your surplice back on and come walk with me," Abbot Ambrose invited, though Charlie heard it as an order.

Charlie angrily grabbed his surplice from Howard's bed and put it back on over his black cassock.

Abbot Ambrose held out his hand to Charlie but Charlie avoided his touch and slipped past him, heading for the door.

"This way," Abbot Ambrose said and directed Charlie toward the central staircase.

Obediently, Charlie complied and followed his great-uncle down the stairs toward the first floor and the Abbot's office. Once inside the room, Abbot Ambrose closed the door behind them and walked across the room to the two chairs that sat to the left of his large oak desk. He motioned for Charlie to sit in the other chair.

Charlie looked around the familiar office and avoided looking at the Abbot.

"Son, I'm sorry Master Miller had to leave," Abbot Ambrose said breaking the silence.

Charlie didn't answer. He tightened his jaw and continued to stare at the pictures on the wall above the other end of the desk.

"Don't you have any questions?"

Charlie turned his head and stared at his great-uncle.

"Son, please, talk to me."

"Why? Why should I? You don't care about me," Charlie snapped.

Abbot Ambrose looked surprised by Charlie's tone. "But I do, son."

"Then why didn't you stop Howard from leaving? You knew he was my best friend."

"I wish I could have—"

"His father didn't want him."

"Who told you that?"

"Howard did. He said his father stuck him here because his new wife didn't want children. He told me his father signed papers so Howard could be adopted by someone."

"I see," Abbot Ambrose nodded his head. "Well, it's a bit more complicated than that. Mr. Miller went through some rough times after Howard's mother died. He turned to alcohol to numb his pain. After several months he lost his job. With the Child Protective Services threatening to take Howard away from him, Mr. Miller brought him here."

"See, he didn't want him."

"No, Charlie, there's a difference between not wanting something and not being able care for it properly. Howard's father was grieving and had no one to turn to for help. So, he brought Howard here to me. Yes, he signed guardianship papers at the time and said if anyone wanted to, they could adopt

Howard but I realized he was speaking it out of pain."

"What about his father's new wife?"

"Howard made that up. His father didn't remarry."

"Why would he do that?" Charlie snapped.

"Son, sometimes it's easier to be angry and blame someone else for situations you have no control over, even if that person isn't real, than to be angry with the one person who is real and here."

Charlie looked away again. What his great-uncle said made sense, but he was not ready to let go of his own pain and anger.

"In fact," Abbot Ambrose continued, "Mr. Miller stayed in touch with us, checking in to see how Howard was doing. When he learned that Howard was doing well, he decided to let him stay with us."

"Then why did he come back now?"

"Because I called him."

"You what?" Charlie's voice shrieked.

"Son, you're aware of the changes happening. As I do for all of the boys in my care, I look out for what's best for each of them."

"But you said Howard's dad is a drunk. How's that doing what's best?"

"Howard's father has been sober for years now. He has turned his life around."

Charlie didn't know what to say. He was still wanted to be angry. He looked at Abbot Ambrose. "Why couldn't he stay here?"

"Because the state stepped in. It was either he went back to his father, or be sent away with the others."

Charlie felt tears pushing against his eyes. He looked away.

"Howard said you two were searching for the lost angel statue?"

"He shouldn't have told you."

"Why not?"

"Because you'll just tell me to forget about the note."

"Note?" Abbot Ambrose said.

"Yeah, the note I found in the pocket watch my grandmother gave me. It just said the dark angel."

"Are you sure that's what it said?" Abbot Ambrose asked.

"Yes, I'm sure. I asked Father Ignatius about it and he said after the fire, some of the boys started calling the statue of Saint Michael the dark angel."

"I see. And you're looking for it?"

"Yes. Mr. DeVries said it has something to do with my family's fortune."

"Did he now?"

"Yes. He's the only one who has given me a clue as to what the key is for. No one else has."

Abbot Ambrose nodded. "I know telling you from the start would have been the easy way, but you wouldn't have understood. Sometimes the wisest course is to wait, to let you discover the answers on your own. But, son, be careful. Sometimes the truth is not what we expected it to be."

Charlie eyed Abbot Ambrose. He remembered another vague clue his great-uncle had given him out on Black Butte. He looked away.

"Son," Abbot Ambrose said. "About Master Miller, believe me when I say, if there were another way to keep him here, I would have done so. But, as much as I love all of the boys entrusted to me, I know that they aren't really mine. They have been given to me on loan either by circumstances or by the state. At any moment each one of them could be taken away. It pains me to see them go, just as it pains you, but I have to remind myself to focus on the good times I've had with them and be thankful for those."

Charlie wiped the tears from his cheeks. He looked down at his feet. "May I go back to my dorm now?"

Abbot Ambrose nodded.

Charlie stood up. He walked across the room and opened the door, then stopped. "Good night, Father Abbot," he said without looking at him.

"Good night, son."

Charlie closed the door behind him.

Walking up the stairs, Charlie kept thinking about what Abbot Ambrose said, that he called Mr. Miller. Charlie no longer wanted to be there. He had the urge to call his grandmother, have her take him away from there, but knew she could not.

The dorm was quiet when he entered. The dim light from the lounge in the center of the dorm provided enough for him to find his way back to his cubicle without bumping into anything. He pulled off his surplice and laid it on Howard's bed. Charlie sat down on his own bed and picked up his camera.

Why didn't I take his picture? He quietly lamented.

He set the camera on his nightstand and in the dim light that shone through the window above his bed, he noticed something on the floor by Howard's nightstand. He bent down and picked it up. It was a roll of spent film. Howard must have dropped it, he thought. He opened the drawer in his own nightstand and dropped it inside.

BEACH TRIP

Charlie stood on the front steps of the Abbey, beneath the portico with the other boys. He clutched his tattered suitcase in his hands and took a deep breath of the crisp morning air. He could not believe that in a couple of hours he was going to see the ocean for the first time. He wished Howard were still there to enjoy it with him.

The laughter of the other boys rose above the din. Charlie turned his head to see what was so funny. Apparently, an older boy was teasing a younger boy.

"You excited about the trip?"

Charlie jumped and took a step away from Dougary. "Yeah," he said.

"Me too. You ever see the ocean?"

"No. You?"

"Once," Dougary answered and set his suitcase down. "My parents took me."

"Really?"

"Don't sound so surprised. They could be nice to me once in a while."

"Sorry, I didn't mean—"

"Forget it. They were jerks to me the majority of the

time. Anyway, that day was a good day. My dad took me out on one of those fishing boats that has a long projection on the front. You could walk out there and watch the water beneath you and all around. It's almost like flying. It was really fun. I don't think we'll get to do anything like that this time, though."

"It does sound like fun."

The Abbey's old yellow school bus sputtered and chugged along the west road toward the portico. With a loud screech and a hiss, it slowed to a stop in front of the boys. The doors opened and Brother Simon stepped out. Brother Conrad motioned for the boys to form a line at the back of the bus.

"Are you sure this bus will make it to the beach?"

"Don't worry about the bus, Vicar, she can make it." Brother Simon said.

"Before you board, make sure Brother Owen has your suitcase," Brother Conrad instructed. "He'll be loading it in the back of the bus. You'll notice we've removed several of the seats in the back to make room. So, it will be tight, some of you will have to share a seat. Remember the rules: no hanging out of the windows, no standing up or moving seats once the bus is in motion. Keep your voices down, otherwise we will make this a silent trip. Now please step forward and no pushing!"

The boys did as they were told. Charlie handed his tattered suitcase to Brother Owen, who apparently still blamed him for Dale being attacked two summers ago. He glared at Charlie and flung his suitcase through the emergency door in the back of the bus.

"Welcome to Fly-By-Night Airlines, in case of a water landing, your seat can be used as a floatation device," Ted greeted everyone from the front row seat as they boarded.

After the fifth greeting, Brother Simon turned around in the driver's seat. "Master Wilson, that is enough."

"Yes, Brother Simon," Ted answered and sat down in his seat.

Charlie stepped up, into the bus. He found an empty seat near the back, four seats behind Rick, who ignored him. He slid into his seat and looked out the window. He watched while the rest of the boys boarded the bus.

Dougary was the last one to board. Charlie looked around. All the seats were occupied, which meant someone would have to share. Charlie closed his eyes and kept repeating to himself, please not with me. He opened his eyes when he felt someone bump against him.

"I hope you don't mind," Dougary said. "No one would share with me."

"No, it's fine," Charlie answered. He noticed the empty seat across the aisle. Before he could point it out to Dougary, Brother Conrad walked up and sat down. Charlie spotted Brother Owen sitting in front, directly behind Brother Simon. "Isn't Father Vicar coming?" he asked.

"He's riding with Father Mark and Abbot Ambrose in the car," Dougary answered.

"Oh," Charlie said.

Dougary bounced on the seat and wiggled in an attempt to get comfortable. Charlie moved over, pressing himself against the side of the bus, to give him a bit more room.

"Thank you," Dougary said, and settled down.

Brother Simon looked into the mirror at the top of the windshield. "Is everyone ready?" he asked.

"Yes, Brother Simon," they all responded as one.

"Then, we're off."

The bus creaked and the engine revved. Charlie felt the bus shimmy before it lunged forward and stopped. The boys were nearly jolted out of their seats.

"It's okay," Brother Simon said. The bus began to move. Brother Simon turned the steering wheel and the bus responded by heading back along the road on the east side of the Great Lawn. Finally, they were on their way.

Charlie stared out the window at the passing trees while the bus wound its way down the long driveway toward the main road. His thoughts immediately turned to the lost angel. He wondered where it could be.

The bus sputtered and slowed. Brother Simon shifted gears and a loud noise caused Charlie to cringe.

"If you can't find 'em, grind 'em!" a boy toward the front of the bus called out while others laughed.

"That will be enough," Brother Owen reprimanded the boys.

At the end of the driveway, the bus slowed to a gentle stop. Brother Simon opened the passenger door, then closed it before turning the bus west toward town. The houses along the road didn't look all that different than the houses on Tam O'Shanter Drive, the street where Charlie had lived with his grandparents. Some had picket fences, others had wire fences and still others, none at all. One thing they all had in common was a tall shade tree in their front lawn.

"I'm sorry about Miller," Dougary said when the bus turned onto the highway, heading north.

Charlie looked at Dougary, surprised by his comment. "Really?"

"Yes. I actually liked the guy. I met him my first day here. Father Abbot had him show me around."

"Why would he have someone from Saint Nicholas do that?" Charlie said, sounding skeptical.

"I started out in Saint Nicholas dorm. I was there almost a year before I moved to Saint Peter. That was before Father Vicar was prefect and before the rivalry between the two dorms began."

"What about Saint Sebastian and Saint Thomas dorms?"

"Everyone got along back then. It was Father Vicar who started this whole superior dorm competition. If you haven't noticed, he's not a nice monk."

"Oh, I've noticed. But I thought you liked him."

"I don't."

Charlie's head jerked back in shocked surprise. "But aren't you his pet?"

"Ha! Father Vicar doesn't have any pets. He reminds us

practically daily that he doesn't like kids."

"Then why's he a prefect?"

"Beats me. I think Father Abbot asked him to do it," Dougary said with a shrug. "I'm sure Father Vicar thinks if he follows orders, he'll get to be Prior or even Abbot someday."

"That'll never happen. Abbot Ambrose would never make him Prior."

"How do you know that?"

"I don't, really. I just gather from the way Abbot Ambrose is always correcting him."

"What do you mean?"

Charlie suddenly realized that he only knew this because of his eavesdropping. He didn't dare tell Dougary the truth. "You've heard it, I'm sure. Anyway, Father Vicar is too mean."

"Tell me about it," Dougary said. "I'm glad he's not on the bus, but I'm sure he'll be trying to convince Father Mark to make him his assistant dean all the way to the coast."

"Assistant dean?"

"Yes. Father Vicar told me that one of the changes still to come is there will be an assistant dean. There won't be monk prefects once school starts. One of the seniors will be given that position for the year."

"Really?" Charlie said. He glanced out the window and then back at Dougary. "Will they stay in the prefect room?"

"I don't know all the details, just that it will be one of the students."

"There isn't a senior in Saint Nicholas," Charlie said.

"I'm sure when they assign the dorms, they'll make sure there's one."

Charlie looked at the other boys in front of him. Aside from Dougary, there were only two other boys that would be seniors starting in the fall.

"Boy, I hope Father Mark doesn't pick Father Vicar for assistant dean."

"That makes two of us," Dougary said. "So, I take it you

want to be a priest or monk since you're still here?"

"No," Charlie said and then cringed when he realized what he had just said.

"You don't?" Dougary asked, sounding surprised and a bit confused.

"Well, I don't know," Charlie stammered. "I'm still considering it." He did not dare to look at Dougary for fear that Dougary would see through his ruse. "What about you?"

"Actually, I going to submit my request to join the monastery after graduation."

"Really!" Charlie gasped. "I would have never guessed you for a monk."

"I know. I've been a bit of a jerk—"

"A bit!" Charlie scoffed.

"Okay, maybe so. But, that's not the sort of person I want to be."

Charlie listened. Thoughts of his many run-ins with Dougary and the bullies of Saint Peter dorm, Travis, Austin, and Larry, came to mind. "Well, I wish you success. I can't wait to tell Howard."

"No, don't. Keep this between you and me, please," Dougary said. "I don't want anyone else to know."

"Well, they're going to know something because you're still here."

"They only know that I'm thinking about a vocation, not the details of my plans. I don't want to jinx my chances of being accepted."

"A bit superstitious, are we?"

Dougary smiled. "Maybe a little. But, when all of your hopes and dreams get crushed, you learn to keep them to yourself."

"So, why are you telling me?" Charlie looked at Dougary.

"I don't know," he answered. "Maybe it's because I've noticed how other guys seem to confide in you."

"Oh," Charlie said. He tried to think of who Dougary

was talking about. The only boys who had talked to him were Howard, Gus, Dale and Ted. "Well, your secret is safe with me," he assured Dougary.

Charlie settled back in the seat and looked out the window. After a bit, he began to fidget. "These seats sure aren't made for long trips," he said.

"I hear that," Dougary answered and shifted in his seat.

Charlie looked at the other boys and caught bits of their conversations about building sand castles, wave jumping and collecting seashells.

Brother Owen turned in his seat so his voice would carry over the rumbling of the bus's engine. "I'll give a dollar to the first boy who sees the ocean," he announced.

Suddenly everyone on the bus became silent as they looked out the windows. Charlie looked out his but wasn't sure where or what he was looking for. The bus rounded a corner. The trees parted.

"There it is!" Ted announced, pointing straight ahead.

Charlie craned his neck to see over the heads of the other boys but he didn't see anything. No trees, no hills, just a grey-blue haze.

"I don't see anything," Charlie said to Dougary.

"Congratulations, Master Wilson!" Brother Owen announced and handed him a dollar bill.

"Of course, he'd win. He's sitting in the front of the bus," Charlie heard a boy in front of him grumble.

"A dollar," Dougary whispered out of the corner of his mouth, "big woo. Make it five or ten and that's something to get excited about."

Charlie laughed.

The bus passed a sign on the side of the road. Welcome to Look-out Bay it read.

The bus slowed and turned down a side street. That was when Charlie saw it. Directly in front of them, at the end of the road, a flat, grey-blue, undulating horizon. Charlie's mouth dropped open. His heart beat faster.

"Look, Dougary, there it is!" he said pointing at the ocean.

"Yep." Dougary answered and nodded. "That's the Pacific Ocean."

The bus turned left. Charlie looked out his window, trying to see the ocean view between the houses. The bus slowed even more.

"Everyone, stay in your seats," Brother Simon called out. "I'm going to turn the bus around."

He pulled into a short driveway and stopped. Shifting gears, the bus began to back up into the street again. When Brother Simon shifted again, the gears complained loudly. Slowly the bus moved forward and closer to the curb. With a loud screeching noise, it stopped, jolting the boys forward. A hissing sound came next and then everything was quiet and still.

Brother Owen stood up and raised his hands as if to silence the already quiet boys.

Charlie looked out his window. The bus was parked beside a retaining wall made of large stones. Above it, set back from the road, a large, weathered grey, two-story house rose. The short but wide driveway, cut into the hillside, led to a basement garage.

"When you disembark, line up at the back of the bus. Brother Conrad and I will begin unpacking your suitcases. Claim your bag before proceeding into the house. Go directly to the second floor where you will find three bedrooms. You are free to choose your own room. The bedrooms on the main floor are reserved for the dean and prefects. There will be no fighting and no saving beds for others. Is that clear?"

"Yes, Brother Owen," the boys answered collectively.

"Remember, when you are inside, keep your voices down and get settled. We will meet in the living room in thirty minutes."

Charlie sat back and waited while the other boys scrambled off the bus.

"Aren't you coming, Charlie?" Dougary invited, while

waiting for him in the aisle.

"Sure," he answered and stood up.

Outside a stiff breeze blew in from the west, across the ocean. The air smelled different than on the hill back at the abbey. It smelled clean, not at all like the fishy scent Dougary had warned him about.

Charlie heard a high-pitched noise and looked up. Seagulls hovered overhead. The sight reminded him of a scene from a movie he once saw. That scene didn't end well. Charlie quickly retrieved his suitcase and hurried into the house through the basement door.

Unlike the air outside, inside, the house smelled old, damp and musty. Charlie followed Dougary upstairs to the second-floor bedrooms. He stopped at the first room. To his surprise, it was large compared to his cubicle back at Saint Michael's. A set of bunk beds sat against the wall on opposite sides of the room. Rick turned around and looked at Dougary.

"We're full in here," he said.

"That's okay," Charlie answered and they moved to the next room.

It was the same story at the next room.

At the last room, Shawn Chambers, a senior, tried to halt them. "The room is full."

"No, it's not," Charlie said and started into the room.

Shawn stepped in front of him. "I said, there is no room."

"And I said you are a liar," Charlie responded, not backing down. "We've been to the other rooms and they *are* full. That means there are three empty beds in this room. So, move aside."

"Is there a problem here?" Brother Simon asked, standing in the hallway, behind Dougary.

"No, Brother Simon," Shawn said, and stepped aside.

Charlie entered, followed closely by Dougary.

"You two can take that bunk," Shawn said.

"That's fine with me," Dougary said and turned to

Charlie. "Top or bottom?"

"Bottom," Charlie said, and put his suitcase on the bed.

"Let's not ruin this trip with arguing," Brother Simon said. "Trust me, returning to the hill with work crew for the rest of the summer would not be fun."

"Yes, Brother Simon," Shawn answered.

Charlie opened his suitcase. He took out his camera and hung it around his neck. Walking into the hallway, he turned around and took a picture of the room before heading downstairs to the living room.

Charlie was the last to arrive. He surveyed the room. A drab green vinyl sofa sat beneath the big window that looked out over the ocean. Across from it was a matching sofa. Two reclining chairs faced a brick fireplace with their backs toward Charlie. A large console television sat in the corner between the stone fireplace and the sofa that was beneath the window. On the floor in the center of the room was a braided rug. It looked similar to the one in the lounge of Saint Nicholas dorm back at the abbey. Even the old steamer trunk-turned-coffee table reminded him of the one back home.

To Charlie's dismay, every seat was taken. He noticed Dougary leaning against the wall behind one of the recliners and decided to join him.

Brother Conrad stood in front of the fireplace. Dressed in blue jeans and a checkered short-sleeved shirt, he looked even thinner than he did in his habit. He kept looking around the room and marking a paper on his clipboard.

Charlie heard a noise and looked toward the arch entranceway to the living room as Brother Owen, also dressed in civilian attire, and Brother Simon, still wearing his habit, entered. They began handing out a slip of paper and an envelope to each of the boys.

"May I have your attention, please," Brother Conrad said in a loud voice. The room went silent. "You each have in your hands the program for this weekend's retreat."

"Retreat? I thought this was a vacation?" Shawn

protested.

"Master Chambers, another outburst like that will earn you work crew," Brother Simon said sternly.

"While this is a vacation," Brother Conrad continued. "Our service to God never takes a holiday. We will still have daily Mass along with morning and evening prayers. Now, we will go over the schedule so there are no misunderstandings. Let me warn you right now, there will be no excuses for being late or missing any of the scheduled gatherings. Is that understood?"

"Yes, Brother Conrad," everyone answered.

Charlie followed along while Brother Conrad read off the daily program. They would begin each day with Morning Prayer and then have breakfast in the basement dining room. After breakfast they would tidy up their bedrooms and the rest of the house. Mass would be held at nine in the dining room after which they would have two hours before lunch for recreation. After lunch they were be free to explore the beach or town, but everyone would meet back at the house at five for evening prayer before dinner. After dinner, they were once again free to explore, but, come sundown, they were to be back at the house and remain indoors. Lights out was still at ten.

After Brother Conrad concluded, he asked if there were any questions. Charlie looked at Rick, who did not disappoint.

"Yes, Master Walters," Brother Conrad said, not even trying to hide his exasperation.

"Brother, what is the envelope for?" Rick asked.

"I'm getting to that, Mr. Walters," he said. "Each of you have been given an allowance of twenty dollars, a gift from Abbot Ambrose. You may use it to buy souvenirs or whatever you wish."

There was the sound of ripping paper as the boys tore open their envelopes and pulled out their money. A bit of excited chatter began to rise but Brother Conrad quickly stifled it when he cleared his throat noisily.

"Before you are dismissed, lunch will be at noon. So, don't be late. Let us close with prayer."

After Brother Conrad offered a prayer, the boys quickly cleared out of the living room. Charlie lingered a moment and opened his envelope. In it he was surprised to find not twenty but thirty dollars. He approached Brother Simon.

"Excuse me, Brother Simon, I think there is a mistake."

"Yes, Master MacCready?" he said and looked at the money in Charlie's hands.

"I have ten dollars too much."

"There's no mistake," Brother Simon said. "Your grandmother sent you a little extra when she learned about the trip from Abbot Ambrose."

"She did?" Charlie said, sounding both surprised and happy.

"Yes. Now go on and have fun," he said and turned back to Brother Owen. "What happed to Vicar? I thought he was supposed to be here for this."

"I don't know. He was going to take Mark and Abbot Ambrose by the parish rectory, and then join us," Brother Conrad answered. "Perhaps he's decided to stay there?"

"What? The beach house isn't good enough for him?" Brother Simon sneered.

Charlie turned aside and went down the stairs to the basement exit. As he opened the door, a black van from the Abbey pulled into the driveway.

"Ah, Master MacCready," Sister Patricia from the abbey's kitchen called to him from the driver's side window. She opened the car door and stepped out. "You're just in time to give us a hand with unloading the van."

"Sure," he answered with a smile. "I didn't know you were coming," he said while he followed her to the back of the van.

"Who did you think was going to fix your meals?" Sister Patricia asked.

"I guess I never really thought about it," Charlie answered.

"Well, we did. We couldn't leave our boys to fend for

themselves. Take this into the kitchen." Sister Patricia handed him a wooden crate of groceries. "And snag a couple other boys, too."

"I will," Charlie said and headed back through the door.

The basement consisted of two rooms. The larger one, just inside the door, had two long wooden tables with benches for seating toward the back of the room. Toward the front, near the entry door, was a foosball table, a ping pong table and a pinball machine. A door between the two tables led to a smaller room. Charlie carried the box toward it. Inside he found a fully equipped kitchen with a commercial grill, large ovens and a double-wide refrigerator-freezer.

"You can put that down on the counter over there," Sister Faith instructed, when Charlie entered the kitchen.

"Sister Faith!" Charlie said, surprised. "What are you doing here? I mean, I didn't know you were coming."

She chuckled silently and continued to unpack a box of groceries onto the large island in the center of the kitchen. "Sister Mary Margaret asked me to help Sister Patricia," she said. "I'm happy to see you are in a better mood since the last time we met."

Charlie looked down, feeling slightly embarrassed. "I'm doing okay," he said. "I better find help."

He rushed upstairs to find someone but the house was empty. Returning to the van, Charlie noticed Sister Patricia had enlisted the aid of Dougary and Ted. Each had already been given a large box.

"There's more," Dougary said and nodded toward the back of the van.

"I see you already found help," he said to Sister Patricia while he waited for her to hand him another box. "I looked inside but everyone was gone."

"That's quite all right. Master Duggan and Master Wilson came along and I enlisted their help."

With three boys helping, the van was unloaded in no time. Sister Patricia thanked them and set them on their way.

With less than an hour before lunch, Charlie decided to write Howard a letter. He wanted to tell him about Dougary, everything except the part about his wanting to join the monastery. He returned to his bunk and opened his suitcase. Taking out his pad of paper, he settled back and began to write. When it was time for lunch, Charlie hid his money in an inside pocket in his suitcase, grabbed his letter to Howard and headed downstairs.

After lunch, Charlie asked Brother Simon where he could mail his letter.

"There's a mailbox at the end of the street. You can drop it in there," Brother Simon informed him.

Charlie lagged behind a group of boys heading down the street. They turned left toward the stairs down to the beach. Charlie spotted the large blue mailbox bolted to the sidewalk on the corner. He dropped his letter inside and then crossed the street. At the top of the wooden stairs that led down to the sandy beach, he stopped. He looked out at horizon where a blue haze disappeared into the sky. Charlie could not see where one ended and the other began. It stirred a strange feeling inside him, a feeling of being small and powerless. He noticed some of the boys playing at the water's edge and raised his camera to capture the moment but they were too far away. He looked at the stairs and suddenly felt queasy as he had been the first time Howard had taken him to the top of the bell tower. He quickly backed away. Noticing a bench on a small patch of neatly trimmed lawn to the right of the stairs, he went over to it and sat down.

High above the beach but away from the cliff, Charlie felt himself relax. A wooden, split-rail fence at the edge of the grass provided a barrier between him and the steep cliff. He looked out at the ocean and wished he had brought along a telephoto lens. He let his gaze drift down toward the waves but quickly looked up again.

"Don't look down," he said aloud to himself and grabbed the armrest.

"Why is that?" a gentle voice behind him asked.

Charlie turned, but kept his grip on the bench. "Oh, hi, Sister Faith," he said.

"I didn't mean to startle you," she said but tried not to laugh. She walked around the end of the bench and sat down beside him. "I see you have found my favorite spot," she said and looked out at the view.

"You've been here before?" he said sounding surprised.

"Oh yes, many times," She answered and smiled while she took a deep breath of the salty air. "I find when I sit here, I can't help but think of our wonderful Creator."

"God?"

"Yes. When I see the waves crash against the rocks out there," she pointed to a cluster of dark rocks jutting up out of the water in the distance, "the waves hit that rock again and again with such great power that over time it eats away the rock, reshaping it, but when the waves reach the shore, look how gently they wash across the sand. I am in awe."

"I see," Charlie answered, nodding his head.

"So, Master MacCready, why aren't you with your friends?"

Charlie looked at the boys on the beach. "All of my friends are gone," he said.

"Isn't Master Walters your friend?"

"I don't know anymore."

"Why?"

"Because he said some hurtful things and has been ignoring me."

"What was so bad?"

Charlie hesitated to answer. He put his hand over the locket beneath his shirt. "He said if my parents were coming to get me, they would have by now. Since they haven't, they aren't going to."

"I see."

"But he's wrong. They will come for me. My mom promised," Charlie said and patted his chest causing his key to hit against his medal and locket with a tink sound.

"What was that?" Sister Faith asked.

"Oh," Charlie said and pulled on the gold chain around his neck until his treasures popped up out from under his collar.

"Oh my, looks like quite a collection."

"Yeah," Charlie agreed. "My grandma gave them to me."

"That's a pretty locket. Was it hers?"

"No. It belonged to my mom," Charlie said and opened it. "She gave it to my grandmother to give to me." He took the chain from around his neck and showed the locket to her.

Sister Faith took the locket along with the other treasures. She smiled at the pictures.

"Your parents look like nice people," she said.

"Thank you. I like to think they are. My dad's name is Patrick and my mom's—well, I already told you her name is Faith. I don't remember them, though."

"Why is that?"

"I was two when they left."

"Left?"

"Grandma said they dropped me off in the middle of the night."

"I see," Sister Faith said. "I'm sorry."

"Oh, it's okay. They'll come back for me. I know they will. They promised."

Sister Faith looked at him but didn't say anything. She looked at the other objects on the chain.

"What is this?" she asked turning the Saint Christopher medal over and squinting to read what was on its back.

"It's a map," he answered. "I found the spot it leads to but there was nothing there. My grandma gave me that, too." He reached into his pocket and pulled out the pocket watch. "She also gave me this." He opened it and gave it to her.

"What a beautiful watch," she said.

"When I got it, it wasn't working. I opened the back and found a piece of paper stuck in it. On the paper was written, the dark angel."

"Oh my," Sister Faith said with a gasp.

"It's okay. Father Ignatius helped me figure it out. It refers to the statue of Saint Michael that was damaged in the second abbey fire."

"Interesting," she said.

"I haven't found the statue yet. Howard was going to help me but then—" he looked at the ground.

"Sounds like you have quite a mystery to solve," she said, handing him back his treasures. "You're a smart boy. I'm sure you'll be able to figure it out on your own."

"I hope so. I just wish Howard were still here," Charlie said, looking at the objects in his hands.

"You will be just fine. Don't give up. Search and ye shall find. That's what the Bible says and it's never wrong." She glanced at her watch. "I best be getting back to the kitchen. Sister Patricia will be needing help soon with dinner."

She stood up and left him alone with his thoughts.

~§~

That night while preparing for bed, Charlie noticed that someone had been in his suitcase. He quickly stuck his hand into the pocket where he stashed his money and found it empty.

"No!" he said out loud and looked at Dougary.

"What's wrong?" he asked.

"Someone stole my money," he said.

"You're kidding, right?" Dougary asked, climbing down from the top bunk.

"No," Charlie said. "I stuck it in here before lunch and now it's gone."

"Did anyone know you did that?"

"No. I was alone."

"We should tell Brother Simon," Dougary said.

"What's he gonna do?" Charlie said already giving into the loss and depression.

"He could ask the others."

"They aren't going to own up to it. It's gone."

"Well, I'll share mine with you."

"No, you don't have to do that."

"I know but there's really nothing I want. You could use it to get some postcards or something."

Charlie thought for a moment. It would be nice to send his grandmother a postcard. He looked at Dougary and shook his head. "No, thank you for offering."

"Well, I'm going to keep an eye out to see who seems to buying more than they should. I think we can find the culprit."

"I suppose," Charlie said.

"Lights out in ten minutes, boys," Brother Conrad said from the doorway.

"Okay," Dougary answered and climbed back up to the top bunk. "We'll figure it out, don't worry, Charlie," he said, leaning over the edge of his bed.

"Thanks, Dougary."

Charlie quickly changed and crawled into bed.

END OF SUMMER

With the beach trip now a memory, Charlie sat at his desk in the photo lab waiting for Brother Claude to arrive. He looked at two small canisters of film on his desk. One from his trip, and the other found under Howard's bed. He was not sure which he wanted to develop first.

"Hey, Charlie," Dougary said when he walked into the room. He quickly sat down in the seat that used to be Howard's and leaned across the aisle. "I just overheard Shawn talking with another kid. He was bragging about all the stuff he bought at the beach. Stuff that he couldn't possibly get for the twenty bucks we were given."

"Really?" Charlie said.

"Yeah," Dougary said and nodded. "I think we know now who stole your money."

"For all the good it does."

"Well, now at least we know who to watch out for."

"I suppose," Charlie said. He picked up the canister he found under Howard's bed and looked at it.

"What's so interesting about that?" Dougary asked.

"Nothing really. I think Howard dropped it when he was leaving. I found it on the floor by his bed."

"I see. I wonder what's on it?"

"I thought I'd develop it and make prints. Then send them to Howard as a gift."

"Good idea." Dougary said.

Brother Claude entered and closed the door behind him. "Good morning. I trust you both completed your final assignment?"

"Yes, Brother Claude," the boys answered.

"Wonderful. Before we adjourn to the darkroom so you can develop and print your film, bring your cameras up and I'll check them back in." He sat down at his desk and took out his ledger.

Charlie took the camera strap from around his neck and waited while Brother Claude checked in Dougary's camera. After nine weeks of having carrying it around, Charlie was going to miss not having it anymore.

"Very well," Brother Claude said, closing his ledger and placing the cameras in the box beside his desk. "Grab your film and let's head to the darkroom."

Charlie placed his two canisters of film on his workstation and began preparing the chemicals. He took extra care to follow the developing instructions. He did not want anything to ruin the film.

"Two rolls of film?" Brother Claude commented while he watched Charlie from a distance.

"Yes, Brother," Charlie answered.

"You may want to use another developing tank and transfer both rolls while the lights are out."

"Good idea," Charlie said. He waited for Brother Claude to walk away before he took the developing tank from Howard's old workstation. When the lights went out, he quickly transferred the two rolls of film to their canisters and sealed them.

Once they finished developing their film, Brother Claude excused himself and left the darkroom.

Charlie turned to Dougary and asked, "Since there's

only one enlarger, do you mind if I go first? I'm really anxious to see what is on this roll of film."

"You took the pictures," Dougary responded with a puzzled expression. "You should already know what's on it."

"Actually, this is the roll of film I found under Howard's bed after he left." Charlie said.

"I thought you already processed that," Dougary said. "Sure, go ahead. Mind if I watch?"

"No."

The first picture Charlie printed was of the construction site, one of the brothers was pushing a cart with sheets of plywood on it. The next was of a birdhouse nailed high up on the trunk of a tree. Charlie recognized it as the one that marked the start of the path down the hill.

"You said Howard took these pictures?" Dougary asked, looking over Charlie's shoulder at the image in the rinse water.

"Yeah," Charlie answered.

"He's really good at this."

Charlie hung the next photo to dry on the cord suspended above the printing station.

"How did he get so close to that squirrel?" Dougary said. "He makes my pictures look like a kindergartner took them."

"Mine, too," Charlie said and laughed. He continued to print several more. There were landscape shots with rays of sunlight streaming through the branches of the trees, illuminating the undergrowth, shots of birds, and even one of a small clearing.

"What was he going for in this one?" Dougary asked.

Charlie looked at the photograph. Sunlight shone through the trees and spotlighted a mound of undergrowth.

"Beats me," Charlie said. "I don't see anything interesting about that."

"Maybe you should blow it up a bit more? Focus on this area," Dougary suggested, pointing at the mound.

A few minutes later, Charlie hung the wet photo on the cord to dry and the two boys took a closer look.

"Look," Dougary said, "Something is sticking out of the bushes."

Charlie pulled a magnifying glass out of the tool drawer and took a closer look. A shiver ran down his back and into his legs.

"I can't believe it," he said out loud.

"What? What is it?" Dougary asked trying to see through the glass but Charlie quickly lowered it.

"Oh, nothing," Charlie said.

"It didn't sound like nothing," Dougary said and nudged Charlie aside. He took the magnifying glass from Charlie and used it to examine the enlargement. "You got excited about something."

"Really, it's nothing," Charlie said, feeling nervous.

"I'll say," Dougary agreed and handed the magnifying glass back to Charlie. "I don't see anything."

"I guess Howard isn't so great at taking pictures after all."

"How many more do you have to print? I've still got mine to do."

"Just five more. It shouldn't take too long," Charlie said.

"Fine. Hurry up. I'd like to finish before lunch."

"Sure thing." Charlie said.

After finishing the last five prints, Charlie collected his things and returned to his work area. Dougary took over the printing station and began making prints of his negatives.

When he finished, it was time for lunch. The boys emerged from the darkroom and found Brother Claude at his desk. He looked up at the boys and smiled.

"Finished?"

"I am," Dougary said and handed his dried prints to the monk.

"I still have to make prints of my roll," Charlie said.

"Can I come back this afternoon and finish?"

"Sure," Brother Claude said. He took a key from his pocket and handed it to Charlie. "You can leave your prints on my desk. Be sure to lock up when you leave and slide the key under back under the door."

"I will. Thank you," Charlie said and followed Dougary into the hall.

"Why didn't you just turn in Howard's pictures?" Dougary asked.

"That would be cheating," Charlie said. "Besides, Brother Claude would know I didn't take them."

Dougary laughed. "I was kidding, MacCready. I've got to run, see you at lunch."

Charlie waited by the museum door until Dougary was gone. He looked at the folder in his hand before giving the doorknob a try. Locked. He knocked. No answer.

"Dang!" he said out loud. He was hoping to run into Father Ignatius and show him the enlargement he made. He wanted a second opinion about what he saw, but the curator was not there.

~§~

After lunch, Charlie stood on the second floor of the monastery wing. He knocked on the door and it opened.

"Come in, Master MacCready," Father Cecil greeted him before turning around. Charlie was still amazed how the blind priest could walk across the room to his chair in the corner as if he could see.

Charlie entered and closed the door. The room was plunged into darkness. Charlie felt the wall for the light switch and, finding it, flipped it on.

"Ah," Father Cecil said with a smile when he heard the click of the light switch. "A bit dark in here for you?"

"Yes, Father," Charlie answered. "May I open the curtain?"

"Sure," Father Cecil said.

Charlie reached across the small table by Father Cecil's chair and opened the blind. The afternoon sunlight filled the small room. Charlie retreated to the chair at the table across the room.

Father Cecil's eyebrows raised. He nodded his head. "Something bothering you?" he asked. "Still angry at Abbot Ambrose?"

"I don't know," Charlie said, caught off-guard by the priest's perceptiveness. "I mean, yes, I'm still upset. Hurt more, I guess."

"I see," Father Cecil nodded.

"I don't know. I'm mad at Abbot Ambrose because he knew Howard was my best friend and—did I tell you he called Mr. Miller and told him to come and get Howard?"

"Yes," Father Cecil said.

"How could he betray me like that? We're fa—" Charlie stopped. He almost slipped.

"You're what?" Father Cecil said and smiled.

"Nothing," Charlie said and tried to sound indifferent so Father Cecil would not question him more. "If he were my friend, he never would have sent Howard away. He could have let Howard stay here."

"Charlie, be fair." Father Cecil turned his face toward the sound of Charlie's voice. "Deep down I think you knew this day would come. I mean, you and Howard couldn't stay together forever. In another year, you both would leave here and each of you would make your own way. Just because you're not here together doesn't mean your friendship has to end, too. You can still write to each other."

"I know," Charlie said. "It's just, now I don't have any friends."

"What about Master Walters?"

"Rick?" Charlie's pitch raised. "He's not my friend. At least, he's not acting like it."

"Oh-oh, what happened?"

"He's been ignoring me and, in the refectory, he's

sitting at another table."

"I see. And that upsets you?"

"Yes. If he was truly my friend, why would he do that?"

"Maybe he's going through a hard time himself," Father Cecil said. "Didn't his best friend leave, too?"

"Howard wasn't his best friend."

"No, Master Kuegle."

"Oh," Charlie said, and looked at the floor. "I didn't think of that."

"But there's more," Father Cecil said.

"Yes," Charlie admitted. "He said some hurtful things."

"Like?"

"He said my parents were never coming for me, and that I need to grow up and face the truth."

"I see. Tell me, are you upset because he's wrong, or is it more that you think he's right?"

Charlie's chin quivered. "I don't know," he said.

"Charlie, son," Father Cecil said in a gentle fatherly tone. "I can't imagine how you feel. But you're not a child anymore. Soon you'll be sixteen, then seventeen. You're a young man."

"You sound like Sister Faith," Charlie said.

"Sister Faith?"

"She works in the kitchen. I've talked to her a couple times."

"Does she think Rick is right?"

"She doesn't know. No one knows."

"What do you think?"

Charlie tried to swallow the lump that rose in his throat. He wiped the dampness away from his eyes. "I don't know. I just want to find out what happened. Why they had to go away and why they couldn't take me with them."

Father Cecil could hear the tears in Charlie's voice. "I wish I knew, son. I would tell you."

"I know," Charlie said.

"So, how was your last photography class?"

"It was okay. I developed the roll of film I found under Howard's bed."

"Find anything interesting on it?"

"I'll say. He took a picture in the woods of some trees and a mound. When I enlarged it, it looks like it might be the lost angel statue."

"Really?"

"Well, I don't know for sure. I need to show it to Father Ignatius, and see if he agrees."

"Why not call Howard and ask him?"

"I don't know, do you think I should?"

"He's the one who took the picture and he did give you his phone number. . .. Maybe he'll even tell you where it is so you can go take a look."

"I'll do it," Charlie said, his mood rising.

The rest of Charlie's visit passed quietly. While Father Cecil read his prayer book, Charlie busied himself tidying up the small room. All the while, he kept thinking about what Father Cecil had said. When he finished with his chores, he bid the monk goodbye and hurried back to his dorm.

Saint Nicholas was quiet and empty. Charlie went straight to his cubicle. He took the prints he made out of the pocket of his cassock and tossed them on his bed. He retrieved the slip of paper with Howard's address and telephone number from his nightstand. Rushing downstairs to the first floor, he hoped no one else would be using the phone, then he remembered that none of the other boys had anyone to call.

The telephone was in a small, paneled closet between the old college refectory and the high school's. Inside, a telephone sat on a small shelf. There was a seat, a piece of wood, affixed to the back and side wall across from the shelf so the caller could sit. Charlie had only used the phone booth a handful of times in the past three years. Even though it was big enough for two boys, Charlie still felt a little claustrophobic. He pushed aside his feelings and closed the door.

Taking the paper from his pocket, Charlie dialed the

number and waited. He'd never talked to Howard over the phone, and wondered if he would recognize his voice.

"Hello?" a familiar voice answered.

"Howard! Hi. It's me, Charlie."

"Charlie!" he said sounding excited. "It's so good to hear your voice. How are you? I got the postcard you sent me. Wow, the coast must have been fun. I'm sorry about Shawn stealing your money. You have to watch out for him. He's sneaky. I caught him several times trying to get into other people's stuff. How's photography class? How was it being alone with Dougary? Is he still a jerk now that he doesn't have his thugs around?"

"That's why I'm calling," Charlie said.

"Oh? Is everything okay?"

"Yes."

"That's good to hear."

"Howard, today I developed the roll of film you dropped. I was going to surprise you by making prints of your pictures—"

"What film? What are you talking about?"

"The roll of film I found under your bed after you left."

"It wasn't mine. I turned all my stuff over to Brother Claude before I left."

"You mean, you didn't drop it by accident?"

"No. Is something wrong?"

"No. I guess not. It's just that when I printed the negatives there was one of a small clearing in the woods. I think it's of the lost angel."

"Really?" Howard's pitch raised.

"I have to ask Father Ignatius, but I think so. The statue is covered with what looks like ivy of some sort so it's hard to tell."

"I wish I were there to help you look for it."

"Me, too," Charlie agreed. "So, how are things going with your dad?"

"Good. I'm officially enrolled in my first public high

school. It starts in two weeks."

"Yeah, that's about when the new kids are supposed to arrive. Do you think you'll come back?"

"I don't know, Charlie. My dad is teaching me to drive his car. He said when I graduate, he'll buy me a car. Won't that be neat?"

Charlie felt the familiar sinking feeling in his chest.

"After graduation we can hit the road and see if we can find your parents. Would you like that?"

"Yeah," Charlie said, trying to sound happy but inside he felt otherwise.

"My dad just walked in the door. I gotta go. Hey, I really like your letters and I will write back, I promise."

"Okay."

"Bye, Charlie. Thanks for calling."

"Bye." Charlie said, and hung the receiver back on the base. He sat still for a moment as tears blurred his vision. He rubbed his eyes and wiped them dry.

Returning to his cubicle, Charlie gathered up the photographs and put them in the drawer of his nightstand, along with the piece of paper with Howard's address. He sat on the edge of his bed and looked at the bare mattress across from him. Howard was not coming back. In the hall, the bell rang for dinner. Charlie did not feel hungry but still headed down to the refectory.

After dinner was finished, Father Mark stood in front of the head table. He looked at the boys and smiled.

"We have a final count of the number of students that will be arriving," he announced. "It's a modest forty-five, but it's a beginning," he quickly added. "So, that means the number of new boys will be nearly five to one of you. I hope we can rely on all of you to help them adjust to life here on the hill."

Charlie looked at Dougary. He was nodding his head in agreement. Charlie wondered if Dougary's transformation from bully to whatever he was now was real or just another ploy to get stick it to him somehow. He looked back at Father Mark.

"To that end, we will be rearranging the dorms. Some of you will be asked to move but all of you will be asked to pitch in when the new bunkbeds arrive. We need to remove all of the old beds—"

Charlie was confused. Lost in his thoughts about Dougary he missed part of Father Mark's announcement. What was he talking about? Charlie tried to stay focused but thoughts of Howard and the film and having to talk to Father Ignatius crept into his mind.

"That is all," Father Mark said. "We'll close with prayer."

After the short prayer, the boys all stood and made their way out of the refectory. Charlie still felt as though he were in a fog. The other boys were talking wildly with each other as they made their way up the stairs to the fourth floor.

"It'll be nice to not have to go to the dungeon for classes," Charlie heard one of the boys say.

"He said the new classrooms won't be ready until sometime mid-year," another boy said.

"What was that?" Charlie asked.

The boys looked over their shoulder at him when they reached the second-floor landing.

"Weren't you listening?" one said.

"The brothers are building classrooms for us on the second floor. We won't have to go to the basement anymore."

"When they're finished," The other boy reminded his friend.

"Oh, yeah," Charlie said, trying to cover up for not hearing the announcement.

The boys shook their head and continued up the stairs. Charlie looked at the fire doors. The glass was still covered with heavy, brown, sack paper.

Once back in his dorm, Charlie headed for his cubicle, only to be stopped when he reached the lounge in the center of the dorm by Rick.

"Where're you going?" he said in a bossy tone.

"What's it to you?" Charlie answered.

"Father Mark said we are supposed to meet with our prefect."

"Oh yeah," Charlie said, still beating himself up for not listening more closely. He sat down in the chair opposite Rick, who had taken over Howard's favorite chair, the one facing the dorm's doors.

Brother Simon walked into the dorm, clipboard in hand. He looked at Rick, then Charlie, then tucked the clipboard under his left arm.

"Our numbers have dwindled," he said, stating the obvious. "Since Saint Sebastian dorm will become our new chapel, we will be moving boys around. Master Wilson and Master Dugan will be moving to Saint Nicholas."

"What?" Rick shrieked.

Brother Simon looked at Rick. His lips pressed thin and his jaw tightened while he exhaled through his nose. It was obvious to Charlie that Brother Simon was angry.

Rick ducked and tried to sink into the chair.

"Master Kaufman and the other boys from Saint Sebastian will be moving to Saint Peter," Brother Simon continued. "Are there any questions so far?" he asked.

Rick did not dare to raise his hand. In fact, he tucked both of them under his leg and kept his head down.

Charlie raised his hand.

"Yes, Master MacCready?"

"When will they be moving?"

"They should be packing as we speak."

"Do you know which cubicles they will take?"

"I'll be posting the floorplan momentarily. You can take a look. The new beds will start arriving Monday. Therefore, we will need your help dismantling the vacant beds in here before then. The brothers will take them away so you don't have to worry about carrying them down the stairs. That is all for now."

Charlie again raised his hand.

"Yes," Brother Simon said.

"Has a decision been made about the new assistant dean?"

Brother Simon nodded. "It has, and it will be announced at the start of the school year. This evening you two can help Masters Wilson and Duggan get settled. Tomorrow we will begin clearing the beds."

"Yes, Brother Simon," both boys said while the prefect left the dorm.

"I can't believe Dougary is moving in here!" Rick spat once the door closed behind Brother Simon. "Next they'll be making him prefect."

"It won't be so bad," Charlie said. "Did you know he was originally a member of Saint Nicholas dorm?"

"No way," Rick said.

"Must have been before you came here," Charlie said. "He's really not a bad guy when you get him away from Father Vicar."

"I still don't trust him."

Charlie shrugged. He headed to the bulletin board in the lounge to check out where his new dormmates would be living.

SAINT MICHAEL'S SEMINARY HIGH

The next two weeks passed quickly. Charlie had little time to himself, let alone time to speak to Father Ignatius or search for the lost angel. He and the other boys were kept busy cleaning and preparing for the arrival of the new students.

"Slave labor," Rick muttered constantly under his breath while he cleaned the sinks in the common bathroom area of the fourth floor.

"Stop complaining," Charlie said. "At least you weren't assigned to clean the urinals and toilets." Actually, his assignment was not all that bad. Armed with gloves and a toilet scrub brush, his hands never touched anything disgusting.

At lunch, Father Mark announced that the new boys would be arriving after lunch, and everyone needed to be available to assist them. Brother Simon already gave the four members of Saint Nicholas the names of the boys they would be assigned to assist. Charlie looked at the note with his charges. He was to show them to their cubicle and locker, then give them a tour of the fourth floor. Afterward, he was to be available if any of them had questions. Charlie was not looking forward to it.

The first group of boys arrived at two. Charlie stood between Ted and Rick at the main entrance with Father Mark and Brother Simon and Father Vicar.

"What're they doing here," Rick said, nodding toward to two prefects. "I thought we were finished with them?"

"I guess until they make the formal announcement tonight at dinner, they're still on duty?" Charlie whispered back.

Two boys with matching suitcases ascended the front steps. That was not all that matched. The twins were identical, same light brown hair trimmed neatly, same blue eyes, same slender build. Charlie looked at his note and read the names Robin and Robert Muster. These have to be them, he thought.

Sure enough, Brother Simon motioned for Charlie to step forward.

"Masters Muster," Father Mark greeted the twins. "Master MacCready will show you to your dorm and help you get acquainted with your new home, at least for the school year."

"Come on, this way," Charlie said. He led them into the main foyer and through the door on the left to the student wing. "So, which one of you is which?" he asked, eyeing them.

"He's Robert and I'm Robin," one answered.

"No, I'm Robin and he's Robert," the other said.

Charlie was not amused. He nodded to himself and pulled open the fire door on the fourth floor. "To your left is Saint Peter dorm and to your right is Saint Thomas the Doubter dorm," he said as he walked down the corridor. He passed through a doorway. "This is our lounge," he said showing them the newly remodeled room. The walls had a fresh coat of off-white paint. The curtainless windows overlooked the Great Lawn. Beneath them was a two-shelf bookcase that spanned the entire length of the room. At one end was a library table and chairs. Magazines were placed in the center. At the other end was another table and chairs. Boxes of puzzles and games were placed on it. In the center were a couple sofas that faced each other and four overstuffed chairs. Charlie recognized them. One set of sofa and chairs came from the former Saint Sebastian dorm, the other was already in the lounge.

"This is the bulletin board where all the announcements are

posted along with our daily schedule. It doesn't change, so you won't have to keep looking at it once you get the hang of it." Charlie turned to face the row of sinks. "As you can see this is where everyone gets ready, brushes their teeth, combs their hair. The door there is to the showers. The other one is to the restroom," he said pointing at the doors at either end of the row of sinks.

"Everyone uses the same—" one of the twins said.

"Yes," Charlie interrupted. "Come on."

The three passed through another doorway into a hall that looked like the one by the other dorms. Charlie stopped when he reached the dorm doors. Turning to his left he said, "This is our new chapel. We meet here three times a day. In the morning before breakfast, we have Morning Prayer. After breakfast but before class, we have Mass. And then before dinner, we have evening prayers." Charlie turned around to face the doors to their dorm. "This is Saint Nicholas. This is our dorm," he said. He opened the doors and walked inside. "As you can see," he said, motioning to the wall on either side of the doors. "These are our lockers. You put your clothes and everything in there. You've have been assigned to the two right here next to the door." He pointed at the two lockers on his left. "Come on, I'll show you to your cubicle."

Charlie led them to Gus's old space. A new set of bunkbeds was set against the partition between their cubicle and his. "Here's your cubicle," he said, standing at the foot of the bunkbeds. "You can decide who gets which bunk. Any questions?"

"Yeah," one said. "Why are you wearing that? Are you serving Mass?"

Charlie looked down at his surplice and cassock, then back at the twin who asked. "No. This is our uniform. Although, for guys not in the Altar Boy Club—"

"Altar Boy Club?" the twin interrupted and snickered. "What is that, a snooty little clique?"

Charlie expression drained and he glared at the boy. "No.

It's a—Just forget it, you'll learn about it later."

"You wouldn't happen to be Charlie, would you?" the other, more serious-looking twin asked.

Charlie felt a jolt deep inside. "Yes, why?"

"Oh, nothing," he answered.

Wary, Charlie looked at them. "I guess if there are no more questions, I'll let you unpack. We meet downstairs for dinner at six," he said and slowly walked away, curious about how they knew his first name.

"So, what did you think of those guys?" Dougary asked when Charlie walked into the hallway. "I heard them jerking you around when you asked them their names."

"Yeah," Charlie said. "It was like meeting two of you. Well, the old you." He grinned.

"Was I really that much of a jerk?" Dougary asked.

Charlie eyed Dougary. He still was not sure what to think about this seemingly sudden transformation. He still did not trust him one hundred percent. "We've all grown up a bit," he answered. "I best get back downstairs. I still have to meet my new bunkmate."

"Yeah, I'm gonna check my cubicle and see you later," Dougary said.

By dinnertime, Charlie's new bunkmate had not arrived. Father Mark shrugged and turned to Charlie. "We'd best go to dinner."

"I wonder what happened to him?" Charlie said while they headed toward the refectory.

"I'm sure he'll be here," Father Mark said.

Charlie took his place in line. He checked the seating chart earlier that day and saw he was at the same table with Dougary and Dale, but the twins and his new bunkmate were new. When the doors opened, the boys filed into the refectory.

After Grace, the boys took their seats. Father Mark remained standing. He walked to the front of the table and surveyed the boys. A smile spread across his lips and he took a deep breath.

"Before dinner is served, I want to welcome you all to Saint Michael's Seminary High School. My name is Father Mark. I am your dean. Brother Simon," he said and motioned behind him to Brother Simon. "Is your assistant dean. If you have any concerns, you may see either of us. Brother Simon has an office and room on the fourth floor by Saint Nicholas dorm. The next person I would like to introduce you to is Father Vicar, our new school principal."

Charlie's mouth dropped open. He looked at Rick, who was seated at a neighboring table. Rick appeared as surprised and worried as he felt.

"Father Vicar will have responsibility of you during school hours. Currently, the second floor is still under construction, but once it's complete, he will have an office on that floor along with your new classrooms. Brother Owen," Father Mark looked behind him but Brother Owen was not present. "Uh, Brother Owen seems to be absent this evening. You will meet him later. He is the new vice-principal.

"Now that you have met everyone, let's eat." He winked at the boys and returned to his seat.

"I can't believe it," Charlie said out loud without realizing it.

"Can't believe what?" one of the twins seated across from Charlie asked.

"Oh, nothing," Charlie said, glancing at Dougary whose lips curled slightly.

"So, while we're waiting for our server to bring our dinner," Dougary said, looking straight at Dale who sat at the opposite end of the table. When he heard Dougary, he jumped up and hurried to the kitchen. "Let's go around the table and introduce ourselves. I'll begin. My name is Dougary and I'm the prefect of Saint Nicholas dorm. I'm also a senior this year." He looked at the twin to his left.

"My name is Robin. I'm a sophomore and I'm in Saint Nicholas dorm," he said, while he looked around the table and smiled at everyone. That was when Charlie noticed a small mole on Robin's neck.

"My name is Robert. I'm Robin's older brother by forty-five seconds. I'm also a sophomore and in Saint Nicholas dorm."

Robert appeared to be more stoic than his brother. After his introduction, he looked down at the table and did not make eye contact with anyone.

Dale returned to the table with the tray of bowls and a platter. He placed them in the center of the table and took his seat at the end.

"D-d-did I m-m-miss anything?" he asked.

"This is Robin and his brother Robert," Dougary introduced the twins. They nodded in response. "You're next. Tell them who you are, what dorm you're in, and what year in school."

"I'm D-d-dale. I'm in S-s-saint T-t-thomas dorm and I'm a ja-ja-junior."

"Nice to meet you, Dale," Robin said.

"Since my bunkmate hasn't arrived, I guess I'm next," Charlie said. "My name is Charlie, but you two already knew that. I'm in Saint Nicholas and I'm also a junior."

"What do you mean they already knew you?" Dougary asked.

"Oh, we just guessed, that's all," Robin said, but Charlie thought he looked nervous. He kept glancing at his brother who was ignoring him.

The boys ate their meal and chatted. When everyone was finished, Father Mark stood up to make his final announcements.

"You may be wondering why some of the boys are dressing in a cassock and surplice. This was our previous uniform."

"I'm not wearing that," Robert grumbled quietly to his brother but Charlie heard him.

"Beginning tomorrow morning, you will each see Brother Felix who will fit you for our new uniform. It will be a white shirt, black slacks and a black blazer. You will be issued a tie.

The stripes will correspond to your dorm. The boys in Saint Nicholas will be green and gold. Saint Thomas will be navy blue and gold, and Saint Peter will be deep purple and gold. Uniforms are required for all meals, services and school classes. If you are not in uniform, you will be assigned work crew as punishment. Work crew is time taken from your recreation to assist a brother with a task. Brother Simon will post the fitting schedule on the bulletin board. Are there any questions?"

Rick's hand shot up. Father Mark cringed. "Yes, Master Walters."

Rick stook up by his chair. "Will the members of the Altar Boys Club still wear their current uniform?"

"Yes, Master Walters but only when attending to Mass. At all other times, you, and they, will wear the new uniform."

Rick sat back down. The look on his face, Charlie thought, was one of disappointment. Charlie knew that Rick loved wearing his cassock and white surplice. It was a badge of honor to him. Charlie, however, was looking forward to not having to wear it. The new uniforms did not sound like they would be as uncomfortable.

DOUBLE TROUBLE

The afternoon sun was warm, and being dressed in his new uniform did not seem to help. Charlie tugged at the collar of his white shirt in an attempt to cool himself, but the tie around his neck seemed to trap the heat. Charlie hurried down to the outside steps to the basement of the monastery wing. His earlier attempts to speak to Father Ignatius had failed, but with the leaves on the trees changing and beginning to fall, Charlie needed to know if the image in the photograph was really the lost angel statue.

When he reached the museum, the door was closed but Charlie could see through the milk-glass window a on inside. He knocked. A shadowy figure moved into view and drew nearer. The door opened.

"Well, hello, Master MacCready. Don't you look dapper in your new uniform," Father Ignatius greeted Charlie with a huge smile. "Come in."

Charlie looked down at his clothes and then back at the monk. "Thank you?" he said, not sure if it was a compliment. He followed the elderly curator into the museum. "Wow!" he said as he looked around. "This place looks amazing. You did an excellent job."

"No, Master MacCready, *we* did an excellent job. I couldn't have done it without your help. Thank you," Father Ignatius said. "So, what brings you here today, besides the grand opening this afternoon?"

"I wanted to talk to you about this photograph." He pulled it out of his pocket and handed it to the monk. "It was from a roll of film I found in my cubicle. I was wondering if you could tell me what it is?"

"You don't know?" Father Ignatius said and gave Charlie a confused look.

"No. I didn't take it. I thought Howard did but he said he didn't. If you look closely at the mound, could it be the lost statue of Saint Michael?"

Father Ignatius's expression turned serious. He glanced at the photograph and then back at Charlie. "Come over here, the light is better."

Charlie followed him to the history corner. Father Ignatius laid the photograph on the glass top of the display counter and pulled a magnifying glass from the pocket in his habit. Leaning over the photo he moved the lens up and down over it and then stopped.

"Mmm," he hummed. "Very interesting. Maybe—no." He straightened up and looked at Charlie. Slowly a smile spread across his thin lips. "I think you have found it," he said.

"Really?" Charlie said, sounding excited by the news. But then his expression and enthusiasm drained. "Now, if only I knew where it was taken?"

"What was on the roll of film before and after this picture?"

"Some other pictures of the hilltop like the gymnasium, the birdhouse at the start of the path down the hill, stuff like that."

"Then use it as a map. Retrace the photographer's steps using the photographs."

The excitement Charlie had felt began to return. He had not thought to do that. Taking the photograph back from the curator, he asked, "Do you mind if I skip the grand opening this afternoon?"

"Not at all. I have enough brothers to give me a hand. You have your mission. Bring us back the lost angel," he answered with his large grin.

"Thank you," Charlie said as he rushed out of the museum.

The rest of the photographs were still in his nightstand drawer. Charlie headed back to his dorm. At that moment he missed having Howard there to share in the search with him. Another mystery was about to be solved, and Charlie wanted to share it with someone. He thought of Rick, but quickly dismissed him. Rick never really supported him in his endeavors to solve the mysteries of his medal, watch, and key. And the times that he did tag along, he complained the whole time. No, Charlie was on his own with this one.

When he reached his dorm, Dougary called him to his cubicle. Charlie debated for a moment whether or not to comply but Dougary's tone and expression drew him away from his mission.

"What?" Charlie asked.

"Where've you been?" Dougary asked. "I've been waiting here for an hour."

"I was down—why? What's wrong?" Charlie asked.

"After lunch I decided to take a nap. I came back to the dorm and spotted one of the twins standing at the foot of their bunk acting a little strange. He shook the bunk, bumping against the partition. That's when I noticed the other one in your cubicle."

"You did? What was he doing?"

"He said nothing, just looking out the window, but I don't believe him. I thought I heard him closing a nightstand drawer."

"My pictures," Charlie said and rushed to his cubicle. He opened the drawer and seeing the stack of photographs, albeit, disheveled, heaved a sigh of relief.

"Did they take anything?" Dougary asked.

"No, not that I can tell. He was snooping around, though."

"Well, be careful around them. I don't trust them."

"Oh, I will," Charlie said. "And thanks, Dougary. I mean

it."

"No problem," Dougary said and returned to his own cubicle.

Charlie took the photographs from the drawer and placed them on his bed. Carefully he laid them out in order but stepped back. Counting them he realized that one was missing. He took a closer look at the pictures. He needed the negatives to compare them with to be sure. He looked in the drawer. The negatives were gone. He gathered up the photos and put them into his pocket. At that moment, he missed Howard more. He needed someone to talk to, someone he trusted.

Moments later he knocked on the door of Father Cecil's cell. The door opened and the blind monk stood in the doorway.

"Yes?" he said.

Charlie noticed Father Cecil looked as though he had been napping.

"Hi, Father, it's me, Charlie."

"Charlie?" Father Cecil repeated sounding confused. "Were we supposed to meet today?"

"No, I'm sorry. I just needed someone to talk to."

"Oh, I see, well, come on in," he invited and turned around. While he walked to his chair, he straightened his habit and ran his fingers through his hair. "So, what's on your mind?" he asked as he sat down.

Charlie closed the door and turned on the light before taking his usual seat at the small table by the door. "You remember I told you about the roll of film I found and the photographs I printed off it?"

"Yes," Father Cecil nodded.

"Well, today, Dougary caught one of the new guys, one of the twins, in my cubicle. I think he may have taken the copy of the photo showing where the lost angel statue is."

"I see."

"I was wondering what I should do?"

"Well, that is a dilemma. No one actually saw him take it did they?"

"No."

"Do you know which boy it was?"

"Dougary still can't tell them apart."

"Well, I'm afraid there's only one thing you can do, find the statue before they do."

"But I don't know where it is exactly. Father Ignatius said for me to use the other pictures as a guide to retrace the photographer's steps—"

"Then you have a plan. What time is it?" Father Cecil interrupted.

"It's almost three in the afternoon."

"That gives you two hours before evening prayer. I suggest you see what you can find."

"Do you want to go with me?"

"I'm afraid I would only slow you down."

"Okay," Charlie said, trying to hide his disappointment from his tone. "Thank you, Father. I'll let you know how I make out."

"I'll be here, son."

~§~

Charlie could not stop the feeling of nervous anxiety from spreading. Father Cecil's rushing him off did not help matters. Charlie looked at the pictures while he started across the Great Lawn. He skipped the first one of the construction site and moved to the next, the bird house. When he reached the head of the path down the hill, he was stopped and looked up. Holding the photo high, he compared it to the actual birdhouse on the trunk of the tree. They matched.

"Wait up, Charlie."

Charlie turned around and quickly tucked the photos into the pocket of his blazer. His anxiety exploded inside him when he saw Robin running toward him.

Robin was out of breath by the time he reached Charlie. "Where're you going?"

"Just for a walk," Charlie answered.

"Mind if I join you?"

"I guess not," Charlie answered, wondering if this was a ploy to spy on him or draw him away from finding the statue first. "Let's go this way," he said, turning back to the path and starting to walk down the hill.

"Rick says you've been here for three years," Robin said.

"What else did Rick have to say about me?"

"Not much."

"Oh, I'm sure Rick said a lot more. He loves giving his opinion on everyone else," Charlie said, while they walked slowly.

"He told me," Robin said, his voice revealing his uneasiness. "You're an orphan?"

Charlie gave a slight, disbelieving laugh. "He did, did he? I suppose he told you I'm delusional because I still think my parents will come for me?"

"He may have mentioned it," Robin said sounding a bit more nervous.

Charlie stopped and turned around to face Robin. "Here's the deal. When I was two, my parents left me with my grandparents. My mother promised to return for me, and my grandmother and I believe her. On the other hand, my mother's brother, my Uncle Chester, doesn't think she will. That's why, after my grandfather died, he had me sent here and he had my grandma put in an old folks's home. But, he's wrong."

"How long were you with your grandparents?"

"Ten years or so," Charlie answered.

Robin nodded as though to soften his reply. "So, that's why Rick doesn't think they'll be coming back for you."

"Rick's a jerk. He's just unhappy because his parents are getting divorced, so he wants to make everyone else miserable." Charlie turned back to the path and began walking and searching.

Robin followed close behind. "So, are you looking for your lost angel?" he asked.

Charlie stopped suddenly and turned around, causing Robin to bump into him. Charlie shoved him away. "Who told you—Rick! I should have known better than to ever trust him to keep a secret."

"Why the secret? It's just a statue, isn't it?"

"Yes."

"So, why's it so important to find it?"

"It's not. It's just something Howard and did. We'd pretend it was a mystery and try to solve it."

"Playing detectives," Robin said and grinned. "Can I play?"

Charlie eyed Robin. Thoughts of Dougary telling him not to trust the twins came flooding back. Charlie wanted to accuse Robin of stealing his photograph but he did not have any proof. "Can you keep a secret?"

"Yes."

"Even from your twin brother?"

Robin laughed. "Sure. Contrary to popular belief, he doesn't know everything about me and I don't know everything about him. We don't share everything."

"Fine. You can help me look."

"What happens if we find it?"

"We tell Abbot Ambrose. Father Ignatius wants it for the museum."

"Oh. Is that all?"

"Yes. Why? What did you think it was?"

Robin fidgeted again. "Oh, nothing. I didn't really have a clue."

Charlie turned back around and started down the hill.

"So, why are we looking here?" Robin asked.

"According to Father Ignatius, the museum curator and historian, some guys from the town tried to steal it but never made it off the hilltop with it. So, it has to be hidden somewhere in the woods, otherwise it would have been found by now."

"Why do you think it's it this part?"

"I don't," Charlie said, not wanting to give him more

information than necessary. "Howard and I have searched the butte and now I'm looking here. Sort of a process of elimination."

"Oh, so you really don't have a clue?"

"Nope," Charlie answered.

"This really is a mystery."

Charlie nodded and kept looking.

They reached the bottom of the hill without Charlie locating the spot in the picture.

"I don't think it's here," Robin said.

"It has to be. We're just not looking in the right place."

"Are you even sure they followed the trail?"

"They had to," Charlie said.

"What about the woods on the other side of the road?

"This side is the closest to town. It has to be on this side," Charlie said, thinking out loud.

"Well, we better get back. It's almost time for evening prayer."

While heading back to the abbey, Charlie searched the ground for any sign that someone left the path. He wondered if the person who took the picture had ventured into the woods at some point before returning to the path. The fading sunlight cast too many shadows, making it hard for Charlie to see. Finally, he gave up searching and focused on getting back on time.

When they reached the abbey and started down the hall on the main floor toward the stairs, Father Mark opened his office door.

"Master MacCready, may I see you a moment?" he said.

"Sure," Charlie answered.

"I'll see you later," Robin said and continued on his way.

"Come in," Father Mark invited and stepped back into his office. Charlie followed.

"Master MacCready, I'd like you to meet Master Gonzales. Your new bunkmate has finally arrived."

Charlie looked at the young boy who stood up from the chair in front of Father Mark's desk. The boy was shorter than

Charlie, coming to Charlie's shoulder. He had nicely trimmed dark, almost black hair and brown eyes. He kept his head lowered when he looked at Charlie.

"Hi, I'm Charlie," he said and held out his hand.

"I'm Jose," he said, while he gave Charlie's hand a brief shake.

"I'd like you to give him a quick tour and help him get settled. You may skip evening prayer, but make sure you are on time for dinner."

"Yes, Father Mark," Charlie said.

"You are excused."

Charlie grabbed the old, tattered, carpetbag from the floor beside the chair Jose was seated in and directed him to the door. "Where'd you get this," he asked when they entered the hall. "I've never seen anything like it."

"It was my father's. He's had it since he was a boy."

"Wow, that's cool," Charlie said and directed Jose toward the stairs at the end of the hall. "We're on the fourth floor. After a while, you'll get used to them," he said while they made their way up.

Charlie gave Jose the tour of the fourth floor. Showing him the dorms, the lounge, the shower room and restroom. They skipped the chapel and quietly entered Saint Nicholas dorm.

"Our cubicle is in the corner, over here," Charlie said after showing Jose his locker.

"It's so big," Jose said, looking at all the cubicles that lined the walls to the right and left.

Charlie smiled and remembered his first day at Saint Michael's. Father Emmanuel had shown him to the dorm. Charlie felt overwhelmed and lost. He wondered if that was what Jose was feeling.

"You'll get used to that, too," he said. "Here's your bed."

"My bed?"

"Yes," Charlie said, a little confused.

"I never had my own bed," Jose explained while he sat down and bounced on the mattress. "Back home, I had to share a bed with my two brothers."

"Wow," was all Charlie could think to say. "I'll help you unpack after dinner. Right now, we better head downstairs to the refectory."

"The what?"

"That's what we call the dining room."

"Oh," Jose said. "Re-fec-tory?"

"Yes," Charlie said.

As the boys made their way down the stairs, the others began to rush past them. Charlie ignored them. "If you don't mind my asking, where are you from."

"California," Jose answered. "Fresno."

"Oh," Charlie said, not sure where Fresno was exactly. "Did your parents bring you?"

"No. It's too expensive. It was cheaper for me to take a bus."

Charlie's mouth dropped open. "It took you almost two weeks on the bus?"

"No," Jose laughed. "It took only twelve hours. My parents got the date wrong and so, I'm late."

"Phew, that's good. Father Mark told me you're a freshman?"

"Si." Jose nodded. "Are you?"

"I'm a junior this year."

Jose continued to nod. "You've been here a long time?"

"I came here four years ago."

"Four years?" Jose's eyes widened. "Where are you from?"

"Here, I guess," Charlie answered. "It's a long story."

When they reached the first floor, they took their place in line. Charlie looked ahead of him to see if he could find another freshman to introduce Jose to but the doors opened and they began to file into the refectory.

"We're over here," Charlie said and directed Jose to their table.

After the prayer, they sat down. Robin quickly brought the bowls and plates of food to table.

"Tonight, we are having a delicious meal fit for a dog. We begin with Gaines Burgers with cheese," he said as he placed the platter of meatloaf topped with a slice of cheddar on the table in front of Dougary. "A lovely peas and carrots combo." He put the bowl down. "And—"

"That's enough, Muster," Dougary said, silencing Robin's show.

Robin set the bowl of steamed red potatoes and the gravy boat down on the table in front of his brother before taking his seat.

"What? No dinner rolls or bread?" Dougary asked.

"I was thinking—"

"Well, don't. May we please have either," Dougary said.

Robin jumped up from the table and returned in seconds with a plate stacked with sliced bread and another with a cube of butter. He dropped them on the table close to Dougary. Glaring at him, he asked, "Is there anything else?"

Dougary looked at the table nearest them before he answered. "No, I think that is all for now."

Robin sat down again.

"Thank you," Dougary said in a kinder tone.

"Yeah," Robin said.

"Guys," Charlie spoke up. "I'd like you to meet Jose Gonzales. This is Dougary, our dorm prefect and a senior—"

"I'm Robert Muster, a sophomore," Robin interrupted.

"No, he's not, I'm Robert Muster," Robert said.

"No, I am," Robin continued.

"He's Robin and this is his twin brother, Robert," Charlie told Jose while the twins kept arguing between them.

"Hi, I'm d-d-dale," Dale said and held out his hand to Jose.

"Dale is the only one not from our dorm," Charlie explained.

"Glad to meet you," Jose said to them all.

After the meal, the boys returned to their dorm. Once he helped Jose get started unpacking, Charlie returned to his cubicle. He noticed a large envelope on his bed and picked it up.

Reading the return address, he smiled. It was from Howard. He tore it open and pulled out a new comic book along with a short letter. He sat down on the edge of his bed and began to read it.

"Another comic from Howard?"

Charlie looked at the foot of his bed. "Yes," he answered Rick.

"I noticed it was still in your mail slot after dinner, so I thought I'd deliver it," Rick said.

"Thank you," Charlie answered.

"Can we go somewhere and talk?" Rick asked.

Charlie set the comic down and sat up. "You doing okay?"

"No," he answered.

"Sure," Charlie said and put the comic book under his pillow. "Where do you want to go?"

"Just walk," Rick said.

Rick remained silent all the way down the stairs. Charlie was concerned. It was not like Rick to not have something to say. They walked out the back door and headed toward the baseball field. The sun was nearly set and the sky was ablaze of pinks and red toward the west. They sat down on the wooden bleachers.

"Is something wrong?" Charlie asked.

"I don't think I want to be here anymore," he said.

"Why is that?"

"There are too many changes. Gus is gone. Howard's gone. Everything is different, even our uniforms."

"Yeah, I know," Charlie said.

"I just don't want to be here anymore. I miss the way things were."

"I do, too. But, Rick, Father Cecil told me that life is all about change. Nothing ever stays the same, not even you. You're not the same as when you came here. You've changed."

"I know all that," Rick said. "I just—"

"Don't you want to be a priest anymore?"

"Yes. More than anything."

"Then, give yourself time. Time to adjust. It's been a crazy summer. Just hang on a few more weeks.”

Rick nodded. “I see your bunkmate has finally showed up. What happened?”

“He said his parents misread the date.”

“That’s a little odd, don’t you think?” Rick said.

“What do you mean?”

“I just find it strange that two adults would not know what day school starts. There has to be another reason.”

“Maybe so,” Charlie said. “I’m just glad he’s here.”

“Glad?” Rick scoffed. “Well, that’s where you and I differ. I can’t believe I have to share my cubicle. Ever since I came here, I’ve always had my own.”

“Really?”

“I don’t know why they couldn’t leave Saint Sebastian a dorm. Then we wouldn’t need to double up so much.”

“True.”

“Did you notice that Dog-boy gets his cubicle all to himself?”

“I think all the seniors do.”

“Well, it’s not fair,” Rick said.

Instantly Brother Simon’s voice rang in Charlie’s ears, life is not fair. Charlie bit his tongue. He knew better than to repeat them to Rick, especially now. He could tell the situation was upsetting and rather than comforting those words would be like gasoline on a fire.

“So, you don’t like your bunkmate?” Charlie asked.

“Terry’s okay. I mean, it’s not his fault.”

“True. None of us got to choose our cubicles.”

“I don’t know why I have to be paired with a freshman. Can’t they put two of the same class together? I mean, like you and me. Let your bunkmate share with mine. It’d give them a chance to get to know each other better.”

“Maybe you could ask Brother Simon. See what he thinks of the idea, but be prepared for him to say no.”

“Well, why bother asking then.”

“Because, he could say yes,” Charlie said. “I guess, it’s like

Father Cecil said, hope for the best but prepare for the worst."

"Well, it can't get any worse," Rick said.

Charlie did not respond. He looked at the darkening sky and then over his shoulder at the abbey. "We should probably get back inside."

They headed back to their dorm.

As the reached Saint Nicholas, the doors burst open and Terry, broom and dustpan in hand, came face to face with Rick. His eyes were wide and his jaw dropped. "Oh," he said and remained frozen in place.

"Do you mind?" Rick said and acted like he was about to walk through his bunkmate.

Terry quickly stepped to the side. "Before you go in," he said, halting Rick whose hand was on the doorhandle.

Charlie looked at the contents on the dustpan and noticed shards of colored glass and what looked like a bottle top. He looked at Rick who must have seen them too.

"What have you done?" Rick shrieked.

Terry began to tremble. "I'm sorry," he said. "I accidently bumped the bottle while I was trying to make my bed."

"Accidently, my foot," Rick said.

"I'm really sorry," he repeated.

"It's okay. I've only had that bottle since I was. . .your age."

Charlie looked at the dark-haired boy and saw the tears in his brown eyes. "Wasn't that the bottle you got at the fair? The one you said you were thinking of throwing out?"

Rick looked over his shoulder at Charlie and glared. "That's beside the point. It was mine and he broke it."

Charlie heard the crack in Rick's voice and realized it was not about the bottle or Terry. "Come on, Rick. I'll let you read my comic book."

UNCLE

"How are your classes going?" Father Cecil asked, holding onto Charlie's arm as they walked across the Great Lawn.

"Okay, I guess. I'm really liking chemistry and think I'm doing well."

"That's good to hear. How about your other classes?"

"Don't ask." Charlie sighed. "I'm doing so-so in most of them but Lit class has way too much reading. I really messed up. I didn't finish our reading assignment and there was only one question on the test about it and I was the only one who got it wrong."

"Oh?"

"Yeah, and Brother Clarence loved telling the whole class that I got the wrong answer. With all the other classes and homework, how does he expect us to be able to read a whole book in a week?"

"It does sound like a lot," Father Cecil said.

"Reading is hard for me. Well, not reading, just remembering what I read. Sometimes I read a page and then when I get to the bottom, I forgot what I just read."

"Sounds like you have other things on your mind."

"I guess," Charlie said. "We're here. Do you want to sit

down?"

"Sure."

Charlie escorted the priest to the bench and wiped the fallen leaves from it before they sat down. In the pond in front of them, Charlie could see the goldfish swimming around.

"Tell me, how goes your search for the lost angel?" Father Cecil asked.

"Not good. Every time I try to go looking, Robin shows up and wants to help."

"He does? How did he find out about the statue?"

"Rick told him."

"Is that okay?"

"I don't know. There's just something about him. . .I mean, he seems nice and all."

"But he's not Howard," Father Cecil said.

"No, he's not, but there's something more. He's seems too eager. Like he wants to find it more than I do, almost."

"Oh?"

"Dougary warned me a couple weeks ago to be careful around the twins. He said they seemed shady, and he should know given his history."

Father Cecil smiled and continued to hold his head still while he blindly looked straight ahead. At least with his dark glasses on, no one could see his eyes.

"Well, maybe you will get a chance to do some more looking this afternoon?"

"I suppose so. But with the leaves on the trees falling, the pictures aren't going to be much help anymore."

"True, but at least you have an idea where to search," Father Cecil said. "So, is there any news from Howard this week?"

"Yes," Charlie said, his tone sounding more cheerful. "He's liking his new school. He said it is strange and a little distracting going to school with girls."

Father Cecil laughed. "I'm sure it is."

"He said he's almost convinced his dad it's okay to let him

come for a visit."

"That would be nice for you."

"Yeah, I really miss him."

"Well, I think I should get back to my room. Do you mind cutting our walk short today?"

"No. Are you okay?"

"Yes, I'm fine. Just a bit chilly out is all."

Charlie returned Father Cecil to his room and while heading back to his dorm, he decided to slip away and search for the lost angel on his own.

He reached the head of the trail and no sign of Robin. Slowly he started down the hill. He searched the woods to the left, away from the road, still looking for signs of someone leaving the trail.

Suddenly, he stopped and looked around. The sound of male voices shattered the quiet of the woods. Charlie looked around to determine where they were coming from. Slowly he crept along the path, keeping low so he would not be spotted. As he moved along, the voices became clearer.

"What do you mean you haven't found it?" a deep voice said. "What have you been doing?"

"We do have to go to school," Charlie recognized that voice, it was Robert's.

Charlie inched closer in the direction of the voices being careful to stay hidden among the bushes and undergrowth.

"Of course, but you do have some free time, don't you?"

Charlie ducked sharply when he spotted the trio standing in a small clearing between the trail and the road. The twins stood facing the third whose back was toward Charlie. The man was a head taller than the twins and very thin. He was wearing a short-sleeved shirt and blue jeans.

"Some, but—" It was Robin's voice this time.

"No buts. I paid you good money to find it. Now find it." Charlie noticed a tattoo of something on the man's forearm when he shook his finger in Robin's face.

"We're trying. It's just that Charlie—"

"No more excuses. There are two of you and one of him. If he gets in your way, teach him a lesson."

"Are you saying to beat him up?" Robin shrieked.

"If you have to."

"That's gonna cost you more," Robert said. "We need compensation if we're going to risk getting into that sort of thing."

"Fine, if it comes to that, you'll get paid. But you have one week to get it or you're the ones who will be sorry."

"What's that supposed to mean?"

"You don't want to know."

"That's a nice way to talk, Uncle."

"How many times do I have to tell you to stop calling me that? Now, when I come back here next month, you better have some good news. Am I making myself clear?"

"Yes." Robert said.

"Yes, Uncle." Charlie heard Robin mutter.

"Well, your best isn't good enough. I paid you good money to find that box and my dad is not happy you are taking forever."

"We'll find it."

"You better and before that brat finds it or you'll be sorry." The man shook his fist at them and then headed toward the road.

The twins stood silently as they watched and waited for the man to leave. The rev of a car engine rumbled through the trees and then trailed off in the distance. Robin and Robert looked at each other.

"We have to get that key," Robert said.

"But where does he hide it?" Robin asked.

Charlie felt the chain beneath his shirt and grasped the key tightly.

"I don't know, but we have to get it," Robert said. "He seems to like you. Why don't you help him search for his lost angel? Then maybe hint around and find out where he's hiding it."

"I don't know," Robin said. "He's pretty secretive about things."

"Well, try, damnit. I don't have fifty bucks to give him, do you?"

"No," Robin answered. "Fine."

Charlie did not wait around to hear anymore. He quickly and quietly headed back to the abbey. All the way, he could not stop thinking about the twins' uncle. He had heard that voice before, somewhere. He just could not place it. But one thing was for sure, Dougary was right. The twins are not to be trusted.

THE LOST ANGEL

A week had passed since Charlie overheard the twins and their uncle. To his surprise and relief, either of the twins had made any attempts to get his key.

Charlie sat with his legs over the arm of the overstuffed chair in the lounge by his cubicle in Saint Nicholas dorm. He flipped the pages of the latest comic book Howard had sent him. He was not reading it so much as looking at the pictures.

Rick walked into the dorm. Charlie looked up. Rick hurried over to the sofa and sat down at the end nearest Charlie.

"I talked with Brother Simon and presented my case about trading cubicles," Rick said.

"And?" Charlie said, still holding the comic book at the ready in case Rick's news was short.

"He said I made a good point and if everyone involved was in agreement, you could move into my cubicle."

The comic book closed. Charlie turned around in the chair and put his feet on the floor. "Hold on a second. I don't want to move. You can trade with Jose but I'm staying put."

"Come on, Charlie," Rick whined. "My cubicle is already set up."

"So's mine. No, I like where I am."

"But there's not enough room for my stereo in yours."

"Oh well," Charlie said, not giving in.

Rick pursed his lips and glared at him. "Fine, I'll move but we have to stack the beds."

"No way," Charlie said.

"Why not?"

"Because I like looking out the window before I go to sleep."

"Well, if you have the top bunk, you can still see out the window. Plus, you'll have a better view of the Great Lawn in case your parents come for you."

"I thought you said they weren't coming?"

"Now you're just being mean," Rick said. "It was your idea for me to ask Brother Simon and now that he's agreed, you're backing out."

"Fine, we can stack the beds," Charlie said.

After sharing the news with Jose and Terry, the boys began the move. Lifting Charlie's bed on top of Jose's old bed was heavier than either of the boys thought.

"Why don't you try taking the mattress off, first," Robin said, from his perch on the top bunk in his cubicle.

"Good idea," Rick said.

Once the bedframe was secured on top of the other, they returned the mattress. While Rick packed up his stereo, Charlie remade his bed. He glanced out the window and had to admit to himself that Rick was right. He had a better view of the Great Lawn. However, when he turned around, he noticed that the partition was only about a foot higher than his mattress and directly on the other side of it was Robin's bed.

"Hey, neighbor," Robin greeted and grinned.

"Hey," Charlie said, less enthused about it.

By the time the move was finished, Charlie's cubicle no longer looked the same. Rick had put a rug down on the floor, his swivel rocker in the corner under the window, and connected his stereo and speakers beside it across from the bed.

"There," Rick said while he surveyed his new home. "This

is going to be so much fun."

"Yeah, yeah," Charlie said while he lay on his bed watching.

"What time is it?"

Charlie pulled out his pocket watch. "Almost time for lunch," he answered.

"Great. Let's go get in line early. I'm starving," Rick said.

Charlie jumped down from his bed and followed Rick out of the dorm. He could not wait to write Howard and tell him about his new bunkmate. Howard was not going to believe it. First, however, he had to get through lunch.

As waiter for the week, Charlie excused himself from Rick and went into the kitchen to prepare the tray for his table.

"Hi, Sister Faith," he said when he saw her dishing up heaping bowls of egg noodles.

"Hello, Master MacCready. You're a little early, aren't you?"

"I wanted to get a head start," he said. "Plus, I needed to get away from Rick."

"Master Walters?"

"Yeah, he's my new bunkmate as of now." Charlie rolled his eyes then shook his head.

Sister Faith smiled at him. "Well, you know where everything is," she said and resumed her duty.

~§~

After lunch, Charlie returned to his dorm. When he opened the door, he noticed the twins sitting on the sofa in the lounge. Quietly he let the door close. This was the perfect time for him to slip away and resume his search for the lost angel.

He took the stairs two at a time and reached the first floor quickly. Glancing toward the back door of the abbey, he decided to take the direct and faster route through the front doors. He kept looking over his shoulder to make sure the twins weren't following. Dougary's warning not to trust them was still fresh in his mind.

Reaching the tree with the birdhouse, Charlie pulled the photographs from his pocket and moved the first one to the back of the pile. He looked at the next picture, at the foliage and began to walk down the path. He held up the picture and looked around while he walked. Suddenly, he stopped.

"Ha!" he said and grinned. "I found you." He put the picture on the bottom of his stack and took the next. Following the same procedure, in no time he located the spot of the third picture. The next picture was of the lost angel partially covered by the undergrowth. He searched the ground on either side of him for any sign that someone had left the path.

He walked another ten feet and stopped. To his left, away from the paved road up the hill, Charlie found what he was searching for. The mossy ground looked trampled on and the smaller shrubs had broken branches.

Charlie glanced over his shoulder to be sure no one had followed him before he left the path. His pulse quickened as he made his way through the trees, following the signs that someone had left. He glanced at the picture and at the forest around him.

"Where is the clearing?" he muttered to himself.

He was about to give up when it appeared in front of him.

The afternoon sun shone through the branches of the trees and illuminated the golden leaves of the shrubs and undergrowth. In the distance Charlie spotted a dark shape of what he thought resembled an angel's wing. It was covered in the same ivy that had overtaken the ground and tree trunks nearby.

"I can't believe it," he said aloud and then ducked when he heard his voice bounce back at him. He cautiously made his way closer being careful on the uneven ground.

When he reached the spot, he began pulling the ivy away as though he were opening a present on Christmas morning. The more he saw of the statue, the more he grinned and faster he pulled at the ivy. Once he had uncovered it, he stood back and looked at it. The statue of Saint Michael was as tall as him, with wings that rose above his head. In his right hand he aimed a long sword toward his feet. Charlie examined the statue closer. Beneath Saint Michael's feet was another angel with a chain around his neck and an angry scowl on his twisted face. Charlie knew it represented Satan, the devil. The entire statue was covered in a mottled matte black.

Charlie pulled the ivy from around the broken base of the statue. The base was made of brick and mortar which crumbled as he pulled the ivy away. A metal plaque was askew, held to the bricks by a screw on the right side. The one on the left had been removed. Behind it was an empty pocket where bricks had been chiseled away to make a small opening the size of a shoebox, but it was empty.

"No!" Charlie said. "I don't believe this." He stepped back and sat down on a moss-covered tree stump. He looked at the picture again and then back at the angel. He glanced at the ground in disappointment and felt a jolt deep inside when he noticed a piece of paper partially covered by the undergrowth.

Retrieving it, he turned it over. "It can't be!" he said, staring at the print he had lost. His disappointment turned to anger when he remembered Dougary had caught one of the twins in his cubicle. He stomped back to the path and ran up the hill toward the abbey. Sweat beads formed on his forehead and he wiped them away with the back of his hand.

Once he reached the Great Lawn, he slowed to a walk. Thoughts of Howard came to him. He wished his friend were there to talk to. He would know what to do. Charlie thought of Dougary and wondered if he could be trusted.

Entering the main foyer of the abbey, Charlie entered the monastery wing and headed to Father Cecil's cell. He wasn't Howard, but he would know what to do.

Charlie knocked on Father Cecil's door. The monk answered almost immediately.

"Yes?" he said and then a smile spread across his face. "Master MacCready, Charlie, come in." He turned around and walked back into his room. "To what do I owe the pleasure?"

"I need to talk to you," Charlie said and closed the door behind him.

"Uh-oh, what is it?" the blind priest asked and sat down in his chair.

"You remember I was looking for the lost angel statue?"

"Yes."

"Well, I found it."

"You did?" Father Cecil sat forward and looked excited. "And?"

"Nothing," Charlie answered. "There was nothing. I mean, I found a plaque on the base and behind it there was an opening, but it was empty. Nothing was there."

"Are you sure?" A worried expression replaced Father Cecil's joy.

"Yes. Remember the picture I was missing, the original print of the place where the lost angel was?"

"Yes."

"I found it."

"Where?"

"It was by the lost angel. I think it had to have been one of the twins. Dougary caught them in my cubicle. They said they were just looking out the window but I think they took the picture."

Father Cecil remained silent but he nodded.

"What do I do now? I am certain whatever was in there has something to do with my key."

"You have to find out who took it. You need to find that box."

"Box?" Charlie repeated. "Then you know what it is."

"Yes, son. I do."

"What's in it?"

"I don't know. I just know that it's a heavy, metal box."

"How did it get there?"

"Years ago, your father and Abbot Ambrose, before he was the abbot, chiseled out an opening in the pedestal and put the box there behind the plaque. That's all I know.

"When the boys from town stole the statue and hid it in the woods, rather than retrieve it, Abbot Ambrose said to let it stay *lost.* It was safer that way."

"So, it wasn't really lost. Abbot Ambrose knew where it was all the time?"

Father Cecil nodded.

"Then the film, the pictures, they must have come from Abbot Ambrose," Charlie said as he thought out loud.

"Yes. That is what I would assume as well."

"So, he wanted me to find the statue and the box."

"It would appear so," Father Cecil said. "Son, it is imperative that you find out who took it before they open it."

"I will and I know just where to start," Charlie said. "Thank you, Father. I'll see you later."

Before Father Cecil could stop him and warn him to be careful, Charlie was out the door, and on his way back to his dorm.

Saint Nicholas dorm was buzzing with several boys huddled around Rick and his new cubicle when Charlie arrived. He ignored them and went straight to Dougary's cubicle.

Dougary lay on his bed reading a book. Charlie recognized it was from the basement library. Dougary looked at Charlie and closed the book.

"Hi, what's up?" he asked.

"You were right about the twins," Charlie said and threw the photograph he had found onto the bed beside Dougary.

"What's this?" Dougary asked and picked it up. "Oh, this is the photograph you printed last summer. I've seen it before. So?"

"It's a picture of where I could find the lost angel statue. I was missing after you saw the twins in my cubicle a while back."

"So, where did you find it?"

"They must have dropped it in the woods by the statue."

"You found it?" Dougary said and sat up.

"Yeah, but they took whatever was hidden in the base of the statue."

"Really? What?"

"I don't know. All I do know is, it's a metal box."

"What are you going to do?"

"I don't know. I was hoping you could tell me which twin was in my cubicle."

Dougary frowned. "I don't remember. I still have trouble telling them apart."

"Darn!" Charlie said and sighed.

"Why don't you go to Brother Simon?"

"No, they'll just deny it was them who took it and then I'll never find it."

"Yeah, I suppose you're right," Dougary said. "On the other hand, you could turn the tables on them. What's good for the goose. . ."

"What are you talking about?"

"Why not wait for them to leave their cubicle and then do your own snooping?"

"I couldn't," Charlie said.

"Why not?"

"What if they caught me?"

"I don't know, say you dropped something or something?"

Charlie thought for a moment. It could work. He could accidently drop a comic book over the partition and then go to get it.

"I don't know," Charlie said, uncertain and a bit nervous. "Thanks."

He headed to his cubicle and climbed up onto his bed. Rick was still showing off his stereo to some of the new guys but the crowd had thinned considerably. Charlie lay down on his side and propped his head up with his hand.

Behind him, Robin popped up over the divider and said, "Hey."

Charlie was startled and felt his body jerk. He turned his head and looked over his shoulder at Robin.

"Sorry. I didn't mean to scare you."

"You didn't," Charlie answered. "What's up?"

"Where'd you disappear to?"

"Nowhere, why?"

"Just wondered. Did you go looking for your lost angel again?"

"Maybe. What's it to you?"

"Is something wrong?" Robin asked.

"No," Charlie said, then turned back toward the window.

"Oh, I bet there is something."

Charlie felt the partition shake and his bed shimmy. He looked back at Robin who had climbed over the partition and was sitting on the foot of his bed. "What are you doing?" he said and pulled his feet back and sat up.

"What's bothering you?"

"You are," Charlie said.

"I'm serious, Charlie."

"Fine," Charlie said. He glanced down over the edge of his bed and saw his cubicle was empty. He turned back toward at Robin. "I found the lost angel," he whispered.

"You did?" Robin said out loud, sounding surprised.

"Keep your voice down."

Robin ducked his head and looked around the dorm before turning back to Charlie. "Sorry."

"Yes, I found it. But someone beat me to it. They stole something that was meant for me."

"They did?"

Charlie saw through Robin's feigned surprise. "Yes, and I know who it was."

Robin's body tensed and he looked nervous. "Really?" he said. Charlie heard the fear in his voice.

"Yep," Charlie said. "I'm betting it was Dougary."

Charlie noticed Robin's shoulders relax. "Dougary? Why him?"

"Because ever since I came here, he's been after my key," Charlie answered and pulled the chain and its ornaments from beneath his cassock. "But he'll never get it so he'll never be able to open the box."

Robin's eyes widened as he looked at the trinkets hanging from the chain. "Where did you get that stuff?"

"From my grandmother, but that's not important. I have to get that box back. You were here this morning, did you notice Dougary acting strange or hiding something?"

"No. He's been in his cubicle reading that book all morning."

"Well, maybe he hid it earlier."

"Wow," Robin said, still trying to cover his nervousness. "I'm really sorry. I hope you find the box. I guess I should go see what Robert is doing."

Charlie watched Robin climb back over the partition to his own bed and heard him hop down to the floor. He grinned to himself when a moment later, Robin left the dorm. Stretching his neck, he looked around the dorm. It was empty. Quickly, he climbed down from his bunk and tiptoed around the corner to the twins' cubicle.

"Where would they hide you?" he said under his breath as he began to look around. He knelt down and looked under the bottom bunk. Nothing but a duffle bag shoved into the corner. Charlie reached out and grabbed it. He pulled it close and unzipped it. Glancing over his shoulder, he looked inside. Nothing. Empty. He zipped it up and shoved it back where he had found it.

"You know—"

Charlie jumped and turning around fell onto his rear. He sat looking up at Dougary who was trying not to laugh.

"Dougary! Don't do that," Charlie whispered harshly.

Grinning and swallowing his laughter, Dougary said, "You can't possibly think they would leave whatever it is laying out in the open. They had to have locked it up in their locker."

"Then why did you tell me to search their cubicle?" Charlie said and climbed to his feet.

"To see if you would."

"That's pretty lame, even for you."

"I was trying to see if you trusted me," Dougary said. "You better come out of there before they come back."

The two moved to the lounge in the center of the dorm.

"Of course, I trust you," Charlie said. "I mean—"

"I know," Dougary said, interrupting him and letting him off the hook.

"So, what is your brilliant idea on how to get into their lockers?"

"We can't. We have to be patient and watch them. They are bound to slip up."

"We?"

"You asked for my help. Why else would you come to me about the missing box?"

Charlie looked at Dougary. He appeared different and not just because he had grown taller, thinner. His dark hair was cut short and looked wet. Charlie knew it was only the hair cream he used. His once devious eyes looked kinder. He was not as threatening as he was when they first met.

"Yeah," Charlie nodded. "I suppose you're right."

The bell rang, signaling it was time for evening prayer. Dougary returned to his cubicle and grabbed his blazer. Charlie looked himself over and felt his necktie. The two walked out of the dorm together and headed to the chapel.

FAILURE

Charlie stood in line outside the refectory doors with the rest of the boys. It had been nearly two weeks since he had found the lost angel. After informing Father Ignatius about it, some of the brothers retrieved the statue and it was now in the basement workshop next to the photography lab. The museum curator was busy trying to restore it. Charlie, on the other hand, still hadn't found any leads as to who may have taken the box.

Charlie stared at the back of Robin's head, four boys ahead of him in line. Robin was alone. It was Robert's week to wait on the table.

"Hi ya, Charlie," Rick said, standing beside him.

Charlie jumped and took a step out of line. "Don't do that!" he said.

"Seriously, you need to relax," Rick said. "What has you so distracted?" He looked ahead of them at the line.

"Nothing. Just thinking."

"Well, I heard you found the statue."

"Oh, everyone knows that," Charlie said, dismissively.

"But not everybody knows someone beat you to it."

"Where'd you hear that?"

"From someone in the dorm," Rick answered.

"Robin?"

"Maybe," Rick said but his uneasiness told Charlie he was right.

"What else did he say?"

"He said you were pretty upset because whoever it was stole a box from the statue."

"He did, did he," Charlie said glanced at Robin again. "Well, don't worry about it. I'm probably just being delusional or something."

"I thought we talked about that. I told you I was sorry for what I said about your parents." Rick's tone softened. "You know I was just upset thinking about Gus leaving. I didn't really mean it. I hope your parents do come for you."

"Yeah, I know." Charlie said. "Sorry. It's just that I never mentioned a box to Robin. So, how did he know it was a box that was taken?"

"Oh," Rick said, his eyes widened and he looked at Robin.

"But you have to keep it quiet. Dougary and I have a plan."

"Dougary?" Rick said, sounding surprised. "Since when have you two teamed up?"

"Since everything changed and he's now in our dorm. He's not like he used to be."

"Don't trust him," Rick said. "He's a snake. He'll stab you in the back when your guard is down."

Charlie shook his head and laughed quietly. "You're wrong about him."

"No, I'm not and I'll prove it to you, somehow."

The refectory doors opened, interrupting them. Rick slipped into line behind Charlie much to the upset of the boy he cut in front of.

Father Vicar walked into the hallway.

"What's he doing here?" Rick whispered in Charlie's ear.

Charlie shook his head.

Father Vicar raised his bony hands and the boys quieted down. Tucking his hands behind the folds in his habit, he tilted his head back and looked down at the boys.

"You may enter," he said in a monotone.

Charlie ducked his head when he passed in front of the school principal. Once inside the refectory, he glanced at the head table. Father Mark and Brother Simon were not there.

"Oh brother," he groaned and took his place at his table, standing behind his chair.

After the prayer, the boys took their seats and the servers brought in their trays of food. Father Vicar left the stereo off, much to the surprise of many of the boys. Charlie leaned toward Dougary.

"Does this mean we aren't supposed to talk?" he whispered.

Dougary shrugged his shoulders.

The boys ate in silence and when they were finished, Father Vicar concluded the meal with a prayer. He stood at the head table and watched the boys quietly leave the refectory.

Once in the hallway, Rick rushed up to Charlie. "What was that all about?" he asked.

"Beats me," Charlie said.

"Well, he ruined dinner. Why couldn't we have music?" Rick said. "Wanna go for a walk?"

"I guess," Charlie answered.

The two boys slipped out the back door and into the brisk evening air. The sky was already dark. The winter sun had set. The outside lights on the abbey illuminated the ground around the building. Charlie folded his arms over his chest to ward off the chill.

"What's up?" he asked Rick while they stood at the edge of the lighted area.

"I miss Gus," Rick said.

"I miss him, too."

"At least Howard writes you regularly. Gus doesn't."

"Have you written him?"

"Yes, nearly twice a week."

"I got a letter from him about three weeks ago."

"That's about the time I heard from him last, too," Rick

said. "How'd he sound in your letter?"

"Okay, I suppose."

"Something must be wrong," Rick said.

"If there is, what can we do about it? He's miles away from here."

"I know, it's just. . .." Rick hung his head and was quiet.

Charlie looked at him and could tell, even in the dim light, that he was crying. "He's going to be fine, Rick," he said and put his hand on Rick's shoulder.

"I hope so," Rick said, sounding weepy.

"It's cold out here, do you want to go inside?"

"Sure."

The two turned around and headed toward the back door. Once inside, Charlie noticed the twins by the phone closet.

When they spotted Charlie, Robert left, heading upstairs. Robin approached them.

"So, what are you two talking about," Robin said.

"Nothing," Charlie answered. "Just talking."

"Oh, I thought I heard you talking about the missing box and your key," Robin said.

"No, we weren't," Rick said, giving Robin the stink face. "And who told you about Charlie's key?"

"Charlie did."

"Charlie?" Rick said in disbelief. He looked at Charlie.

"Yeah, I told him," Charlie admitted.

"But I thought your grandmother told you not to tell anyone?" Rick whispered without moving his lips.

"He told you," Robin said to Rick.

"That's because we're friends," Rick said in a snooty tone.

"So are we," Robin answered back. "Tell him, Charlie."

"I suppose," Charlie said. "I mean, sure, we're all friends."

"Well, thanks a lot," Robin said. "I guess I won't tell you what I found out."

"About what?"

"About who took your box."

"You know who has it?"

"Well, not exactly. But I do know they aren't able to pry it open. They need your key."

Charlie grabbed the chain around his neck through his uniform. "Well, they aren't getting it. You can tell them that."

"That's what I told him. You never take it off."

"Only when he showers," Rick blurted.

Charlie looked shocked at Rick. "But I lock it away, so it's safe," he added quickly.

"Well, don't let it out of your sight," Robin said and glance at something behind them. "Hey, wait up," he called and raced off.

"Don't be telling people that," Charlie said and slapped Rick on the shoulder with the back of his hand.

"What?"

"That I take off my chain when I shower."

"Why? It's only Robin and you two are supposed to be friends."

"That's what I want him to think," Charlie said.

"Why?"

"Because he and Robert are the ones who stole the box."

"No," Rick said, stretching out the word in disbelief.

"Yes," Charlie said. "I never told him the item stolen from the statue was a box."

Rick's eyes widened. "You didn't?"

"No," Charlie scoffed. "So he and his brother have to be the ones who found it."

"Now what are you going to do?"

"I don't know, but I'll think of something," Charlie turned around toward the stairs and the two headed to their dorm.

The next morning Charlie dressed and went into the hall. He didn't sleep well the night before because he kept thinking about the missing box. He wondered if he should try harder to see Abbot Ambrose and tell him what happened.

He walked across the hall to the new chapel and went inside. He took two steps into the room and stopped. It was hard to imagine it used to be a dorm. Metal folding chairs were arranged in neat rows on either side creating a center aisle. A wooden altar was set up in front of chairs and decorated with a white altar cloth and two gold-plated candlesticks. Behind the altar, the windows were coated with a nearly transparent paint to resemble stained glass. Above the windows was hung a burlap banner with colorful letters sewn onto it that read, Praise the Lord!

The door opened behind him. Charlie glanced over his shoulder as the assistant dean entered.

"Don't let me interrupt you," Brother Simon said.

"You're not," Charlie answered. "I'm just looking around."

"So, what do you think of our new chapel?"

"It looks great," Charlie answered. "How'd the brothers get the altar through the door?"

"In pieces," he answered and walked over to the stereo in the back corner of the chapel. "They assembled it in here."

"But it looks so solid."

"It's deceiving. It's actually quite hollow."

"Huh," Charlie grunted.

Brother Simon put a record on the turntable and placed the needle on the edge. The chapel was filled with a soft melody.

"Here," Brother Simon said, handing Charlie a book of matches. "Light the candles on the altar for me, please."

"Sure."

While Charlie lit the candles, the other boys began to fill the room. Charlie returned the matches to the supply locker in the corner by the stereo and then took a seat in back between Rick and Dougary.

Brother Simon walked to the head of the chapel and bowed in front of the altar. He took a seat at the side and opened his prayer book. The boys all stood while the assistant dean offered the opening prayer. When Dougary stood up to do a reading, Charlie was a bit surprised. He glanced at Rick who was looking intently at the prayer book in his hands.

Once Morning Prayer was concluded, the boys exited and

headed downstairs to breakfast. Charlie and Rick lagged behind.

"Have you thought of a plan, yet?" Rick asked when they started down the stairs.

"No."

When they reached the second-floor landing, Rick leaned over the handrail to look down the stairs. He then motioned for Charlie to come over to the fire doors. Part of the paper that covered the windows had fallen off. Rick cupped his hands on either side of his face and leaned against the glass to look inside.

"Wow," he said. "You gotta see this." He stepped back to let Charlie have a peek.

Charlie stepped forward and, putting his hands on either side of his face to block out the light, he put his nose to the glass.

Inside, the once-gutted floor was now a bright hallway with doors on either side. The walls were painted two shades of tan; light tan on the top half and a darker shade on the lower half. There was another hallway immediately inside, to the left, but Charlie could not see what was down it.

"Do you think they are finished?" Charlie asked and stepped away from the door.

Rick went in for another look. "I don't know, but it looks like it," he said.

"They won't be finished for another three months," a deep voice said.

Both boys jumped and turned around. Rick let out a yelp.

Brother Simon tried to hide his smirk and appear stern. He took a deep breath, folding his arms over his chest beneath his robes and straightening his back a bit more than usual. He raised his chin and looked down his nose at them, trying to appear disapproving.

"We were just looking," Rick said. "We weren't going inside."

"I should hope not," Brother Simon said.

"Really?" Charlie said.

Brother Simon's lips curled upward ever so slightly. "I trust you," he said. "Come on, or you'll be late."

The three continued down the stairs.

"This is one change that I don't mind," Rick said.

"Yeah, I can't wait," Charlie said.

"Once the floor is completed, we'll have a dedication ceremony and your classes will be moved up there."

"I can't wait," Rick said.

All through breakfast, Charlie seemed preoccupied. He was the last person at his table to finish, which upset Robert, who was becoming impatient.

After the meal, Charlie headed back to his dorm to get ready for Mass. It was Rick's and his turn to serve as altar boys. Charlie traded his blazer for his black cassock and surplice, then headed to the chapel. Father Mark was offering the Mass and was waiting in the back, dressed in his vestments. Charlie retrieved the matchbook and relit the altar candles.

"I think I figured out a plan," he said to Rick while he put the matches back into the closet and shut the door. "I'll fill you in later."

"Okay," Rick said.

All through Mass, Charlie went through the motions. His mind kept drifting to fine-tuning his plan. Luckily, it was Rick's turn to take the lead and ring the bells at the appropriate time during the consecration portion. When the service was finished, Charlie returned to his dorm to change back into his blazer and head to the basement for class.

"So, what's the plan?" Rick asked when Charlie took his seat at the desk beside his.

"I'll tell you at lunch break," he said. "We can meet at the bleachers."

"Okay."

~§~

After lunch, Charlie and Rick met outside by the baseball diamond. They sat down on the bleachers. Charlie pulled the collar up on his blazer to keep his neck warm. There was a trace of chimney smoke in the air from the houses in the town below. Memories of the fires from the year before stirred in Charlie's head. He shook them off.

"Cold?" Rick asked.

"Yeah."

"Well, talk fast and we can get back inside."

"Robin and Robert's uncle wants them to steal my key."

"And how do you know that?"

"I overheard them talking to him in the woods nearly a month ago," Charlie answered. "He told them they better have the box by the time he came back in a month, or they would have to come up with fifty bucks."

"Fifty bucks? Why?"

"I guess he paid them to steal my key. Anyway, they don't have it and he's due to come back this weekend. So, I'm sure they are going to make an attempt to get it, even if they have to beat me up to get it."

"Beat you up?" Rick said, turning to face Charlie. "How can you sound so cavalier about it? You should tell someone."

"They aren't going to do anything."

"How do you know?"

"Because, they haven't tried anything so far."

"Maybe they are waiting so they can get rid of the key before they get into trouble," Rick said. "I don't like this."

"That's why I want to set a trap for them."

"Okay. I'm listening."

"I'll accidently leave my locker ajar when I go shower. I'll have a fake key on a chain hanging on the hook inside the door. Then I'll wait and see."

"So, they take the fake key. What good will that do? Aren't you afraid they will give it and the box to their uncle?"

"No. I think they'll try to open the box themselves."

"What makes you think that?"

"Because they haven't told their uncle about the box."

"How do you know?"

"Because Robin said they couldn't open the box. They

need a key, my key."

"Oh," Rick said.

"So, I'll make sure they get a key but also, watch them to see where they have stashed the box. Then I will be able to get it back."

"Brilliant," Rick said. "When are you going to do this?"

"As soon as I can get another key. Father Ignatius has a bunch of old keys. I'm sure he wouldn't mind lending one to me."

"Well, I'm freezing and it's nearly time for class. Come on." Rick jumped up and headed back to the abbey.

Charlie followed close behind.

~§~

That evening Charlie pulled Rick aside after dinner. They waited in the hallway outside the refectory until the other boys headed upstairs before they slipped out the back door.

The sun had set and the air was cold. The few leaves that still clung to the trees rustled in the breeze. Charlie tucked his hands under his armpits to keep them warm.

"I got it," he announced.

"You did?"

"Yes," Charlie answered. "This afternoon I saw Father Ignatius and he was more than willing to loan me an old key."

"Cool. Do you have it on you?"

Charlie reached into his pants pocket and pulled out the key. He held it up.

Without asking, Rick snatched the key away from Charlie and took a closer look. "What's it to?" he asked.

"Does it really matter?"

"I guess not," Rick answered and handed the key back to Charlie.

"He said it was to an old suitcase he had once," Charlie said. "He also let me borrow this chain to put it on." Charlie held up the beaded chain.

Rick gave it a cursory glance. "Did you tell him what's going on?"

"Yeah. It's okay. He's not going to tell anyone."

"I hope you're right."

"I am. Now, I just need to set my plan in motion. Wear it for a few days and let them see it. Then leave it in my locker. Once they take it, I'll follow them and take back the box."

"How do you intend to do that by yourself?"

"I don't, you're going to help me, aren't you?"

"I'm not sure you've noticed but I'm not a fighter," Rick said.

"Who said anything about fighting?"

"Oh, you think they're just going to hand it over to you? If that was the case, why haven't they given it to you already?"

"Good point," Charlie said. "I'll have to think about that one."

"You do that. I'm going inside before I freeze to death."

Again, Charlie followed Rick back into the warmth of the abbey and up to their dorm.

~§~

The following morning, Charlie put his plan into action. Before he left to shower, he took off his real chain with his treasures and rolled them into the long edge his towel. He then wrapped the towel around his waist. He put Father Ignatius's chain around his neck, and let the key hang freely on his bare chest. Glancing over his shoulder, at the lockers on the other side of the doors, he noticed Robert standing by his locker. Charlie turned back, removed the chain and hung it on the hook. Leaving his locker ajar, he left the dorm. He waited a second and then pushed the door open a crack to watch what happened.

"Psst," Robert hissed from the other side of the door to get his brother's attention.

"What?" Robin said.

"MacCready just left and his locker is open."

"Master MacCready?"

Charlie jumped and let the door close. "Yes, Brother Simon."

"Spying again?"

"Well, sort of. I'm watching to see if Robert and Robin try to steal my key."

"What?" Brother Simon said and pushed through the doors, taking Charlie with him. He looked toward Charlie's locker just in time to see Charlie's locker door open, and Robert putting something into his pocket. He walked across the room toward the twins. "What are you doing?" he demanded.

"Nothing," Robert answered.

"What did you put in your pocket?"

"Nothing," Robert repeated.

"Let me see it," Brother Simon said, holding out his hand.

Robert stuck his hand in his pocket and pulled out the chain and key. He handed it to Brother Simon.

"Where did you find this? Choose your words carefully," the assistant dean said while he examined the key.

"It was hanging in Charlie's locker."

Charlie was shocked that Robert would admit to it so fast. "Did you ask Master MacCready if you could take it?"

"No."

"So, you stole it."

"Yes, Brother Simon."

"Why?"

Robert looked at his brother and then at Charlie before looking at Brother Simon. "I don't know."

"I think you do know," Brother Simon said. "You both will have an hour of work crew each day until you can tell me the truth."

"But our uncle is coming to visit this Saturday," Robin protested.

"Then I suggest you call him and let him know you won't be able to see him."

"But—"

"Yes, Master Muster?" Brother Simon said, looking at Robin.

Robin looked at this brother who shook his head. "Never mind," he answered.

"Very well. Now get ready for Morning Prayer, and don't be late."

"Yes, Brother Simon," the twins answered as one. They sulked away to their lockers to finish getting dressed.

"Master MacCready," Brother Simon said with his voice lowered to just above a whisper. "Where is your real key?"

"Safe," he answered and gripped the towel around his waist.

Brother Simon nodded. "May I suggest you not leave your locker open in the future?"

"Yes, Brother Simon," he answered.

"I'll return this key and chain to Father Ignatius," he said and left the dorm.

"I knew Father Ignatius would tell," Rick said when he joined Charlie at his locker.

"Yeah, well, so it didn't work."

"Maybe you should tell Brother Simon you think the twins took the box from the statue."

"Then I'll never get to find out what is in it," Charlie whined.

"Well, how are you going to get your hands on it now?"

"I don't know." Charlie answered.

~§~

At breakfast, neither of the twins said a word to anyone. Robert glared at Charlie while he ate his meal. Robin did not look up from his plate.

"W-w-why's everyone s-s-so qu-qu-quiet?" Dale asked.

Robert glared at him.

"Just tired," Jose said.

"I guess we all are," Dougary said looking at the twins and

then at Charlie.

"Sorry, I'm lost in my head," Charlie said. "I'm not looking forward to our speech class test today."

"Oh," Dale said. "I f-f-f-forgot." Now he looked worried.

After the prayer, the boys were dismissed. Charlie noticed that Robin stayed behind while Robert cleared the table. Once in the hall, Charlie slipped into the college's unused refectory next to theirs. From there, he could spy on the twins through the glass window in the doors as they came out of the refectory.

The twins seemed to be taking their time. Charlie watched the other waiters leave and head up the stairs. He was beginning to wonder if he had missed them. He was about to give up when the refectory door opened and the twins came out. Instead of heading for the stairs, they went directly to the phone closet. Robert went in first, and Robin followed.

Curious, Charlie cautiously slipped back into the hallway and inched closer to the phone closet. Luckily, Robin was standing with his back against the glass window in the door. Charlie listened.

"Hi Uncle—" Robert sounded as if he had been interrupted. "We almost had the key, but we were caught." Again, he paused. "It wasn't our fault. He must have tricked us."

"Tell him about the box," Robin whispered, yet loud enough for Charlie to hear.

"No, that's ours," Robert whispered to Robin. "Yes, I'm still here," he said a bit louder. "There's more. You can't come to see us this weekend. I know, but Brother Simon won't let us have any visitors until we tell him why we tried to steal MacCready's key." Robert paused again. "We don't have the money anymore. Where do you expect us to get it? No, don't tell your father. We'll try again. We just need more time. One week? But—" Robert stopped. "Okay, see you then."

"What'd he say?" Robin asked.

"Let me out of here," Robert said.

Charlie felt panicked and looked around for a place to hide. He slipped back into the college refectory and out of sight. He heard the phone closet door open and the twins' voices became louder.

"He said he will postpone his visit for one more week. We are to have the key by then or he has to tell his father."

"Let him," Robin said.

"Do you want his dad going to our parents?"

"No, I guess not."

"Exactly. So we have to come up with a plan to get that key away from MacCready."

"Why didn't you want to tell him about the box?"

"I told you, it's ours. When we get the key, we'll open the box. If it's nothing, then we'll tell uncle and he can have it. But, if it's worth anything, we're keeping it. We can give him the empty box and key. It'd be too bad they went to all that work for nothing."

"You're so smart," Robin said.

Charlie waited until he did not hear them anymore before he slipped out of the refectory and hurried up the stairs.

When he reached his cubicle, Rick was waiting. "Where have you been?" he said.

"I was downstairs," Charlie whispered. The twins were in their cubicle next door. He did not what them to hear him.

"Why are you whispering?" Rick asked.

In his peripheral vision, Charlie saw Robin's head raise above the partition. "Who died and made you my guardian?" Charlie said in a regular volume.

"There's no need to get snippy. Father Mark wanted us to serve Mass again."

"What happened to Dougary and Ted? I thought they were assigned to do it today?"

"I don't know. Come on," Rick said.

IT'S GONE

A week passed since Charlie overheard the twins talking on the phone with their uncle. Neither Robin nor Robert had made any attempt to get his key. Brother Simon made sure of it. He kept them busy every afternoon after school doing odd jobs around the abbey. That meant their evenings were spent doing their homework. They were too tired to do anything.

Saturday arrived and the twins' uncle was coming to visit. Charlie lay on his bed writing a letter to his grandmother, asking her once again to tell him what the key was for and what she knew about the missing box. In the cubicle next door, he heard Robert's voice.

"He's going to be here any minute."

"What are we going to do? I've only got ten bucks left of the money he gave us."

"That's better than me, I've got five."

"We're dead."

"Unless you could convince Charlie to give you the key."

"We both know, that's not going to happen." Charlie smiled at Robin's comment. "Besides, we need the key for ourselves, first," Robin continued.

"Well, we have to figure something out before he gets

here."

The sound of the dormitory doors opening and the noisy chatter of a couple boys made it impossible for Charlie to hear what the twins said next. When there was a lull in their conversation Charlie didn't hear Robin or Robert. He popped up and looked over the partition. They were gone. Putting his letter aside, he jumped down from his bed and began his pursuit.

By the time Charlie reached the hall, the twins were at the other end, starting down the stairs. Charlie picked up his pace to an almost run. When he reached the end of the hall by Saint Peter and Saint Thomas, Father Mark was coming out of Father Vicar's old room.

"Master MacCready." His voice was stern. "You know the rules, no running."

Charlie skid to stop. "Yes, Father. I'm sorry, it won't happen again."

"See that it doesn't."

Charlie did not answer. He hurried down the stairs. When he reached the first floor, the twins were heading out the front. Charlie turned and rushed out the back door. He hurried around the building to the front. Peeking around the corner, he saw the twins on the steps beneath the portico. They were watching the road to the west. Charlie darted across the roundabout and ducked behind a fir tree.

Suddenly he heard the sound of a car's motor. The twins heard it too. They walked down the steps to the sidewalk. Charlie watched the road where it bent around the new gym. As the sound grew louder, a dark red sporty-looking car came into view and zipped along the west driveway, stopping short of the portico.

Charlie hurried to get a closer look. He ducked behind another tree as the driver's door opened. A man, surprisingly tall for the size of the car, stepped out. His hair was somewhat long, blonde and windblown. His shirt had the top two buttons undone but the shirttails were neatly tucked into his tight bellbottom jeans. Even with his mirrored-lens sunglasses on,

Charlie felt a shiver of recognition. The twins' uncle reminded him of his Uncle Chester's son.

The visitor was the first to speak. "Where is it?" He held out his hand.

Robert took something from his pocket and put it in the waiting hand.

"What's this?"

"It's the key," Robert said.

Charlie put his hand over the key beneath his shirt.

"You must take me for a fool," the man said.

"What?" Robert said and took a step back, beside his brother.

"This isn't the key. This is a piece of crap." He flung the object across the driveway toward the Great Lawn. Charlie heard the faint sound of metal hitting the asphalt.

"That was the only key we found," Robin lied.

"Then you're not looking hard enough. I heard he wears the damned thing on a chain around his neck."

"But—"

"I don't want to hear anymore excuses. Either get me the key or give me back my money."

"We don't have that either," Robin said.

"Oh my, then you do have a serious problem." The visitor clenched his fists. Charlie could tell he was about to lose his temper. The man pointed a finger at Robert's face. "I hired you two dimwits because you said you could get that key. It's obvious you lied to me."

"We just need more time," Robert said. "If we rush it, we'll get caught and could get kicked out of here."

"And we came here to become priests," Robin said.

"Ha!" the man threw his head back and laughed. "Are you serious? You two, priests? From devils to saints? That's funny." He laughed again.

"You're the devil!" Robin said in an angry tone, pointing his finger at his guest.

The visitor's body tensed. He took a step forward and

grabbed Robin by the shirt collar and pulled him up onto tiptoes. "Well, you haven't seen anything yet. Get me that key or else!" He shoved Robin away.

Robin lost his footing and fell onto the grass behind him.

"You try that again and you can forget about the key," Robert said. "We'll go straight to the abbot."

"Don't threaten me, little man. The abbot's my great-uncle."

Charlie's jaw dropped. Any doubts that this was his cousin Niles were now dispelled. Now his mind was flooded with questions.

"Is there a problem here?" an elderly monk asked as he slowly approached from the path to the basement. He looked at Robin, who was once again standing beside his brother.

"No, Father Mathias," Robert said. "Do you need help?"

"No, No, I can manage," he said and inched his way between the twins and Niles.

Again, Charlie was shocked. For the past couple of years, he had tried to get a glimpse of Rick's Altar Boy assignment but Rick had managed to keep him a secret. And yet, there he was. Charlie could not wait to tell Howard.

"Carry on, boys. Don't let me interrupt you," the elderly man said once he passed.

Niles watched and waited until Father Mathias was inside. Then he stepped toward the twins, fist raised. "You've got until Spring Break to get that key. I won't be able to make it back here until then. Have it or be ready to pay me back my money with interest!" He turned around and headed back to his car.

"Yes, uncle," the twins said.

Niles stopped and turned back toward them. "I told you to stop calling me that. I'm not your goddamned uncle. Quit horsing around and get me that key. The real one." He opened his car door and slipped behind the wheel. The engine revved. Niles made a U-turn and sped off down the west driveway.

Charlie came out of hiding and rushed across the driveway to the twins. "How do you know that guy?"

"What business is it of yours, MacCready?" Robert said, in an argumentative tone.

"None," Charlie answered. "Just curious. He's got a nice car."

"It's not his. It belongs to his father," Robin said.

"Oh, his dad drives that?" Charlie said and looked over his shoulder at the empty driveway.

"No," Robert said. "His dad bought it. Niles just gets to drive it."

"So, is Niles a relative or something?" Charlie asked.

"No," Robin answered.

"How did you meet him?"

"What's with all the questions?" Robert asked. "You writing a book or something?"

"No. It's just I don't get any visitors and I'm curious, is all."

"Well, he wasn't your visitor, so forget it. He's nobody to you." Robert said and headed back to the front doors.

"Don't mind him," Robin said. "He's just stressed out. Niles is the older brother of a classmate we had before we came here."

"Oh, I see," Charlie said. "Well, we better get ready for dinner."

Charlie walked with Robin back into the abbey. When he reached the stairs, he noticed that some of the boys had already begun to line up outside the refectory. Rather than go back to his dorm, he joined them.

~§~

After Mass in the abbey church next day, Charlie and Father Cecil went for a walk. The sun was shining and felt warm against Charlie's back, but the wind was cold. Charlie stopped at their favorite fish pond and, after brushing the leaves from the bench, the two sat down.

"What's on your mind, son?" Father Cecil asked.

"Remember I told you about the twins trying to steal my key?"

Father Cecil nodded. "Yes."

"Well, yesterday I found out they are trying to get it for my cousin Niles."

"Really? How interesting. Why does he want it?"

"I don't know, but I also overheard the twins admit they have the box and intend on using the key to open it before they give the key to Niles."

"A-ha. The old double-cross. That never ends well," Father Cecil said. "But I wouldn't worry too much about it. Things always have a way of working out."

"I wish I knew what was in that box," Charlie said.

"Give it time," Father Cecil said, and then changed the subject. "What do you hear from your friend Master Miller?"

Charlie smiled. "He told me his dad is teaching him how to drive a car."

"Oh my," Father Cecil gasped. "That would be scary."

"I'll say," Charlie agreed. "He said he nearly had an accident already. After that, his father had him sign up for drivers ed at school."

"Good idea."

"He said he's trying to talk his dad into bringing him up for a visit. I sure hope he does. I really miss him. I still don't understand why he couldn't stay."

"Oh, son," Father Cecil said and shook his head slowly. "I know it's hard but you will find out for yourself as times goes on that people will come along and may stay a while, but eventually they will leave as someone new enters. You have to remember to enjoy the time you have with them while they are here and open your heart to new friendships. Does that make sense?"

"I guess," Charlie answered.

"You know, son, there is one friend who will never leave you, and he'll always be there when you need him. Do you know who that is?"

Charlie thought for a moment and then shook his head. "You?" he answered.

"No. Although, I'm here for you now," Father Cecil said. "It's your Heavenly Father. He will never leave you, and even if you leave him, he will always be there to welcome you back."

"It's just that Howard was the first real friend I ever had." Charlie said.

"I know." Father Cecil said. He patted Charlie's knee. "So, what are your plans for the rest of the afternoon?"

"I don't know, just hang out? Maybe watch some TV?"

"Whatever you decide to do, keep an eye out. You can be assured that those two boys will keep trying to get your key."

"Oh, I will."

"Good. Let's head back inside. It's starting to get a little chilly."

~§~

When Charlie returned his dorm, Rick met him in the hallway.

"Where have you been?" Rick asked.

"With Father Cecil, why?"

"You missed the excitement. Someone stole something that was in Robert's locker."

"What? When?"

"Beats me. All I know is Robert went to his locker and then suddenly began yelling and throwing his things on the floor. He was pretty upset. Even Robin couldn't calm him down."

"How could someone get into Robert's locker without him knowing about it? He keeps it locked."

"There is a master key to all of our locks," Rick said. "Someone has to have one or they figured out his combination. I bet it was Dougary."

Charlie shook his head. "I don't think so. Where is he now?"

"Dougary? Who cares?"

"No, Robert," Charlie said.

"In his cubicle still throwing a fit."

"Did he ever say what was taken?"

"Not that I heard. I got out of there." Rick said, glancing over his shoulder at the doom.

Charlie started for the door.

"Don't go in there," Rick said.

"I'll be fine," Charlie said and entered.

Charlie stopped and let the door close behind him. He looked at the mess of clothes scattered on the floor in front of the lockers. Robert was standing on a step-ladder rummaging through his storage cupboard above his locker, pulling out his suitcase and boxes and letting them fall to the floor.

"Where is it?" he shouted at the cupboard.

"Robert, stop," Robin pleaded, while trying to gather up the mess.

Robert turned and jumped down from the ladder. "It's got to be around here somewhere." He opened Robin's locker.

"No!" Robin said and dropped the armful of clothes.

He was too late. Robert was already emptying the contents of the locker onto the floor.

"Robert, stop it!" Robin shouted and grabbed his brother. "It's gone. The box is gone. I don't have it."

Robert ignored him, and emptied the shelf of Robin's underwear onto the floor. Socks started flying as he tossed them over his shoulder in a rampage.

Robin grabbed his brother and pulled him away. Robert slipped on sock and fell on his butt. "Stop it, Robert!" Robin repeated through clenched teeth. "It's gone."

"We have to find it."

"We will, but now we have to clean up this mess."

"No. I have to find it, now!" Robert stood up. He turned toward the door and saw Charlie standing there watching them. "You took it!" he shouted and started for Charlie.

"Took what?" Charlie said, and backed up, into the door.

"You know full well what. Give it back."

"I didn't take anything. How could I?"

"He's right, Robert. He doesn't know the combination to your lock. Leave him alone." Robin said.

Robert pushed Charlie aside and left the dorm.

"I take it, someone stole the box you took from the statue?"

"You know about that?" Robin said.

"Yes. That box was meant for me."

"Well, we don't have it now." Robin bent down and started picking up the clothes. "What a mess we've made," he said.

"Yeah," Charlie said looking around him at the clothes. He looked back at Robin who was crying while he grabbed at his socks. "Hey, do you want some help?"

Robin did not answer. He wiped his damp eyes with the back of his hand and continued to pick up his things.

Charlie bent down and picked up a shirt. "Why don't we take all of this to the sofa and I'll help you fold it up." He did not wait for an answer. He scooped up an armload of clothes and took them to the dorm's lounge.

A moment later, Robin arrived with his own armload. He dropped him in a heap on the sofa.

"Let's get that suitcase put away," Charlie said. He went back to the locker and standing on the chair, shoved the suitcase back into the storage cupboard.

"Here, these go up there, too," Robin said and handed Charlie a couple of empty boxes.

Charlie put them beside the suitcase and closed the door. Returning the step-ladder to the broom closet, he joined Robin at the sofa. He picked up a t-shirt and folded it.

"Where did you learn to fold shirts like that?" Robin asked.

"Father Emmanuel showed me when I first came here."

"Father Emmanuel?" Robin said. "Who's he?"

"He was our prefect, but he died."

"Oh," Robin said.

The two continued to fold the clothes.

"When I said that about the mess, I wasn't talking about

the clothes," Robin said.

"I gathered that," Charlie said. "I saw you two and Niles. I heard what he said."

"You did?"

"Yes," Charlie said. He put the folded socks down. "I have to tell you something. He's my cousin."

"Niles?" Robin said, looking both surprised and confused.

"Yes."

"Then why didn't he just ask you for the key?"

"Because he knows I would never give it to him," Charlie said and continued folding the clothes. "Our grandmother gave me the key the day Niles's father sent me to live here. I suspect Uncle Chester is behind this."

"I don't think he is," Robin said. "Niles said something once that made me think he's afraid of his father."

"Yeah, I hear that."

"But Niles isn't much better. He's scary. If we don't hand over your key to him or give him back the money he paid us, he'll get us expelled. Then our parents will know about our arrangement. They paid a lot of money for us to come here. It wouldn't be good."

"I can't give you my key," Charlie said.

"We don't need it anymore," Robin said. "What are we going to do?"

"Why don't we turn the tables on Niles? Tell him we will go to his father and tell him what Niles has been up to?"

"Do you think it would work?" Robin said.

"I don't know, but at least it might," Charlie said. "Do you think Robert will go for it?"

"Leave Robert to me," Robin said. "I'll talk to him over Thanksgiving vacation. Maybe by then he'll have calmed down."

HOLIDAYS

The Thanksgiving holiday arrived and the majority of the students returned to their families to celebrate. Charlie wandered the hallway on the fourth floor. It was hard to be thankful for anything, it seemed. Without Howard and Gus, none of the holidays seemed fun to him. Just constant reminders of how much he had lost.

When he reached the lounge, Charlie noticed Jose curled up in one of the overstuffed chairs. He looked like Charlie felt.

"Hey there," Charlie said, while he stood behind the sofa. "You doing okay?"

Jose looked at Charlie and wiped his eyes with the cuffs of his sleeves.

"It's okay," Charlie said. "I feel the same way."

"You do?" Jose said.

"Yeah," Charlie answered. "It's been a rough year." Charlie walked around the end of the sofa and sat down.

"This is the first time I haven't been home with my family for Thanksgiving," Jose said. "I think I want to go home."

"I understand. I felt like that too, my first year, but I couldn't. I lived with my grandma, and she now lives in an old folks home. There's no room for me."

"I'm sorry."

"It's okay. Being here isn't so bad," Charlie said. "They go all out for dinner. It's a lot of fun."

"I just miss my family."

"Have you called them?"

"We can't afford it," Jose said.

"How about I talk to Father Mark, and see if there's a way for you to call them?"

"You'd do that for me?"

"Sure, why not? Wait here, and I'll be right back." Charlie rushed away.

A half hour later, he returned. Jose was still sitting in the same chair, his feet pulled up and his chin resting on his knees. When he saw Charlie, he jumped up.

"What did he say?"

"Come on, he's going to let you call on the phone in his room."

Charlie led Jose to Father Mark's room by Saint Peter. He knocked on the door and waited for Father Mark to answer.

The door opened. "Come in," Father Mark said, with a warm smile.

The boys walked into the office. Charlie thought it looked a lot like Brother Simon's with a desk to the left of the door and a seating area at the back that had two chairs and a small side table between them. However, unlike Brother Simon's office, there were no bookcases. Instead, there were framed paintings and picture of a smiling couple. Charlie assumed they were Father Mark's parents.

"You may use the phone on my desk, Master Gonzales. Take all the time you need. Master MacCready and I will step out to give you some privacy."

"Gracias, Father," Jose said. He looked at the black telephone on the desk and walked around to the chair.

"Come, Master MacCready," Father Mark said, and escorted Charlie back into the hall.

Once in the hallway, Father Mark closed his door. "That

was a really nice thing you did for Master Gonzales."

"He's having a rough time, this being Thanksgiving and all."

"How about you?"

"I'm doing okay, now." Charlie said, with a nod. It was true. Helping Jose feel better actually made him feel better, too.

"Good. I know that being away from family on holidays can be rough, especially the first one. Would you like to call your grandmother?"

"No, I'm good," Charlie said. "She's spending the day with my Uncle Chester and his family."

"Oh," Father Mark said, and gave an understanding nod. "How about Master Miller?"

"He's with his dad. They went to visit relatives. I'm okay."

Father Mark put his hand on Charlie's shoulder. "How about we go downstairs to the kitchen and peek in on the sisters fixing dinner?"

"Sure."

~§~

Charlie was lying on his bed reading a comic when the twins returned after the holiday break. He glanced over the top of the partition as they put their bags down on the floor of their cubicle.

"Hey, Charlie," Robin said.

Robert looked at Charlie. He did not smile, but at the same time, he did not scowl.

"Hey, guys. How was your vacation?" he said.

"It was fun. Our mom always makes way too much food. We had turkey and pumpkin pie all weekend, and there was still more."

"Sounds great."

"How was your holiday?" Robin asked.

"It was okay. Sister Margaret Mary made her special apple, cranberry, walnut stuffing. Jose got to talk with his family. All in all, it wasn't bad."

"Well," Robin said, lowering his voice to just above a whisper. "We talked it over and would love to hear your idea on how to get Niles off our backs," Robin said.

"Good," Charlie said. He put his comic book down and looked around. "But not here, though. How about we meet by the bleachers once you've unpacked?"

"Sure," Robin said.

Charlie looked at Robert who gave no response. "Okay, see you there." Charlie jumped down from his bed and left the dorm.

All during the break, Charlie had been trying to figure out a plan, but nothing seemed to come to him. It had to be something that would be serious enough to cause Niles to back down and forget about the key. Without realizing it, Charlie found himself standing in front of Abbot Ambrose's office door. He knocked.

"Ave," his great-uncle said.

"Hi, Father Abbot, may I talk with you a moment?" Charlie said when he opened the door.

"Of course, son, come in. Have a seat."

When Charlie left the abbot's office a half-hour later, he felt good. He wondered if the twins were already waiting for him outside. He hurried to meet them.

Sure enough, when Charlie reached the bleachers, the two were sitting beside each other with the collars of their coats turned up and their arms folded over their chest.

"What kept you?" Robert snarled, and shivered. "Couldn't we meet inside where it's warm?"

"Too many ears," Charlie said. "I'll make it brief."

He filled the twins in on the plan he and Abbot Ambrose had worked out. They both seemed to like it and did not ask any questions.

"We'll have to wait until Spring Break to put it in motion, though," Robin said. "Niles told us he won't be able to get away until then."

"It's more like his car won't be able to make it," Robert said. "It sits too low and if there's even an inch or two of snow, it would high-center."

Charlie had no clue as to what Robert was talking about. Cars had never really interested him until Howard talked about getting one, and even then, it was beyond him.

"So, we have a plan?" Charlie asked.

"We do," Robin said. "Thank you, Charlie. And I'm sorry about. . .you know, before."

"It's forgotten. We pals now?"

"Yes," Robin answered, and nudged his brother.

"Sure," Robert said, sounding less convincing.

~§~

The next three weeks flew by for Charlie. The school's choir and band began their weekly Christmas concert program. They sang and played at the senior home in town. The following week, they participated in a regional Holiday Concert as one of ten other school choirs. The last concert, before the boys went home for the holiday, was given for friends and family members.

The Abbey Church was decorated with garlands of pine branches with shiny red bulbs and large red bows. In front of the main altar, the nativity set was arranged, minus the Christ Child. He would not make his appearance until Midnight Mass on Christmas morning. The choir's risers were set up in the nave facing the two rows of pews.

This was Charlie's fourth year singing in the choir. He started out in the front row as a first tenor, but now he was in the back with the other first bass singers. Standing on the riser, looking out at the faces of the students' parents smiling proudly, Charlie pretended his parents were watching and hearing him sing. Once the concert was over, that daydream was shattered when the parents collected their sons and headed home for the two-week Christmas vacation, leaving Charlie behind. Adding to the disappointment, Charlie noticed that Jose's family had made the long trip to hear him and take him home.

Christmas was not as much fun without Howard. Charlie returned to Saint Nicholas. This year there was no tree in the dorm. Instead a single tree was decorated in the main lounge on the fourth floor. Saint Nicholas could not look more depressing to Charlie.

"Hey, MacCready," Dougary called to him from his cubicle when Charlie entered the dorm.

"Hi, Dougary," he said. He crossed the room and stood at the foot of Dougary's bed.

"You guys sang well," he said. "I really enjoyed it."

Charlie smiled. "Good."

"You looking forward to Christmas?"

"Nah," Charlie said with a shrug. He looked over his shoulder at the empty dorm.

"Yeah, I hear ya. It's not much fun without the other guys around."

"Yeah," Charlie agreed. He could feel his mood sink even lower. "Well, I guess I'll go to my cubicle."

Charlie grabbed his stationary pad and pen. He returned to the lounge in the center of the dorm and flopped down on the sofa. Putting his feet up on the old steamer trunk-turned-coffee-table, he began another letter to Howard.

~§~

Christmas Eve arrived and Charlie's mood had not changed. He was not excited for the holiday in the least. He felt more alone than he had ever felt before. Suddenly he remembered what Father Cecil had told him. He went to the Abbey Church and sat down in the last pew. Staring at the huge crucifix suspended by chains above the altar, Charlie began to pray. As he did, tears filled his eyes and he knelt with his elbows resting on the back of the pew in front of him.

The sound of talking echoed off the rafters high above. Charlie quickly wiped his damp cheeks and looked around. On the balcony above that encircled the nave on three sides, he spotted Dougary and a novice walking together. He could not hear everything they were saying clearly but it was plain to him that they were happy. Charlie wanted that right then. He wanted to feel happy again, but without his best friend, it seemed impossible. He said a silent amen and then left.

In the foyer, Charlie bumped into Brother Simon.

"Master MacCready?" he said. "Is everything all right?"

Charlie nodded and put on a smile. "Yes."

Brother Simon raised his head and looked down his nose at Charlie. "Come, walk with me."

The two headed out the front door into the brisk winter air. Snow had fallen the night before, and left patches on the Great Lawn. Brother Simon ignored it, preferring to walk on the dry sidewalk instead.

"Having a rough time, are we?" Brother Simon said.

"Sort of," Charlie answered.

"This is your first Christmas without Master Miller and Master Kuegle, and Master Walters went home with his mother."

"Yes," Charlie said, and wondered if Brother Simon was trying to cheer him up or make him feel worse.

"It doesn't feel like Christmas without them, does it?"

"Not really."

"Son, people will come and go throughout your life. You can't base your happiness on others. You have to find your own happiness and that comes from inside. So, the other boys are not here. You are. What makes you happy?"

"I don't know," Charlie said. Then he remembered when he helped Jose at Thanksgiving. Doing something for someone else made him feel good inside. "I suppose, well, I felt good when I helped Jose."

"Yes. The Apostle Paul reminded the Christians in his day of what Jesus said, there is more happiness in giving than receiving. So, when we do something for others it brings us joy."

Charlie felt his mood lift. He now had a mission. He needed to find something to do for someone else, but what?

"Look for a way to help or brighten someone else's day and you will brighten your own," Brother Simon concluded. "We have to go back inside," he said, and shivered. "It's too cold out here without my cape. Come."

The two picked up their pace and hurried back to the warmth of the abbey.

~§~

The next afternoon, Charlie stood in front of Father Cecil's cell. He was not sure the monk was inside, but he had to give it a try. Holding the brightly wrapped gift behind his back, he knocked on the door.

"Merry Christmas!" Charlie greeted when Father Cecil opened the door to his cell.

"Merry Christmas, Master MacCready. Come inside."

Charlie entered the priest's room. He was not surprised by the lack of holiday decoration. Since Father Cecil could not see them, what was the point?

"I brought you something," Charlie said, looking at the colorfully wrapped package in his hands. "I told my grandma about you and she sent you a gift along with mine."

"How very thoughtful of her," Father Cecil said while he sat in his chair.

Charlie placed the package in the priest's hands and stepped back to watch him open it.

Father Cecil took the package and held it to his hear. He gave it a shake and smiled. "Well, it doesn't rattle," he said. His hands felt the package and found the places where the paper had been taped. Gently, he unfastened it without tearing the paper. Charlie was in awe.

"You will have to help me write a thank you card to your

grandmother," he said and removed the top of the box. Inside was white tissue paper folded over the gift. Father Cecil moved it aside and felt the contents. Grabbing hold of it, he let the box fall to the floor. "A scarf," he said and ran his hands along the edge until he found the ends. "Did she make this?"

"Yes," Charlie answered and grinned.

"What color is it?"

"It's your favorite color."

"Blue?"

The smile vanished from Charlie's lips. "No," he answered. "It's green. I thought you told me your favorite color was dark green."

Father Cecil let out a laugh. "It is, son. I was just teasing you." He reached down beside his chair and picked up a package. "I have something for you," he said and held it out.

"For me?" Charlie said, sounding surprised. He quickly took the present and sat back down in the chair by the table.

"I had one of the brothers wrap it for me. I hope you like it."

"I'm sure I will," Charlie said while he tore the wrapping paper away. "A Prayer Book?" he said and then realized it came out as a question.

"I thought you should have one of your own. It's the same one we use for our prayers."

"Wow." Charlie said as he examined the dark brick-red, leatherbound book. "Thank you so much. It's wonderful. It even has ribbons."

"You use those to mark the different parts. There's one to mark the Bible reading for the day. One for daily schedule and one for the prayers for the day. You'll need to have one of the brothers show you how to use it. Since mine is in Braille, I'm afraid I'm lost with yours."

"Okay. Thank you so much, Father. This is really special." Charlie said.

"Now, tell me, how are you and the Muster twins getting on?"

"We're actually doing okay," Charlie said. "I mean, Robin has really opened up but Robert is still a bit cool. We're still waiting to put our plan into action and get Niles off their backs. Rick is a bit jealous, though. He doesn't like that they are being nice to me. I think he feels like I don't need him."

"Friendships are tricky," Father Cecil said. "What do you hear from Master Miller?"

"Surprisingly very little. I don't know, maybe he's busy with school and stuff."

"Stuff?"

"Yeah, I don't know."

"I see. Well, you keep writing to him, and eventually he'll answer."

"I will and am." Charlie turned and set his Prayer Book down on the table. The key beneath his shirt hit against the locket.

"Ah, you still have your key," Father Cecil commented.

Charlie put his and over his trinkets. "Yes," he said. "You heard that?"

Father Cecil chuckled. "You'd be surprised what I hear. When you can't see, you have to rely on your other senses more. Hearing is one of the senses you learn to appreciate more. You should try sitting quietly with your eyes closed, without falling asleep. Pay attention to what you hear, try to identify it. Try it for me, now."

"Okay," Charlie said. He took a deep breath and closed his eyes. He heard the sound of someone walking in the hallway outside the room. He heard a creaking sound. He heard someone tapping softly. Charlie opened his eyes and saw Father Cecil tapping his index finger lightly on the table beside his chair.

"Wow," Charlie said. "I heard someone in the hallway, the ceiling creak and a tapping sound."

"Very good," Father Cecil said and cupped his fist in his other hand while resting his elbows on the arms of his chair. "When you can see, you tend to filter out the little sounds."

"That's so true," Charlie said.

After his visit with Father Cecil, Charlie headed outside. He wanted to get some fresh air and see how deep the snow was that fell overnight.

Walking down the front steps of the abbey, he came noticed a car parked beside the curb. Curiosity overtook him and he casually walked over to it. Stealing a glance, he looked into the car. The front bench seat was devoid of anything that would tell him who owned it. Walking around the end, he headed across the driveway to the Great Lawn. His shoes sank into the snow but only an inch. Not quite enough to build a good clean snowman. He remembered when he tried before with snow this shallow. It looked like a porcupine with green bits of grass sticking out everywhere.

"So, you're not going to say hi?"

The familiar voice stopped Charlie in his tracks. He turned around to see Howard standing beneath the portico. A big cheesy grin on his face.

"Howard!" he shouted and ran, slipping and sliding, to greet his friend.

They laughed and hugged each other.

"I can't believe you're here? I thought your father didn't want you to come back here for a year."

"Yeah, well, it's Christmas, and I couldn't let you celebrate it alone."

"I'm okay," Charlie said. "Well, it was rough at first, but Brother Simon helped me."

"What?"

"Never mind, you're here!" Charlie said. He could not stop grinning. "How long are you staying?"

"We've been invited to dinner with you. So, at least until after that."

"Oh, this is great!" Charlie said. "You won't believe it. You have to check out our cubicle."

"I'm sure Rick has changed it all around."

"I'll say."

The two headed back into the abbey and up to the fourth

floor.

"Nice tree," Howard said and stopped to admire it.

Charlie looked at the tree in the lounge. Even though he had seen it for the past two weeks, somehow it seemed different. It sparkled and glowed. It was pretty almost magical.

"So, how's drivers ed?" Charlie asked as they resumed walking down the hall.

"I feel like such a Gus," Howard said. "I don't think I'm gonna pass the course."

"Why?" Charlie nearly laughed at his analogy. He remembered how clumsy Gus was, and could not imagine Howard being a klutz.

"So far I've managed to run two stop signs, scrape the tires against the curb trying to parallel park, and nearly run over a person in the crosswalk."

"Oh no, you didn't."

"Yep. Call me Gus." Howard said. "Hey what do you hear from him?"

"Not much. The last time he wrote was before Thanksgiving. I think he writes Rick more often. At least that is what Rick says."

They walked into the dorm and Howard stopped.

"Where are all the decorations?" he asked.

"We only decorate the main lounge now."

"But this is Saint Nicholas!"

"Yeah, I know. Seems odd doesn't it?"

"Yes."

"Since there are only three of us, Dougary, Ted and myself, there's not really a point. It's not like it used to be."

"Yeah, I suppose."

As they headed toward Charlie's cubicle, Howard looked at his favorite chair in the dorm lounge. "So, did you take over my chair?"

Charlie stopped and turned back. "No. Rick did. And you know how obstinate he is."

"Yep," Howard agreed. "So, let's see what—oh my God!

You've got to be kidding me. Is this your cubicle?"

"Yes. I have the top bunk. That way I can still look out the window at the road."

Howard pushed his glasses up on his nose and shook his head. "I can't believe how he took over our cubicle. A rug? Seriously? It's too frou-frou for me."

"I ignore it and him most of the time," Charlie said and put his new prayer book on his bed. "He still won't let me touch his stereo. Like I even want to in the first place."

"He's. . .." Howard stopped and shook his head. He walked over to the chair in the corner beneath the window and sat down. "How's the search for the missing box going?" he asked.

"It's not," Charlie answered, and sat down on the edge of Rick's bunk. "There are no clues to who took it. Rick thinks whoever it was had the master key to the padlock."

"Then it had to be Father Mark, Brother Simon or Abbot Ambrose. You know they have the only master keys."

"Well, if it is, then there's nothing I can do about it," Charlie said.

"I still can't believe your cousin is behind stealing it in the first place."

"Oh, I can. My grandma told me stories of the things he's done. Big stuff. I don't know how he didn't end up here when it was a home for juvenile delinquents. But Abbot Ambrose and I have come up with a plan to put an end to his pestering the twins."

"Oh yeah, I remember you wrote something about it."

"Yep. We just have to wait until Spring Break for him to come back, then we'll get him good."

"So, are they being nicer to you?"

"Robin is but Robert is still standoffish."

"Boy, I wish I were still here, but it's nice being with my dad again."

"I bet." Charlie said. "Hey, where's your dad?"

"He's visiting with Abbot Ambrose."

"Oh?"

"Yeah, I think they've become friends or something. He told me to run along. He wanted to talk to Abbot Ambrose alone."

"That's odd, isn't it?"

"Not really. He still treats me like I'm five, sometimes. Tells me to go play in my room." Howard let out a laugh. "He forgets that I'm sixteen and in six more months I'll be seventeen. But I don't mind, I guess."

The bell in the hallway rang. Charlie jumped.

"They still ring that thing when there's so few of you here?"

"Oh, yes," Charlie said and stood up.

The two headed downstairs to the refectory for dinner.

"I know you've said he's changed," Howard said while they walked. "But I'll have to see it to believe it. As long as I've known Dougary, he's been a bit of a troublemaker."

"I'm serious, he's changed. You'll be surprised, trust me."

"I'll wait and see."

"So, how do you like public school?"

"It's okay, but I sure miss this place. Now I know how you must have felt when you came here. The guys at school aren't a lot of fun. You're either a jock or a nobody. And the girls are only interested in the jocks. Still, some are pretty to look at."

"I wouldn't know. I've never been to a public school. My grandmother taught me everything at home. Did I ever tell you she's a retired teacher?"

"Really? You never said anything about your grandma being a teacher."

"It was before I was born."

"Why didn't she just let you go to regular school?"

"I don't know. Maybe she thought my parents would come back sooner, and I'd have to switch schools or something?"

"Yeah, something," Howard said and sighed. "I miss our mystery solving."

"It's not as much fun on my own. Rick thinks it's all a big joke."

"Rick's the joke," Howard said and shook his head. "I can't imagine he's any help."

"Not as much as you, that's for sure."

"Well, keep writing me, and I'll try to do better about helping you as much as I can."

"I will."

The refectory doors were open when they reached the first floor.

"Oh crap!" Howard said.

"Howard!" Charlie said and frowned.

As it turned out, the boys were not late. Father Mark had opened the doors early. Charlie's mouth dropped open when he saw the decorations. Between brunch and dinner, the refectory decorations had been enhanced. There were centerpieces of pine sprigs, red poinsettia flowers, small shiny gold bulbs, and a candle in the middle on each of the three tables. The dishes were not the usual white crockery, each place setting was a shimmering white porcelain with a gold band around the rim. Even the drinking glasses were upgraded to nice crystal. Charlie noticed on every plate was a large cylinder-like object wrapped in holiday paper and tied at each end with ribbons.

At the head table, Father Mark sat talking with Howard's father, who was seated beside him in Brother Simon's usual seat. Brother Simon sat at the end of the table on the other side of Howard's father.

Charlie let Howard have his old place back at the table while he moved over a chair. Dale and Ted claimed the twins' seats across from them, and both appeared happy to see Howard again.

After Grace, Father Mark welcomed everyone, and said that two of the brothers would be waiting on the tables that evening. He then instructed them to set their gifts aside until after the meal.

The brothers brought out the Christmas feast of turkey, baked ham, candied yams, dressing, green beans and mashed potatoes with gravy. Charlie ate heartily. He had not felt so happy in a long time. When the brothers brought out the pumpkin pie with fresh whipped cream, Charlie thought he would burst.

Once the meal was finished, Father Mark stood behind his chair. He looked at the ten boys in front of him. "Merry Christmas," he said. "The gift you see in front of you is called a Christmas Cracker. They are from the sisters in the kitchen. They know you have been though a lot this year with all the changes, so they wanted to give you something special. You open the cracker by pulling on the tied ends like this." He held up his cracker to demonstrate. When he pulled the ends, the paper ripped and there was a loud pop sound. Bits of confetti puffed into the air and rained down on the table in front of him. He laughed. "Now, you may open yours."

The refectory was filled with the sound of popping and the laughter from the boys as confetti burst into the air.

"Hey, there's stuff inside," Ted said.

The boys began to pull from the tube small trinkets, five silver dollar coin, a folded-up paper crown and several strips of paper with jokes written on them.

Charlie looked at Howard who had not opened his cracker. "Go ahead, open it."

"I don't deserve it," he said. "I'm not here anymore."

"It's Christmas. Everybody gets a gift on Christmas."

"That's right, Howard. When we told the sisters that you and your father were dining with us, they were thrilled. They want you to have it," Father Mark said, standing behind Ted and looked around the table. "Don't worry about the mess," he announced to the boys. "The brothers will take care of it."

"See, Howard, it's yours," Charlie said.

Grinning, Howard pulled the ends of his cracker and it burst open with a loud pop.

While the boys tried out their jokes on each other, Father Mark and Mr. Miller continued their conversation unheard. Mr. Miller, an older version of Howard, smiled proudly when he looked at his son.

When the party was over, Charlie and Howard followed Father Mark and Mr. Miller to the main foyer.

"I'm so happy you came," Charlie told Howard. "I was feeling a bit down, missing you."

"Well, I'm glad we came, too." Howard said. "I wish I could stay but my dad needs me, I think." He glanced over his shoulder at his father and smiled. "But, hey, maybe Abbot Ambrose will let you come for a week or two next summer?"

"Don't hold your breath. He's very protective of me for some reason. I haven't been allowed off the hilltop on my own, ever. But I'll talk to him."

"Keep those letters coming and I will too." Howard said.

Charlie gave Howard a hug and then, standing beside Father Mark on the front steps of the abbey, they watched the car until it disappeared behind the gymnasium.

BETRAYAL

"Master MacCready," Brother Simon said just before Charlie entered the refectory.

Charlie stopped, stepped out of line, and waited for the assistant dean.

"Your package arrived early this morning. The brother working in our post office brought it directly to me." He handed Charlie a small, padded envelope.

"Oh, that's great. I was beginning to worry. Thank you, Brother Simon." Charlie said and took the envelope. Without opening it, he stuffed it into his blazer pocket.

"I hope you know what you're doing," Brother Simon said.

"Father Abbot and I came up with the plan. It has to work."

The two entered the refectory and went to their tables.

Robert kept fidgeting in his seat and picking at his breakfast.

"Would you relax?" Robin whispered to him.

"I don't think it's gonna work," Robert said.

"Trust me, I know my cousin. It will work as long as we stick to the plan," Charlie answered.

"What are you three talking about?" Dougary asked.

"Nothing," Robin said, his eyes widened. "Robert is just

nervous about something he has to do today. But there's nothing to worry about."

"Easy for you to say. You're not the one who'll get punched if the brothers aren't quick."

"They won't be late," Charlie said. "What time did he say he'll be here?"

"Ten," Robin answered.

"Wh-wh-what's he g-g-got to do?" Dale asked.

"It's none of your business," Robert snapped.

"Robert, don't be rude," Robin reprimanded. He looked at the other three at the table. "Fine, there's this guy—"

"My cousin," Charlie interjected.

"Yes, Charlie's cousin. He's been hounding Robert and me and Charlie figured out a way to get him off our backs."

"Oh," Dougary said. "Does this have to do with his key and that box?"

"How do you know about that?" Robin asked, sounding surprised.

"Long story," Dougary said. "But everyone has heard about it. And everyone heard about the fit you threw over someone swiping a box from your locker."

"See, I told you, you needed to calm down," Robin said to his brother.

"What key?" Jose asked.

"Wh-wh-what box?" Dale chimed in.

"Nothing," Charlie said. "It's really no big deal."

"So, what's your plan?" Dougary asked.

"I can't tell you, I'm sorry," Charlie said. "The fewer people who know about it, the better. We don't need the whole school showing up."

Dougary eyed the three of them. "Don't go getting into trouble," he said. "I don't want Father Mark asking me why I didn't intervene and try to stop you or something since you three are in my dorm."

"No, you won't get in trouble," Charlie assured him. "Father Abbot already knows."

"I'm sure he does," Dougary said.

After the closing prayer was said, the boys were dismissed. Charlie, Robin and Robert met in the hallway.

"Come on. We can wait on the front steps," Charlie said and led the way.

"When do I get the key?" Robert asked. His nervousness was evident by the way his voice cracked.

"Oh," Charlie gasped, and reached into his pocket. "Brother Simon handed it to me before breakfast." He pulled out the envelope and tore it open. He pulled out the antique key wrapped with an invoice and rubber band. Removing the paper, he looked at the key. "Perfect. This one should fool him." He handed the key to Robert.

Robert examined the tarnished brass key. "How would I know? I've never seen the real key."

"You'll have to trust me," Charlie said. "My grandmother told me never to show it to anyone."

"Why?" Robin asked.

Charlie shrugged. "I don't know. But trust me, this is close to what it looks like."

"I guess," Robert said. He put the key into the pocket of his blazer and sat down.

Charlie looked across the Great Lawn at the gymnasium. The outside was finished and all the scaffolding was removed. There were a few brothers taking advantage of the warm spring morning by working on the landscaping around it.

"It looks like they're almost finished with the new gym," he said to calm his own nerves.

"You can't tell anyone," Robin said. "Ted and I actually snuck inside."

"You did?" Charlie said.

"Yeah, the door was left unlocked so we took a peek around. It's really cool."

"When was that?" Robert asked.

"Last week. They were working on the floor. It's all wood, you know. There's a stage at one end and a big empty room at the other end. When you walk inside, there's a room to the right and left. Above them are bleachers. It's the same on the other side, but we didn't get to see what was under them because someone walked onto the stage. We rushed out."

"Wow," Charlie said, bobbing his head slightly. "Everything keeps changing."

"What do you mean?" Robin asked.

"There used to be a garage where the gym is. It burned down last year."

"Really?" Robert asked. "I heard some of the boys talking about the fires here last year. Is it true you pegged the guy?"

"Yes, but no one believed me."

"How did you know?" Robert asked.

"I don't know. I just knew."

"A bit psychic?"

Charlie looked at him. "No. I'm not crazy!"

"No, psychic. It means you can see the future or read people's minds. That sort of stuff. Not psycho," Robin explained.

"I don't know anything about reading minds or seeing the future," Charlie said. "I just had this feeling that it was him."

"Wish we were here, then," Robert said.

"Speak for yourself," Robin said, and shook his head.

"Trust me, it was not fun. Everyone was on edge and scared."

"I bet. Is it true he lit the crypt chapel on fire?" Robert asked.

"Yes, but it didn't do a lot of damage. Just singed the floor and one edge of the altar."

"He'll go to hell for that for sure," Robert said.

"Hey, what time is it?" Robin asked.

Charlie pulled out his pocket watch and opened it. "It's a little after nine," he answered. "I best go get ready. I'll be waiting inside, listening. Remember, stick to the plan and everything will be fine."

"We will," Robin said.

A half hour later, at a quarter to ten, Charlie returned to the foyer and knocked on the glass door to get the twins' attention. When they looked up at him, he waved. Across the driveway, on the Great Lawn, a brother wandered but stayed close to enough to the portico. Charlie noticed Abbot Ambrose and Brother Simon walking near the front of Xavier Hall, the college seminary building built into the side of the hill just west of the abbey. Everyone was in place.

Ten o'clock came and went. Charlie could see Robert was nervous. He stood up and began to pace. Robin tried to calm him while he walked beside him.

Ten-thirty. The sound of a car approaching stopped the twins in their tracks. Charlie looked at the gym. Niles's sportscar came into view and slowed as it made its way along the west side of the Great Lawn. It was action time.

Niles pulled to a stop under that portico. He shut off the engine and climbed out of the car. Still wearing the mirrored sunglasses, he walked around the front of his car.

"So, where is it?" he asked in a demanding tone.

"It's right here," Robert said. "But before I give it to you, I want your assurance that we're done here."

"Fine, you got it. We're finished. Now, where is it?" Niles held out his hand.

Charlie glanced toward Xavier Hall and saw Abbot Ambrose and Brother Simon approaching. He looked at Robert. He was sticking to the plan. He hesitated before pulling the key out of his pocket. He held the key up by the bow.

"Is this what you want?" he asked.

"Yes. Now hand it over."

"Good morning, boys," Abbot Ambrose said. "Niles? What a surprise." He looked at Robert who quickly put the key behind his back. "What's going on here?" he asked.

"No-no-nothing," Robert pretended to stammer.

"What are you hiding behind your back?" he asked. "Show me."

"Don't do it," Niles said sounding panicked.

Slowly Robert took his arm from behind his back and showed the key to the abbot.

Abbot Ambrose took the key from him. "Isn't this Master MacCready's key?"

"No, it's mine," Niles said and reached for it but Abbot Ambrose closed his fist around it.

"Yes, Father Abbot," Robert said.

"He's lying," Niles said.

"Where did you get it?" he asked.

"From Charlie."

"No!" Niles said sounding angry.

That was his cue. Charlie burst through the door, covering his left eye with his hand. His clothes were disheveled and his blazer even had a tear in it at the shoulder where the sleeve was attached.

"Good heaven," Brother Simon said, completely out of character and if Niles had known him, unbelievable. "What happened to you?"

"Robert stole my key," Charlie answered as he joined them at the foot of the steps. He removed his hand and both Robert's and Robin's eyes widened in shock.

"Who hit you?" Brother Simon asked.

"He made me do it," Robert said, pointing at Niles.

"No, I never."

"He told me to beat Charlie up if that's what it took to get the key."

"That's right," Robin said. "He even said he would pay us."

"No, I didn't."

"I see what's going on here," Abbot Ambrose said, with a nod. He looked at Niles.

"I never said that. I don't want the key." Niles was backing away.

"Is that true?" Abbot Ambrose asked.

"Yes, keep it. I don't want anything to do with it. I don't even know what it's for."

"Very well, then. I don't want to see or hear of you being

on this hilltop ever again without your parents present. Or I will be forced to call the authorities. Is that understood?"

"Yes, Uncle Father Abbot," Niles said, and quickly jumped into his car. The engine roared and he made a U-turn and sped away.

Brother Simon applauded. "Well done, everyone."

"Yes," Abbot Ambrose said turning back to the three boys. "Master MacCready, I believe this is your key?" he said and handed Charlie the fake key. "I think that will be the last time we see him around here. Are you okay, Master Muster?"

"I can't stop shaking," Robert said. "But I'll be fine."

"You did a fantastic job," Charlie said and put his hand on Robert's shoulder.

"Whoever did your make up did a fantastic job," Robert said and looked at Charlie's eye. "When I saw your black eye, I almost wet my pants."

"Good thing you didn't," Robin laughed.

"That's enough of that, boys," Father Abbot said. "Get cleaned up, and I will see the three of you in my office in a half hour."

"Yes, Father Abbot," the three said in unison.

They watched Brother Simon and Abbot Ambrose ascend the steps and enter the abbey.

"Do you think we're in trouble?" Robin asked.

"He's probably going to kick us out," Robert said.

"He won't do that," Charlie said.

"How can you be so sure?" Robert asked.

Charlie frowned. "I'm not. I just hope he won't."

A half hour later, the three boys met in front of Abbot Ambrose's office door. Charlie knocked.

"Ave," his great-uncle called from inside.

Charlie opened the door and led the three inside. To his surprise, Father Mark stood in front of the abbot's desk. Abbot Ambrose stood up from his chair behind his desk. Brother Simon rose from where he was seated behind the door.

"Please, have a seat," Abbot Ambrose said and held out his

hand toward the three chairs to the right of his desk, where Brother Simon was standing.

The boys nervously sat down.

Abbot Ambrose and Father Mark also took their seats. Brother Simon excused himself and left the office. Charlie's anxiety rose.

"I understand from Master MacCready that Niles hired you to steal his key. Is that so?" Abbot Ambrose asked.

"Y-yes," Robert answered.

"How much did he pay you?"

"Fifty dollars, twenty-five each," Robert answered again. He glanced at his brother, who was quietly sitting beside him with his hands between his knees.

"Very well," Abbot Ambrose continued. "You do understand that what you did violates our school code of ethics, do you not?"

"Yes, Father Abbot," they both responded.

"And we would be within our rights to send you both back home."

Robin's jaw dropped and his mouth gaped. Robert nodded silently and to Charlie, looked as if he were about to cry.

"Well, we will not be sending you home. We understand that it was an error in judgement due to your youth. However, it will not go unpunished."

"That's okay," Robin said. "We'll take our punishment."

Abbot Ambrose held up his hand. "Wait until you hear what it is. For the rest of the school year, you will be working for the abbey every afternoon sweeping the classroom floors, dusting the shelves and cleaning the restrooms top to bottom."

"That's six weeks," Robin said.

Again, Abbot Ambrose held up his hand to silence him. "Seven, to be exact, Master Muster. In addition, you will have to pay Niles back the money he gave you."

"But we don't have any money," Robert said.

"You will be paid two dollars an hour for your labor. Half of it will be held back and given to Niles. The other half will be held in trust and given to you when you leave for the summer. Does this sound fair?"

"Yes, Father Abbot," they again answered in unison.

"Very well, beginning Monday after classes, you will report to Brother Gregory and he will instruct in your duties."

"Yes, Father Abbot."

"You may leave. And boys, keep your noses clean. You are on probation. Another incident and I will have not choice but to expel you both. Understood?"

"Yes, Father Abbot."

Charlie watched the twins leave. When the door closed behind them, he looked at Father Mark and his great-uncle and wondered what sort of trouble he was in for.

THE BOX

A knock on the office door startled Charlie.

"Ave," Abbot Ambrose called out.

The door opened and Brother Simon entered the office. "We're ready for you in room three," he said.

"Splendid," Abbot Ambrose said, and rose. He held out his hand directing Charlie to join him and Father Mark.

Charlie quickly stood up and led the way out of the office and into the hall. Brother Simon was standing by the door of visiting room three. His eyebrows pinched above his nose as he wondered what was going on. Once the three were standing together, Brother Simon opened the door.

"Go on in, Master MacCready," he said.

Nervously, Charlie stepped forward and entered the room. The room was decorated with a fireplace set between the two windows that overlooked the Great Lawn. Above the fireplace was a large mirror with an ornate gold frame. In front of the windows was a wingback chair, and in front of the chair stood Charlie's grandmother.

"Grandma," Charlie shrieked and rushed to her with open arms. He hugged her and realized she was shorter than he remembered. He let go and stood back to look at her.

"My sweet boy, you've grown so," she said and smiled at him.

"I can't believe you're here," he said. She still looked the same as the day he left her. Still wearing her white hair twisted in a tight bun on the crown of her head. Still wearing an apron over her red, floral-patterned, house dress. Still smelling of rose petals and Ivory soap. He hugged her again. "I've missed you so much," he said into her ear.

"And I you, dear," Ophelia said. "Come, let's sit down."

Charlie released his embrace and turned toward the sofa that sat with its back to the entrance. That was when he noticed the trunk in the center of the room. The coffee table had been moved aside. Confused, he looked at Abbot Ambrose. "Isn't this the trunk from Saint Nicholas?"

Abbot Ambrose smiled, and nodded. "Very perceptive of you, son." He walked across the room to one of the chairs. Father Mark followed and stood in front of the other, and waited for the abbot and the guest to sit down before he sat.

"Charlie, dear boy," Ophelia said, holding his hands on her knee. "I owe you an apology. Dietrich has told me what has been going on here because of the key I gave you."

"It's okay, Grandma."

"Hush now, let me finish," Ophelia said with a gentle tone. "I never meant to put you in danger. That's why I didn't want to tell you what it was for. I figured if you knew, you would do as your father did and let it slip to the wrong people. Then you would be in danger. But I see now, that not telling you has been worse. So, it's time you knew." She looked at Abbot Ambrose.

"Simon," Abbot Ambrose said, and held out his hand toward the trunk.

Brother Simon stepped forward and took a key from his robes and unlocked the trunk. Carefully, he opened it. Charlie watched intently. The inside of the trunk was lined with fabric that was worn and torn in places. A large metal box sat on the bottom. Brother Simon picked it up and handed it to Father Mark while he closed the trunk. Taking the box back, he placed it on the top of the trunk and stepped back.

"Was that in there the whole time?" Charlie asked.

"Yes, son," Abbot Ambrose answered.

"But. . .then. . .what was the box that Robert took?"

"It was a fake. Years ago, we discovered this box hidden in the base of the statue. We replaced it with one filled with a few lead weights. We couldn't leave this out there," Abbot Ambrose explained.

"So, it was you who took it away from Robert?"

"Yes, we couldn't let him get your key and try to open it. The key wouldn't fit," Brother Simon said.

"Charlie, where is your key?" Ophelia asked.

Charlie quickly pulled the key and the other trinkets from beneath his shirt. He took the chain from around his neck and gave them all to his grandmother.

"No, you do it," she said, and gave them back to him. "Go ahead and open the box."

Charlie looked at her and then at everyone in the room before looking at the box. "No, I can't," he said.

"Yes, you can, dear," Ophelia said and patted his leg for encouragement.

With his hands trembling, Charlie sat forward and inserted the key into the lock. He turned it and heard a click. The lid released and popped up a small bit. Charlie pulled the key out and set it on the trunk. Slowly, he raised the lid. His hands trembled more.

"It's okay, son," Abbot Ambrose said.

Opening it the rest of the way, Charlie's eyes widened. He turned and looked at his grandmother, his mouth gaping. He looked at Abbot Ambrose. The box was filled with gold ingots, and stacks of cash.

"I don't understand," Charlie said. "What is this?"

"It is yours, son," Abbot Ambrose said, and sat forward a bit more. "When your father came to live here, this box was with him, along with a letter from his parents. They said to keep this hidden and safe. When Patrick was old enough, give it to him to start a new life." Abbot Ambrose took a tattered, yellowed envelope from his pocket and handed it to Charlie.

Charlie looked at it. There was no return address or postmark. Carefully, he opened the loose flap and removed the fragile piece of stationary. At the top of the letter, in the center, was a family crest that read O'Sullivan. Charlie felt confused. Carefully, he opened it and began to read.

Dear Father,

It is with great pain of heart that we are sending our son to you. Through bad decisions, I have unwittingly ruined my life and that of my wife. I don't know how much longer we will be able to hold out. That is why we are sending our precious Patrick across the country where no one will know the truth about his parents. Please take care of him. Keep him safe. Also, protect this box and its contents. Give it to Patrick when he is old enough so he can start a new life.

May God bless you.
Danny O'Sullivan

Charlie stared at the letter. His mind was numb and confused. He looked at his grandmother and then at the abbot. "O'Sullivan?"

Abbot Ambrose nodded. "Yes."

"But my dad's name is MacCready."

"Yes, son. I was the Prior when your father was left here. He was about five or so. He had that note pinned to his lapel and this trunk with the box hidden in the bottom."

"Who brought him here?"

"We don't know, son," Abbot Ambrose answered. "Our Abbot made the decision to take him in and he changed Patrick's last name to MacCready."

"But why?"

"Charlie, dear boy," Ophelia said, her eyes glistening with tears. "Your father's parents were involved in the Irish Mafia back east. Your grandfather, Danny O'Sullivan, wanted out, but he knew too much and they weren't going to let him just walk away."

"What happened to them?" Charlie blurted.

Abbot Ambrose shook his head. "We don't know, but I imagine by now, they are either in jail or deceased. I'm sorry."

"Now do you understand why we couldn't say anything?" Ophelia said.

"What about my parents? Where are they?"

"We don't know," Ophelia said.

"Son," Abbot Ambrose said. "Your father found out about who his parents were when he was still here. One of the brothers slipped up and told him about the letter. Instead of keeping it quiet, your father boasted about it to the other boys as if he were proud that his father was in the Mafia. When he left here, against my better judgement, I gave the box to him. It appears for whatever his reasons, he hid the box in the base of the angel and left all of the clues, the medal, the watch and the key.

"After you were born, he came to me, afraid and shaken up. He said he received a threatening letter from someone demanding the box. He said somehow someone had figured out who he was, and threatened to go public with the information if he didn't comply."

"That's when your parents brought you to your grandfather and me," Ophelia picked up the story. "They were going into hiding, and feared that they couldn't keep you safe if you were with them."

Charlie sat in stunned silence. He kept thinking this was all a mistake. That none of it was real. He looked at the open box in front of him, at the stack of money and the ingots of gold.

"Where did this come from?" he asked. "I mean, was it stolen?"

"We don't know," Abbot Ambrose answered. "At the time we did research, but we couldn't dig too deeply or we would endanger Patrick. We scoured the newspapers from back east and nothing was ever mentioned about the money. We're assuming it was obtained legally. Your grandmother was from a wealthy family, and it may have come from them.”

Charlie looked at the box again. It was a lot to take in. He reached out and closed the box. Using his key, he locked it tight.

“Abbot Ambrose, please keep this hidden away,” he said.

“Certainly.”

“Grandma, thank you for telling me all of this.”

“Are you all right, dear?”

“It’s a lot to take in. I don’t know,” Charlie answered.

“Well, take your time, son,” Abbot Ambrose said.

Charlie nodded.

“But, Charlie,” Ophelia said, and squeezed his hand. “You mustn’t tell anyone about this. Not even your friend Howard. No one must know until we can find your parents and be sure they are safe. Understand?”

“Yes, Grandma.” Charlie nodded.

The next six weeks passed in a blur for Charlie. He felt as though he could not concentrate on anything. Even Father Cecil commented on his distracted behavior, but Charlie could not tell him what was troubling him. Surprisingly, he passed all of his finals, some just barely, but it was still a pass.

Charlie readied the wine and water cruets in the Abbey Church’s sacristy. He handed them to Rick and instructed him to place them on the side table in the sanctuary. Walking into the priest’s side of the sacristy, he checked to make sure the vestments were ready for Abbot Ambrose and the other officiating priests.

“You’re doing a fine job,” Father Mark said.

“Thank you,” Charlie answered. “I’m a bit nervous about the two new altar boys. This will be their first procession.”

“They’ll do fine. I’ve watched you train them,” Father Mark said. “Son, how are you doing?”

“I’m doing okay,” Charlie answered.

“Well, if you need to talk with someone, you know that

Abbot Ambrose, Brother Simon, and myself would be happy to listen and help as best we can."

"I know and thank you. I'll let you know."

"Charlie, which of us do you want to carry the incense?" Robin asked.

"Excuse me, Father Mark," Charlie said.

"Certainly," Father Mark said and smiled proudly.

Once back in the altar boys' side of the sacristy, Charlie said, "May I have everyone's attention." The three boys lined up in front of him. "When Abbot Ambrose is ready, we will go outside and make our way to the portico. When everyone is ready, Abbot Ambrose or one of the other officiating priests will add a spoonful of incense to the thurible. Once that is done, Rick will take his place at the front of the line. The two of you will carry your lit candles, one on my right and the other on my left. Does that make sense?" he said, turning to Robin and Robert, "It's just as we rehearsed. Nothing's changed."

"Got it," Robin said. Robert nodded, and Rick did not respond, but Charlie knew he understood.

"Behind us, the senior class will make its entrance," Charlie continued. "The two assisting priests will be next and Abbot Ambrose will enter last.

"Once we reach the sanctuary, Rick will stand to the left, near the pulpit. We will walk up the steps and stand in front of the altar facing the congregation. Once Abbot Ambrose arrives, he will motion for the thurible and bless the congregation. Afterward, he will say the opening prayer. Then you two will place the candlesticks at either end of the altar. Rick will take the thurible back to the sacristy and I will place the cross on the stand by the side table. Rick and I will be the primary servers. You two will sit at the side. At communion, you will help the assisting priests, while Rick and I assist Father Abbot. Is that clear?"

"Yes," the twins answered.

"Pssst!"

Charlie looked over his shoulder at the side door that led to the nave. Dougary was standing in the doorway, dressed in his black graduation gown and holding his mortarboard.

"Can I have a word with you?" he asked.

"Sure," Charlie said after glancing at the clock on the wall by the sink. He walked over to Dougary while the others waited for the priests. "What's up?"

"I just wanted to congratulate you on being named sacristan."

"Thank you."

"And to tell you how much I appreciate your keeping my secret. I know I haven't been the best—well, I was horrible to you, and I'm sorry. I really do like you."

"It's in the past and forgotten."

Dougary smiled. "After I graduate today, I've been accepted as a postulant. I'll also be going to college in the fall."

"That's really great, Dougary."

"So, you can let people know now. They're going to make the announcement at the end of the graduation ceremony."

"Okay. I'm truly happy for you, honest."

"I'll let you get back to. . .," he said, nodding his head.

Charlie watched while he turned around and went back to join his classmates outside.

"What did he want?" Rick asked.

Charlie turned back around. "He just apologized for being mean to me. You'll hear it soon enough, but he's entering the monastery after the ceremony."

"You're joking."

"Nope. Serious as a heart attack."

"I don't believe you."

Father Mark stuck his head through the doorway. "We're ready to head outside."

"Grab your candles and light them. We're on," Charlie said and picked up the processional cross.

ABOUT THE AUTHOR

James M. McCracken spent much of his teenage years away from his family in a seminary boarding school. It was there that his love of writing began. It is his experiences while at the boarding school that serve as the inspiration for the Charlie MacCready series.

James M. McCracken currently resides in Central Oregon. He is a longtime member of the writing group Becoming Fiction and the Northwest Independent Writers Association.